UNEXPECTED PLEASURES

UNEXPECTED PLEASURES

MARY WINE

BRAVA

KENSINGTON PUBLISHING CORP.
www.kensingtonbooks.com

BRAVA BOOKS are published by

Kensington Publishing Corp.
119 West 40th Street
New York, NY 10018

All Kensington titles, imprints, and distributed lines are available at special quantity discounts for bulk purchases for sales promotions, premiums, fund-raising, educational or institutional use.

Special book excerpts or customized printings can also be created to fit specific needs. For details, write or phone the office of the Kensington special sales manager: Kensington Publishing Corp., 119 West 40th Street, New York, NY 10018, attn: Special Sales Department; phone 1-800-221-2647.

BRAVA and the B logo are Reg. U.S. Pat. & TM Off.

ISBN-13: 978-0-7582-4209-9
ISBN-10: 0-7582-4209-3

First Trade Paperback Printing: June 2012

10 9 8 7 6 5 4 3 2 1

Printed in the United States of America

CHAPTER ONE

Whitehall Palace, October 1546

The Viscount Gregory Biddeford was considered to be a handsome man, but Justina saw only his ambition, which made him hideous in her way of thinking.

"You have made me wait upon you, madam."

He touched the tips of his fingers against each other, lightly tapping them together. "For a woman who has so much to lose, I think your tardiness a foolish lapse of attention to the matter of making certain that I am pleased with you . . ."

His eyes narrowed. "In all that you do."

Justina suppressed the urge to cover herself. The viscount had not announced his entrance into her chamber, and she wore only a chemise. The fragile silk was translucent in places from the water that had dripped out of her freshly washed hair, making the thin fabric stick to her body. The viscount considered her curves with a flicker of lust in his eyes. However, she knew the man well enough to know that it would be simple to turn his attention away from her flesh in favor of reprimanding her for being bold enough to argue with him. The man's ego always reigned supreme over his lust.

"The Baron Ryppon is known for his dislike of being

betrayed, my lord. You knew that he would not fail to un-mask me once I had done your bidding and set his bride free during the night."

"You should have followed her out of the fortress. That solution was so simple, it could have been thought of by a child."

Justina had to force her temper down, which was sur-prising. Her time at Amber Hill seemed to have drained away some of her tolerance for the viscount's lashing tongue. The pompous ass always sent others to do his bid-ding while having no compassion for the difficulty of the tasks. He was dressed from head to toe in the latest fash-ions. Velvet sewn with pearls, bits of gold, and jewels was tailored to fit his frame precisely. Around his neck he wore the solid gold knight of the garter order with its Tudor rose medallions and depictions of St. George slaying the dragon. While she had been imprisoned on the border-land, the man who had sent her there had been busy vis-iting his tailor.

"If I had attempted to follow her, the guards would have been alerted to her escape. Once she was gone, I was trapped inside the walls until morning and could not es-cape being caught. The Baron Ryppon refused to allow me to leave once the deed was discovered."

Biddeford stepped closer, his gaze sliding down her body in a slow and insulting inspection. He reached out and touched her cheek, stroking his fingertips across her skin. A single shudder of distaste rippled across her in spite of her years of bowing to his will.

"Your time in that fortress weakened you, my sweet widow. Your feelings show on your face now." He leaned down, close enough that she felt his breath against her cheek. "That will never do."

He peered down the front of the gaping neckline of her

chemise, his gaze drinking in the sight of her nude breasts and nipples. Justina jerked away, revulsion flowing through her in a thick stream.

Biddeford chuckled. "As I stated, you are weak. That body is mine to command, madam. I am your guardian, and you shall be obedient to my will."

She wanted to narrow her eyes, but showing her real emotion was a luxury that she could ill afford. Instead she lowered her eyelashes to conceal the bright flash of her rebellion. "I did as you said, my lord."

The viscount waved his hand. "Ryppon's bride is irrelevant now. Lord Oswald has been given his expected treat in the form of another girl I was forced to find because you failed to deliver Bridget Newbury as I instructed you to. You have failed me."

"I showed Bridget the way from Amber Hill. She was well away. Her escort failed you by not being able to get her to the coast."

The viscount waved his hand again, this time his motion more impatient. "I told you, madam, it is irrelevant. While you have been locked away on the borderland, much has happened here at court. The King will die very soon."

"You should not say anything of that nature. Only God knows such a thing." Justina snapped at him before thinking.

A deadly look entered Biddeford's eyes. "Have you taken leave of your senses, madam? Has it somehow escaped your notice that I am the guardian of your son and his future is entirely within my power to direct? Perhaps you require a demonstration of my control over your future. I will send for Brandon and have him brought to court. For certain there will be something I can think to do with such a pretty little boy."

"You promised me that you will leave my son in the country." Rage flashed through her too hot to ignore but still she fought to conceal it. "I have done much, too much, to earn that from you."

"You seem to have forgotten that my word is good only so long as you obey me, madam." Biddeford drew in a stiff breath. "You shall keep that tongue pleasant when addressing me, and you had better be grateful that your beauty still shines enough to be of use to me. I care not what you think, madam, no one does. You are a woman, a vessel used to please men, You will serve me, and anyone I direct you to, else I shall have your son be brought to court. As we both know, there are men who prefer boys to women."

The chamber was so silent, Justina could hear her own heart beating. Part of her would have liked to die rather than submit, but the memory of her son's sweet face kept her alive. She was his only hope, his one protector, no matter what it took to shelter him from the depravity of the man standing in front of her. The law favored the viscount in every way since her husband had named him the guardian of their son. She was naught but a widow and her own family was gone.

The viscount took her silence as agreement. "Better. At least you seem to be able to learn quickly. Now, dress yourself and attend to the Princess Mary. The ambassador from Portugal has been sitting beside her most of the day, and I want to know what the man is saying to her."

The door closed behind the man, and she heard his escort fall into step with him. Shivers began to move down her back and along her limbs.

She dare not refuse . . .

A side door opened and two maids entered the chamber without a sound. The servants who lived in the palace were always wise enough to disappear when it was in their best interest, but they also heard everything, returning at precisely the moment they were needed. One knelt at her feet to help her into lace stockings secured with satin garters, while the other picked up a silver hairbrush and began pulling it through Justina's damp hair.

Anyone looking into the chamber might think her a lady being attended as her noble blood deserved, but in truth she was no better than any whore walking the dockside out of desperation, to earn enough coin to avoid seeing her children suffer. Just because she had finer clothing and a warm fire at hand did not change how she earned those comforts. The world seemed to hold little good for women. The most blessed gift she had ever received took every bit of her strength to protect.

Her son Brandon.

Justina allowed his face to surface from her memory while the maids continued to dress her. One of them picked up the pair of boy's britches she had used to escape from Baron Ryppon. The maid looked shocked, but Justina offered her no explanation for the male garments. For certain it was considered wrong for a female to wear such things as britches; the Church preached that it was unnatural for any woman to dress contrary to her gender. Only a woman possessed by the devil would do so. Those who liked to hunt witches often used the charge of wearing britches to help condemn their unfortunate prisoners.

Justina didn't plan to say even one prayer of repentance for the wearing of those boy's clothes. No one thought about stopping a young boy on the road. Every villager she had passed had taken little notice of her. They had assumed she was carrying a message and never thought she might be a woman who had bound her breasts to keep them from betraying her. She had even been tossed bread and cheese because the mare she rode was fine, and the woman who offered her the meal hoped that Justina would tell her master of the kindness. Perhaps send her a silver coin or two if she passed that way again.

Guilt did prick her for taking the food, but she had needed the strength to make it to Whitehall. She had to return and protect her son. What did it matter if she hated what she had become, so long as her child remained in the country, far removed from the depravity of court. Her own father was dead and that left her at the mercy of the guardian her husband's will named. The Viscount Biddeford was a relation of her husband and the man embodied the ideal of a noble family. He made sure that not one bit of silver went unaccounted for and that every person under his power did their share to advance his name and fortune.

He didn't care what method was needed, either. Justina refused to allow tears to gather in her eyes. Tears were a sign of weakness, and she wasn't the first woman who had been used to charm information out of a man by acting as his lover. As far as the viscount was concerned, her chastity had served its purpose when she wed a titled man, and whom she slept with now that she was widowed was something for him to direct. It shouldn't bother her, after all, she had never chosen her own lover, never laid down with a man she felt something more than even mild lust for. It shouldn't matter and yet, she discovered herself dwelling on it now. The viscount was correct about one thing; her time away from court had affected her. She wouldn't have thought that distance might cleanse her, scraping away the deceit and sin that felt as though it clung to her skin, but it had, because now she would have sworn that she could smell the stench of those around her who had blackened souls.

She turned and looked into an expensive and rare mirror. It was by far one of the finest things in the room, its surface showing her reflection with the help of the candlelight.

She was a beauty. As long as she could recall, she had been told that her complexion was flawless, creamy and smooth with lips that remained the color of spring berries without paint. Her nose was small and well shaped and her cheekbones high and slanted. She had a head of golden hair with a hint of red. Her father had delighted in her fair looks, clothing her in costly silk to show off her beauty. But he hadn't done it to celebrate her good fortune in being blessed with comely features; no, her sire had dangled her like a rare treat in front of men with bluer blood than his. Marriage offers had begun appearing on her father's desk by the time she was ten and before she saw her sixteenth natal day she was a wife. A coveted bride that her husband, the Baron Wincott, had delighted in parading through the court like a mare won from the auction block. He had lorded her possession over his friends, outlining every detail of their coupling without any concern for her tender modesty. Five of his fellow lords had been invited to the consummation of their union and the tears falling down her cheeks had not stopped her husband from stripping her bare in front of their lustful gazes. It had not been the only night her husband had allowed others to watch him using her. The baron was sick and depraved, and her married life had been one torrid night after the next, the only reprieve coming when she swelled with child and her husband sent her to the country because he found her round belly ugly.

No, she had no time for tears, or weakness, or admiring of her fair features. Her beauty was a curse and one that had brought her much suffering. Her life would have been far kinder if she were plain, for that would have seen her father wedding her to some quiet gentleman of modest means.

The maids brought her fine leather shoes that had been specially made for her feet. They had heels on them for dancing, and one maid fetched a silk ribbon with pearls dangling from the ends to tie each shoe with. Next came a farthingale. The slip was set with steel hoops that would hold out the skirts of her gown and keep the dress in its cone shape. A pair of stays was laced over her chest to raise and support her breasts. The maids lifted a heavy dress up and over her head. Justina raised her arms and the garment fell down in a flutter of brocade and velvet. The viscount made sure she was provided with the most recent fashions, and the gown was no exception. Set with a square neckline edged with costly velvet, the gown was constructed of brocade in hues of blue and silver to set off her blond hair. The neckline exposed the creamy swells of her breasts when the bodice was laced into position.

"A partlet, I believe."

One of the maids looked up and nibbled on her lip. "His lordship did not instruct us to dress you in a partlet, my lady."

The servant looked at the amount of flesh the gown exposed but still remained obedient to her employer's instructions. Justina was well accustomed to such but she had also learned long ago, when she had wiped her childbride's tears from her cheeks and refused to crumple at the feet of the men who felt they owned her, to be clever. She had discovered how to outthink the men around her because that was the only way that she, as a woman, might prevail.

"Yes, and you also heard the viscount tell me to attend the Princess Mary. Her highness is known for her modesty and does not tolerate ladies who do not recall that facet of her disposition. Without a partlet, I doubt I will attend her very long."

The servant's eyes widened with understanding. "Oh yes, you are very astute, my lady. The viscount will be pleased."

Pleased . . . yes, that was what Justina needed. For the man to be satisfied with her. A ripple of something that felt very much like resentment went through her. The emotion surprised her because she had banished such feelings long ago. If she had not, she would have gone insane.

The Church would tell her that she deserved what Biddeford gave her for being so relieved when her husband died. She had been relieved and overjoyed and a hundred other emotions that had nothing to do with grief. But such elation had been short lived. The viscount had sent for her, and the moment she appeared at court, the man had begun directing her to use her cursed beauty to snare the secrets that he desired.

The maid returned with a simple over-partlet that was little more than a yoke, sewn at the shoulders with a collar. It fit perfectly on top of the dress and tied beneath her arms. The maid used pearl-topped pins to secure it at the center front of the neckline. Constructed of silk, the fabric covered her breasts up to her collarbones, leaving only a slim inch of skin on display where the two fronts met. It was set with a collar that had lace edging and more pearls.

"That should meet with her highness's approval." The maid had spoken before she thought, and ducked her chin when she realized that she had indeed uttered her thoughts without being asked for her opinion. She hurried to finish dressing her and Justina remained silent.

They were both caught in the net of rules that held them down. Just because she was addressed as a lady made little difference. She was a servant as sure as the woman fussing with her cuffs.

The other maid had dressed her hair and Justina moved

to the door the moment they both stopped picking at the details of her dressing. At least going to attend the princess was not a horrible thing. She would save her hesitating for times when the viscount pointed her toward truly sordid things.

Brandon . . . she thought of her son and her lips lifted with true joy. No one need know why she smiled.

Curan Ramsden, Lord Ryppon, stood on his front steps to watch his second in command take leave of the castle for the final time.

"I believe I shall miss Synclair. He's served me as a second in command very well, I shall be hard pressed to find anyone as skilled."

His wife, Bridget Newbury, drew a quick jerk from him because he had been so focused on the knight making ready to leave. His wife offered him a slight curving of her lips as she joined him. The minx enjoyed being able to sneak up on him.

"Synclair has performed his duty with honor. It is time for him to return to his family."

"That isn't where he is going." Bridget kept her voice low so that it would not carry. His wife was the model of submission except for when no one else might hear her.

Curan admitted to enjoying that facet of her personality quite well behind the closed door of their chamber.

"Synclair didn't say where he was going, and he owes me no telling of what is on his mind now that his time of service is finished."

His wife smothered a small sound of amusement. "You choose not to ask because we both know full well that he is going to pursue Lady Wincott.

"We do? I am not certain of any such thing."

His wife frowned at him. "I see, my lord husband, then am I to understand that you gave him a parchment, sealed

with your crest, to deliver to the King because you expect
him to ride to his lands and hand it over to a rider there?"

Curan chuckled softly. "I didn't ask him, but in the
event that he does go to court, I sent the missive with him.
You are too concerned with others' affairs, Wife."

Bridget offered her husband a calculating glance; he returned a guarded one that she answered with a widening
of her eyes and a flutter of her eyelashes. Bridget offered
him a sweet smile that held no more meaning, nor intelligence, than a springtime duckling. Curan laughed, his rich
voice full of amusement.

Bridget waved one hand in the air and allowed her features to return to normal. "I am also not simple, and you
like that too much, Husband."

"That is true, even if I find your ability to mask your
thoughts quite entertaining . . . that is when it is being directed at someone else."

Curan reached down to where his wife's belly was gently rounding. Their first child was growing in spite of the
winter closing its grip over the land. Snow flurries drifted
in the air, melting when they made it to the ground. Synclair was tense, the knight intent on checking his horse before he mounted. He reached out to tug on a strap and
then another, walking all the way around the horse before
nodding with approval.

That had always been the man's way. Synclair left nothing to chance, no detail overlooked. He had served out his
time with a diligence that was worthy of the knight's chain
he wore. Synclair lifted one booted foot and placed it in
the stirrup before rising in a single fluid motion to gain
the saddle. His body was powerful and accomplished the
task with ease, giving testimony to the years the man had
trained. Two white plumes topped his helmet, proclaim-
ing his rank to anyone approaching him.

Somehow, Curan didn't think that Lady Wincott needed

to see Synclair riding toward her. Unless he missed his guess, the lady would feel the knight closing in on her. His own sister had gifted her mare to Justina so that she might flee back to court. Curan wished Jemma hadn't interfered. One more day and Synclair would have been free to claim the lady.

Synclair never looked back but set his spurs into the belly of his stallion and leaned down low over the neck of the animal when it lunged forward. A small party of men followed the knight newly released from service. These were Harrow retainers, men who had been waiting for their lord to finish his sworn duty.

"I do hope Justina is looking over her shoulder, Husband."

"Come now, Wife, do you wish her to be any easier to bring to heel than you were?"

His wife frowned at him. "Bring to heel?"

Her complexion darkened as she chewed on his choice of words. "I was attempting to be a dutiful daughter."

Curan felt his own mood darken. "I believe Justina feels she is doing the same, but I for one hope Synclair can interfere in that duty."

His wife lost her annoyed look. "As do I."

For love was worth the sacrifice of pride.

The palace, despite being full of people, was unnaturally hushed. Justina made her way through the hallways, feeling the eyes of the people she passed rest on her. They inspected her, critiquing her poise and every detail about her person from the position of her hands to the angle she held her chin. Fans lifted and ladies leaned closer together to whisper about her, not really caring if she noticed. When one was at court, it was simply best to expect to be talked about; when one did the things that she had done, gossip was sure to follow.

"Lady Wincott."

Francis de Canis drew her name out in a low tone that left no doubt in her mind that the man was debating just how high her price was. He was a dangerous man, one who sold his services to high-born nobles and didn't quibble over spilling blood in the process of delivering what he'd promised.

He didn't wait for her to offer her hand but instead reached out and captured it while she was completing her curtsy.

"I must say, it is a delight to see you gracing these hallways once more."

"How kind of you to say."

Justina didn't tug on her hand; resistance would only encourage a man such as he. He thrived on making conquests, and putting up a fight was sure to cause him to double his efforts to claim her. He raised her hand to his lips and pressed an overly long kiss against the back of her hand, but he stared into her eyes while his mouth lingered over her skin. Lust darkened his eyes along with the unmistakable flicker of arrogant intention to have her at his mercy.

Justina offered him naught save for a bland expression. His fingers tightened around hers before releasing.

"We must see more of each other, now that you are returned. You will have to tell the Viscount that."

"The Viscount Biddeford is my most dear cousin by marriage. His very great kindness to me since my husband died makes it impossible for me to do anything so bold as to tell him what to do."

Justina lowered her lashes to conceal just how revolting she found his suggestion. The man hunted amid the court for any woman he considered to be wanted by other men. Well, she knew a thing or two about how to survive at court, and one was to use formal politeness to gain her way. It pleased her to be able to give a man such as de Canis such empty words because he was a man that enjoyed having women kept beneath the heels of other men. Let him watch that same meekness being used against him for a change.

"But does he show his appreciation of your devotion as well as I might?" There was a hint of a promise in his voice but one she would be foolish to take sanctuary in. She would only be trading one monster for another. De Canis would use her and then sell her without a care to who bought her favors, so long as he was well pleased with the transaction.

"As I said, he is most dear because of the great concern he lavishes upon me. I do not believe there is a single hour of the day that he is not sure of where I am. He is very careful to make sure I am well settled in every moment."

Aye, well settled and well paid for . . .

"Yes, I have heard that he keeps you close, Lady Wincott. Which accounts for my surprise in discovering you here. Quite alone as it seems."

"I am to attend her majesty the Princess Mary."

"Ah . . ." He boldly reached out and trailed one finger across the surface of her partlet. Beneath it, the swell of her breast felt his touch, and she fought the urge to cringe.

"That would explain you covering up such delightful treats."

He was daring her to show her true temper and abandon her meekness. Justina brushed by de Canis but not before she heard him chuckle. The man had a habit of decorating his lovers with expensive jewelry, proving that in spite of his common birth, he was a man of means.

He wasn't the only one walking the halls of Whitehall Palace. There were new men of means who owed their fortunes to the sacking of the monasteries and cathedrals. King Henry Tudor handed out the riches to those who aided him in driving the last of the Catholic Church from England, but he took much of that money back when those common men came to him to buy titles.

It was a petty circle, one fueled by greed, and now that King Henry Tudor was dying, the fighting over what was left was growing more frantic. The King's only son, Edward, was a boy of nine. True power would be held by the men named in the King's will to govern for the young prince whom King Henry had spent so much effort trying to have.

Justina turned a corner and discovered the Princess Mary strolling on the green with her half sister, the Princess Elizabeth. The weather was cold now and the grass more brown than green, but the two sisters walked side by side while surrounded by onlookers.

Justina had to force a lump down her throat before she could walk any further. The onlookers sickened her with their sly glares and whispers. Mary Tudor was a grown woman now, but her father had never seen her wed. Both sisters had spent many years labeled as bastards while the King married again and again in pursuit of more sons. Only now, at the end of his life, was Henry Tudor spending time with his daughters. It was Queen Catherine Parr who urged her husband to do so but Justina couldn't do anything save pity the two princesses for the rough road both had been given by life.

"The Lady Justina, Dowager Baroness Wincott."

The chamberlain announced her and struck the stone walkway with his white staff while Justina lowered herself. Neither princess even looked at her, but several heads turned in her direction as she joined the crowd. Newly arrived daughters stood in their fine dresses near their mothers or guardians while they hoped to be noticed by someone important. Justina moved through the crowd, offering curtsies to many but avoiding engaging in true conversations. People were pressed almost too close in their quest to be near the royals, everyone talking in hushed tones while they tried to think of ways to gain whatever they wanted. Justina moved through them, intent on the same thing, to gain enough of the princesses' attention to satisfy Biddeford.

"Lady Wincott." Another chamberlain struck the stone walkways, startling her.

Justina faltered for a moment because she had not expected her name to be called so soon. She recovered quickly, hurrying to the man wearing the tabard of the King. She lowered herself and waited for the princesses to raise her, but it was an older woman who spoke.

Queen Catherine Parr was much younger than her husband, and she sat beneath a canopy with her ladies. In fact, there was not a single gentleman beneath the fabric, the chamberlain standing a full twenty feet away.

"Yes, Your Majesty?"

The Queen set her embroidery aside, looking disgusted by it. She changed her expression quickly, as though she had made a great error in allowing any emotion to show. A smooth expression appeared on her face as she looked at Justina.

"It is said that you have returned from the high country."

"Yes, I have."

The Queen folded her hands perfectly and sat them in her lap. "Perhaps you might sit and offer us a bit of entertainment with details of your travels."

"Of course. Is there something in particular Your Majesty would like to hear about?"

The Queen tried to sound happy but there was a hint of boredom in her tone. Justina nodded and stepped forward while a chill went down the back of her neck. There was a tension beneath the canopy she had not felt from the

Queen before. Her ladies cut quick glances between one another before they all folded their hands and adopted the same posture that the Queen did. Each looked like a doll that had been carefully dressed and posed by its owner. The rest of the court pressed forward but were kept behind the chamberlain so that no one was near the Queen. Not one of her ladies moved or spoke, they simply waited. The Queen kept her hands folded and seemed to search for a question.

"Were the flowers and clover in bloom?"

It was quite a benign topic and one that stunned Justina. Catherine Parr was well known for her love of books and study. It was one of the reasons Henry the Eighth enjoyed her company. It was known that she often debated theology with the King when they were in privy. She had been heard to say that such debates took his mind off his leg wound and that she was happy to be able to ease his pain.

And today she asked about flowers and clover . . .

There was a hint of fear in the Queen's eyes and a pinched look around her lips. Justina felt the tension wrap around her and she clasped her hands together, just as sedately as Catherine Parr was doing.

"The clover was indeed quite lovely during the summer . . ."

Justina didn't know why, but she could feel the anxiety in the air, so she spoke of springtime foolishness, and noted with unease that the Queen seemed to listen intently.

The Queen retired early, taking her ladies and the princesses with her. Justina forced her expression to be smooth while she walked the distance to her rooms. Being housed in the palace was the doing of Biddeford, but for the moment she was pleased to not need to travel to a townhome for the night. That would have required her to either ride or take a carriage. She might wait quite some time for her carriage or mare to be brought up from the stables because they were an entire city block from the main palace. The only way to ensure her mare was brought forward soon would be to press some silver into the groom's hand.

Her chambers were very nice, if a bit small. She had two windows and they were a very nice luxury for they allowed the rooms to be aired out. Many of the interior rooms had the scent of smoke lingering halfway down their walls from the fires that had kept their inhabitants warm during the winter months.

But her chambers were not as private as she might have liked. The viscount sat at the table in the front room, sipping expensive French wine from a glass goblet. His manservant stood silently behind him which was a reminder to her that Biddeford considered himself worthy of service at all times of the day.

"Do you like it?" He held one of the glass goblets up so that the candlelight shone through it. The wine in the glass was visible, and he tilted the glass back and forth to display its translucent ability.

"A gift from the King." Smug satisfaction coated his voice while he took another sip from the delicate glass. Justina stood and waited while he set the goblet down. There was a flicker of his eyelashes, indicating that he knew she waited on him, but he did not grant her permission to sit. The heels were digging into her feet now and the skirt of the gown had begun making her lower back ache hours ago, but she could not sit in the presence of her better without his leave.

"How did you find our Queen?" There was thicker smugness in his voice now and a satisfied gleam in his eyes as well.

"Her Majesty was very welcoming."

"You mean she was boring and meek." Biddeford

chuckled. "Yes, our dear Queen almost found herself in the tower like so many of her predecessors."

Justina failed to smother her gasp of horror. The viscount tapped the table while smiling at her.

"Chancellor Wriothesley had the arrest warrant penned and the guard marching off to take her away when she somehow learned of the affair and threw herself on the ground at the King's feet to beg for mercy." Biddeford waved his hand through the air. "To beg for her life, actually."

Justina felt her own throat contracting. There was no way to ignore the rising horror that filled her; the look of enjoyment in Biddeford's eyes doubled it.

"The clever woman managed to soothe the King's ego by spouting some nonsense that she had argued with him only to distract him from his festering wound. She burned her books and told her ladies to follow her example. She therefore kept her head, for the moment." He reached out to finger the thin stem of the wineglass. "She has been properly submissive ever since, a rather good example of how a woman should conduct herself if she wants to live."

He took another sip from the wine. "However, Chancellor Wriothesley lost some of his influence over the King during the matter of the Queen's investigation. Edward Seymour has been enjoying His Majesty's company a little too much for my taste since then. Seymour will be hunting tomorrow. Make sure you ride with his party."

"I thought you detested the Earl of Hertford. He must know that I am your servant."

The viscount stood, his enjoyment fading. "I do hate him, which is why I want you to ride near the man. Since you spent so much time with Ryppon, it is possible the man will believe you have changed your allegiances, even if you can do nothing to change the legal fact that I am your guardian. Let him see you looking pitiful and needy.

He's been known to have a softness for pretty women. We shall exploit that if he is foolish enough to take the bait."

Biddeford left, his manservant stepping forward to pick up the wineglass before following his master. Justina felt her heart beating softly, as though it was afraid to make too much noise. Now she realized what it was that she had felt around the Queen and princesses today. Fear, thick and choking, it hung over them like a fog that made everyone want to speak only in the most hushed of tones.

The chamber door closed and she winced at the sharp sound it made. Her heart instantly began beating faster, the feeling of being trapped tightening around her until she felt the need to run. Fast and as far as her legs might carry her away from the hideous man who had just invaded her chambers.

Of course that was the entire point of Biddeford's visit tonight. He knew the art of intimidation well, understood how to upset any sense of balance she might gain for herself. A tremor traveled over her body, followed by another and still more until she was quivering. Fear, thick enough to taste, permeated the air.

The maids returned and helped her disrobe with nothing but pinched looks on their faces. Justina longed for darkness and sleep to give her relief from some of the dread, but when she lay in bed at last, in nothing but her chemise, there was no peace to be found. Instead another face rose from her mind, one that sent tears to burn her eyes. Her fearful mind reached for this memory, needing the strength that shone from his eyes.

Synclair . . .

The man she had no right to long for or even think about. He was her opposite, everything honorable, while she was scarlet with sin. The knight had been sworn to serve Lord Ryppon and he had done so obediently. It had been Synclair who locked her away once her treachery was discovered, but he had not done so with disgust. The knight had boldly claimed a kiss from her that she still felt lingering on her lips.

You feel that kiss because you are too weak to ignore the memory . . .

So true, and still she allowed herself to sink into her mind's recollection of the way the knight had felt against her. Somehow, she had never really thought that a man might feel so good, that she might take pleasure from his harder body. His kiss had been hard and punishing, demanding a response she had been powerless to deny him. For a few precious moments, her mouth had mimicked his, returning that kiss because she longed to, not out of obligation to her husband, or because she had been ordered to by the viscount. One sweet kiss that she recalled because it was genuine, but it was also a cruel torment because after the rush of sweet enjoyment, her mind returned to the times she had used her kisses to deceive. Misery wrapped around her as she saw Synclair standing so stiffly on the walls of Amber Hill, attending to his duty while always casting looks toward her tower-top room.

She had rejected him. Pushed him away and labeled him a blackard.

That was a kindness on her part.

Synclair was noble and pristine. He deserved a wife who matched his virtue with her own. It didn't really matter anymore. She had left the knight far behind and the memory of his kiss was the only thing she would ever have of him.

The tears fell down her cheeks, but the darkness allowed her the luxury of not having to fight them. Instead she wept for the innocent bride she had been and the disappointment her husband had turned out to be. Knowing Synclair made her pain even worse for she knew that there were men worthy of the innocent she had been. There were knights who ladies might save themselves for and have their affections rewarded with faithfulness and honor.

Of course, that was not her lot, and the Church would tell her not to argue with God for what He had given her.

Well, she wanted to do much more than argue; she wanted to rail against the injustice of her life.

But most of all, she wanted to be worthy of Synclair, and she cried with the knowledge that she could never clean away enough of the sin clinging to her body to ever be good enough for him.

CHAPTER TWO

Attending court left little time for sleep. Justina awoke when the horizon was turning dusty rose. Her maids were blurry eyed and rubbed the sleep away from their eyes when they thought she wasn't watching. Anyone who drew their pay from the Viscount Biddeford earned every silver penny, and the slump of both girls' shoulders confirmed that they were enduring the man's harsh demands.

A hunting dress was pressed and ready for her today. No doubt the maids had spent several hours ironing the dress and polishing her shoes for the morning hunt. Even the hat had its feathers steamed and curled and the wool newly brushed free of every speck of dirt. Like everything at court, hunting was yet another time to observe and be observed. Her dress must be perfect down to the smallest details.

How she loathed it. Putting on a pretty dress was fun so long as it was not another chore.

Justina stepped into hose and shoes once again, only this time the shoes were more practical, lacking the high heels. They were tied with sturdy leather, and her garters were wool instead of silk. The dress was much more comfortable. Instead of a slip set with stiff hoops, there was only an underskirt of soft wool to keep her legs warm. The skirt was hemmed just above her toes, and it lacked the pull on her back of the court gown she had endured the day before. Today she wore a doublet buttoned to her neck and a more loosely fit set of stays. There were no pearls to worry about snagging, and the hat the maids brought forward was felted wool and, beside the feathers, only a ribbon to enhance it.

She liked the dress, liked it full well.

Yes, the time in the borderland had certainly left its mark upon her. There had been no need of court fashion at Amber Hill, and Justina admitted that she had a fondness for the lack of pomp and ceremony.

"You'd best hurry, my lady. The earl will be letting his hounds loose soon."

It was a bold thing for a maid to say to her mistress but Justina understood what prompted the woman to speak. If the viscount was displeased, they would all suffer. There was no difference between them, no matter who wore the finer clothing.

The maid had spoken truly, though. Justina neared the south gate and heard the hounds howling with excitement. The Earl of Hertford's household was turned out in large numbers and a great many of the court were also in attendance. The yard was a mass of horses and pages all attempting to ready the animals for riding. The sky was turning rosy pink now with yellow and orange streaking through it. Dark clouds were beginning to drift overhead, promising a storm before afternoon. The sound of trumpets broke through the buzz of conversations and the hounds yelped in response. The large animals pulled against their grooms, knowing the sound of the beginning of the hunt well. A group near the gate surged forward, with the colors of Hertford flying behind them. They took to the road, the hounds leading the way and falcons and hawks perched on arms with their leather hoods still in

place. That didn't keep the birds from showing their growing excitement. They moved their heads with sharp motions in spite of the leather covering them, and they
flapped their wings, causing their handlers to make soothing sounds.

Justina mounted her mare and hooked her knee over
the saddle horn. It was a precarious seat, but since Anne
Boleyn had lost her head, women were wise to avoid riding like men. The former queen had been well known for
her love of riding astride but it had been yet another
charge used to condemn her.

The crisp air turned her cheeks cold and Justina leaned
low over the neck of her mare to ride faster. She left behind her the aspiring daughters of nobles who were only
there to be seen and possibly offered for, along with the
good wives who attended in order to gossip. Riding away
from the palace filled her with joy, and she urged her mare
faster, allowing herself to live only in that moment, when
there was nothing but the open forest. Her heart beat
faster and her shoulders lost much of the tension that had
been keeping her on edge since her return. Once they
reached the woods, the falcons were loosed to spread their
wings out and fly overhead.

Justina tipped her head back, grateful for the long steel
pin that kept her hat in place while she watched the rap-
tors soar over the top of the trees. She envied them, but
smiled as she watched the way they floated far above
everything.

She did know how to smile.

Synclair watched Justina, drinking in the sight of her.

Had it truly been only a few days since he'd seen her
last? His lower back ached from too many hours in the
saddle, but it was worth it because he'd managed to find
the woman he'd spent too many hours thinking about.

Her face inhabited his dreams, and he heard her voice when the morning was still dark but he was walking the walls and searching the night for signs of invaders. Whenever there was nothing for his mind to do, his thoughts filled with her. No amount of discipline seemed able to banish his addiction to her. The thing that doubled his frustration was the way the lady ran from him. This time, she had truly taken to the road to escape him.

That roused his temper because of the risk she'd taken. No woman should be pushed to such lengths; it was dishonorable of a man to do so. True honor was not the pride-filled nonsense that was so often displayed at court. He watched her and drank in the sight of her sitting safely on the side of her mare. It was a fine sight, one that he was determined to see more often.

Some might label it an obsession. Synclair didn't know, but he was sure of one fact—he was going to put whatever was between them to the test. At last, at long last, because the single kiss he'd stolen from her was as fresh in his mind as the ale he'd consumed at midday.

Only far sweeter.

He guided his stallion closer to his prey. He'd spent hours watching her, waiting on her to emerge from her tower at Amber Hill so that he might approach her. Things would be different now. The rules that had governed his behavior while he was sworn to serve the Baron Ryppon were no longer binding him. He could feel something dark rising up inside him. It had kept him awake too many nights to count while his flesh burned for the touch of the woman intent on refusing him.

He chuckled softly. He still felt the sting of her hand across his jaw but all that did was increase his need to taste her honeyed lips once more. There was something between them and it was not just he who felt it. She might

tridge-pleated material, holding her in place when her own movement would have carried her over the side of the mare.

"What are you doing at court?"

She couldn't deal with him back at court when she was forced to remain, too. Something flashed in his eyes, a warning that cut through her like a knife. Her breath became lodged in her throat.

"Following you, Justina."

He spoke her name in a rough voice before stretching out his arm and allowing her body to slide down the side of the saddle. Even as shock held her in its grasp, she was amazed at the amount of strength in his body. He controlled her descent to the ground, lifting one leg up and over her mare so that he sat for a brief moment on top of the animal before he followed her to the ground. He might have simply released her skirt and dismounted from his own horse but he refused to allow her to drop so carelessly. His solid strength supported her all the way to the ground, while he followed her. It happened in a moment but her mind was frozen in shock, making every action slower and more noticeable.

"Did you doubt that I would follow you?" He made a low sound that communicated how frustrated he was. The tone of it made her tremble, an instant response that she neither considered nor controlled. It simply happened, just as heat began burning a path along her arms and up her neck, before it reached her face to set her cheeks on fire. Words failed her, her thoughts centering on the blush staining her face.

To think that she might still be capable of blushing . . . Such an innocent action felt misplaced but it also sent a tingle of excitement through her heart.

Synclair lifted a hand and gently stroked her face before

she shook off her astonishment. "How could you doubt that I would follow, Justina? I spoke my intentions clearly to you at Amber Hill."

"Your intentions?" She stepped away from him, not because his touch offended her, but to escape the sheer enjoyment of having his skin against her own. "You locked me in a chamber."

"Only for a week, and then you were given the freedom of the castle. Considering the peril you allowed Bridget to run into when you showed her the way out of Amber Hill, a week was a small penance. But it was by Lord Ryppon's order and one designed for your protection. Your guardian is unfit. He sent you to deceive us and send Bridget into the night where she might have been harmed. Keeping you in the castle was to prevent you from returning to a guardian who has no conscience about how he uses you." His voice was edged with hard command, but instead of striking her as arrogant, Synclair seemed worthy of the tone. His eyes sliced into hers. "You were the one who kept to your chamber after that, Lady. It was no simple task to meet you outside it."

And yet he had managed it far too often for her faltering self-discipline. Each time he'd managed to intercept her had chiseled away at her resolve to push him away. Now, with his eyes on her again, she could feel every hole in the walls around her heart.

"I had to sequester myself because you lacked the sense to stay away from me." He was too large and too tempting. Justina stepped away from him, needing distance to regain her composure. There were solid reasons why she could not allow him to pursue her; she simply couldn't think of any of them at the moment.

"If either of us lacks sense, Lady, it is you." Synclair didn't follow her. The knight swallowed further words before they crossed his lips, frustration darkening his face. He gripped his wide belt and drew in a deep breath.

"Your guardian is unjust, Justina."

"That is not uncommon nor does it change the fact that he is my guardian."

He took a step toward her. "That does not excuse him." Fury edged his words, noble fire that stole the breath from her lungs. All of her reasons for refusing him flew back into her mind. Her knees nearly buckled beneath the weight.

Justina clasped her hands together, making herself steady and poised for the rejection she must give him.

Synclair didn't give her the chance. He closed the gap between them, his hand cupping her chin and holding it.

"Do not waste yet more of your breath." There was a hard warning glittering in his eyes and his tone was as sharp as steel.

"I must. You cannot champion me."

"I assure you, Justina, I can."

She drew in a deep breath, frustration biting into her. Trust the man to take her words as an insult.

"It is not a matter of your ability; I am not a good match for you."

The fingers clasping her chin tightened to the point of discomfort but he stiffened and forced his grip to relax before true pain needled her. He lifted his hand away and she pulled in a deep breath, determined to cut him with her next words and send him away before he was smeared with the stains of her sins. She couldn't bear that idea, and it tormented her unmercifully.

"That is my choice, madam, and what I have decided is that you shall be mine."

"Synclair—"

He moved lightning quick once more, reaching out to

slide one arm around her waist and pull her against his body. He also stepped forward so that she felt like he was capturing her, and indeed the knight was. She felt his strength wrap around her in a solid curtain that blocked out everything except him.

"Mine, Lady. I swear it to you."

Swear . . . For a man such as he, that was a solemn oath. She witnessed it flickering in his eyes as her breath lodged in her throat. Justina shook her head, every fiber of her being refusing to allow him to come anywhere near her sordid life.

"I have said it, Justina, and I plan to keep my word."

His mouth claimed hers in a motion that was forceful and demanding. She leaned away from him, seeking escape from her own longing for him. The hand that had cupped her chin found the back of her head and held it steady while his mouth reclaimed hers. There was no further way to avoid his kiss. He took her mouth, demanding that her lips part to allow the kiss to deepen.

God help her, she wanted to do exactly that.

Running through her was a current of excitement she had never felt before. In spite of her husband and lovers, a single kiss had never sent her blood racing through her body at such a speed that her head spun in a lightheaded manner. She had never noticed that a man's mouth might taste sweet.

Synclair's did.

A soft moan rose from her chest, somehow escaping through their joined lips, and the kiss changed. Synclair still held her hostage to his demands but his lips began to slip and slide across her own, gently teasing her lower lip before she felt the tip of his tongue flick over the sensitive skin. She shivered. Enjoyment took command of her body, making it impossible to control her responses. For all her experience, she discovered that she was powerless against his kiss because of the sweet sensation it unleashed upon her.

"Your body craves my touch, Justina. I can feel you trembling in my arms."

She clamped her mouth closed against a sharp cry because she had never heard Synclair use such a tone before. It was deep and husky, touching off a moment of panic because she recognized how devastating that voice would be. She would become enchanted by it, in but a few more words.

"I am no stranger to lust."

He growled at her, the hand holding the back of her head tightening while his eyes narrowed with his displeasure. She could see his temper straining against his control and the battle mesmerized her.

"Do not belittle yourself, Justina."

She pushed against his chest, struggling when she knew that the only way she might be free was by his will. "Release me now."

He grunted but his embrace opened, allowing her to place distance between them. She felt chilled the moment she moved, her body lamenting the steps that she took away from him. The skin of her lips was suddenly more sensitive than it had ever been, longing for her to return to him and offer him a kiss in return for the one he had given her.

"I am honest with you, Synclair. I have no more liking for it than you. Yet it is the truth. You must not seek me out."

"And you, madam, would be wise to learn that I am not given to making declarations lightly."

He meant what he said, she could hear the determination in his voice. It was there in his expression, too, and Justina discovered she had too much liking for the way he looked when he was staring at her. It was so tempting to sink into his gaze and allow it to wrap around her like a cloak that could cut the chill of life's injustices.

A blast from a hunting horn broke through the early morning from somewhere back in the trees. The sound startled the horses, sending a twist of fright through her belly as she heard the stallion snort; if the animal reared up they would be directly beneath its sharp hooves. Synclair twisted in an instant and reached for the reins of his stallion, gripping the leather just as the horse was rising up. With a powerful motion of his thick arms, he controlled the huge animal, moving in a slow circle as he soothed it with several long strokes down its face. Justina blew out a stiff breath as relief tingled across her skin.

Hounds suddenly swarmed through the trees, weaving around the trunks while they pressed their noses to the ground.

"Do my eyes deceive me? Synclair, man, when did you rejoin the court? I thought you were with Baron Ryppon."

It was the Earl of Hertford who came through the trees, his voice cutting through the silence. But his attention settled on her, his gaze sharp and questioning.

"Good day to you, Lady Wincott. I had not heard that you were returned to court either."

Justina lowered herself, but Synclair answered the earl before she rose again.

"Lady Wincott passed the summer with Baron Ryppon and myself at Amber Hill."

Edward Seymour, brother of the late queen, Jane Seymour, leaned over to offer his hand to Synclair. It was a mark of high regard from a man who held an extremely high position in England, thanks to the fact that his sister had given Henry the Eighth the son he longed for so much. He was a prince in everything but blood, and since Prince Edward Tudor was only nine years old, the earl would most likely have a great deal of power while the boy grew up.

"Has Ryppon given you leave for your service to him then?"

"I am finished with my time, my vow completed and satisfied."

The earl nodded. "An excellent time to be finished with your training. I can use a man like you by my side."

The hounds began to howl with excitement, and the earl turned his attention to them.

"Join me, man. We'll catch some supper to enjoy together."

The earl didn't wait for them; he kneed his stallion and set off after his hounds.

Justina had taken advantage of their conversation to reclaim her mare. The animal had shied away from Synclair's stallion and was searching through the fallen autumn leaves for grass, but there was little left alive. Running a soothing hand along the neck of the mare, Justina grabbed a handful of her skirt to allow her to place her foot in the stirrup. She was keenly aware that they were once more alone.

A shiver crossed her skin. She was far too sensitive to the knight, one of the reasons she had taken to the road to escape him. She lacked the strength to resist the pull she felt toward him.

Two hands closed around her waist, drawing a gasp from her startled lips. Synclair lifted her easily to the back of her mare, his lips twitching with amusement when she stared into his eyes with astonishment. Many a man boasted of his strength, but there were few who might actually prove it. Among those, she had rarely discovered one who knew how to control his grip such as Synclair seemed able to do. His embrace had been solid, yet pain-

less. She felt her resolve weakening even further because
to have a man that was considerate of his strength for a
lover must be pure delight.

It was something she must not allow herself to taste, but
she saw in his eyes the intention to make his touch intimate. Synclair didn't hide it from her, and let her view the
desire darkening his eyes. A chill went down her back,
spreading out over her skin until it reached her breasts.
Behind her corset, her nipples drew into hard beads, startling her with the quickness of the response.

"You should not." She didn't finish her warning because
it was too difficult to form into words what she wanted
him to refrain from doing, and she feared that her voice
betrayed her growing desire. It was more than his touch,
it was the way his blue eyes probed hers and the way her
belly tightened just because she knew he was closing the
distance between them.

"And you should not protest when you enjoyed my kiss
so well."

Her hand gripped his, where it still sat at her waist, pry-
ing at his fingers to remove them, but he captured only
her hand, pulling his fingers along her bare palm before
relinquishing his hold on her.

"It is a pity we were interrupted, Justina. I promise to
remedy that."

Her eyes widened once again and she scoffed at herself.
Such lack of control was unlike her and destined to land
her in a great deal of misery.

"Do not. There is nothing for us to talk about."

Synclair moved to his horse and gained the saddle in another fluid motion that left no doubt about how much
strength the man had in his body. The stallion turned in a
circle, demonstrating that it was a fit mount for the knight
who rode him. The animal snorted, shaking its head while
pawing at the ground with eager anticipation.

"I disagree, Justina."

Only three words, but they sounded like a sentence being issued by a magistrate. She felt them as much as she heard them, her body quivering with trepidation. Synclair shot a hard look at her before giving his stallion its freedom. The animal surged forward and her mare followed instantly. She tried to pull the reins up to slow the mare, but heard Synclair chuckle in response to her efforts.

"The mare has more wisdom than you, Justina." He turned to look at her. "She does not fight against what she craves."

The mare was increasing her speed to catch the stallion, and the stallion tossed its head again to encourage the mare. Justina felt her face turn red with her temper.

She was not a mare.

Lust would not control her, not now, not ever. She refused to crumple in the face of her emotions. Even if she did enjoy his kiss, there was nothing to be gained from yielding to such pleasure. The only thing that would happen would be more despair when the viscount decided to whom she would be sent. She would be tormented by the lack of enjoyment she found in that bed, because she would now know what it felt like to enjoy being kissed.

Better to never know. It would be far wiser for her to bury the need clamoring inside her so deeply that it might never rise up to tempt her.

Better . . . wiser . . . and more lonely than she had ever felt.

Yet that was the way life was.

Biddeford was waiting in her chambers again. Whitehall Palace had several secret passageways, and she had been placed in her current chambers to ensure that the man might come and go without being witnessed. Still trying to regain her composure, Justina was far from pleased to see him. She needed sanctuary, a place to collect her thoughts and seal them behind her poise once more.

It seemed she was going to be denied that as well. She frowned and turned her back on the viscount under the guise of placing her riding gloves on the table, but she could not remain there for long.

"You did well this morning."

Justina didn't enjoy the compliment. Any form of praise coming from Biddeford always had an ulterior motive. She could see the way the man's eyes shifted while he plotted. In a way, she pitied him, because he never seemed satisfied. He wore the finest clothing and supped on the best food. He didn't reek from hours spent breaking his back in the fields, and still the man struggled to gain more.

"I was quite surprised to see you riding with the Earl of Hertford, but that pleased me greatly. What was he talking about?"

"Hunting."

The viscount frowned at her, his eyes narrowing. A trickle of fear made its way through her.

"He wasn't talking to me but to Sir Synclair, who is newly returned from the north."

"I noticed such." Biddeford paused for a moment while he considered that fact. "Synclair desires your sweet body."

"He does not." The words left her mouth too quickly and too sharply. Justina turned her face away and sat her hat on top of a table to conceal her expression while she struggled to regain her composure.

The viscount clicked his tongue in reprimand. She heard his steps behind her and she stiffened as revulsion went through her. He was going to touch her and she hated his fingers upon her flesh. Today, she had to fight the urge to cringe because her emotions were so unruly.

He turned her to face him and tapped her chin with one finger.

"Yes, you were separated from me too long." He leaned closer, so that she felt his breath against her cheek. "I suggest you find your balance, sweet Justina, else I shall have to design some task that will firmly remind you whom your master is."

He placed a kiss against her neck, and she shivered with distaste. Bitterness filled her mouth to the point that she had to fend off retching. She discovered herself agreeing with him because she had been away too long and now she knew that there were places where life was decent such as it had been when she was with Lord Ryppon. Such knowledge bred a desire to escape from everything at court but her son's fate would not allow such. She swallowed her distaste, forcing it deep so that she might turn to look at the viscount with an expression that was devoid of her true emotions.

"I did as you commanded this morning, my lord."

The viscount snickered. "So you did, but that does not change the fact that our newly returned baron finds you pleasing to his eye."

"Baron?"

Biddeford shrugged and moved to the small door that would lead him to the concealed passageway. "Yes, Sinclair has inherited the title of Harrow from his uncle who died without issue. Since he appears to be in good standing with the Earl of Hertford, you shall allow him to think you find his attentions . . ."

Justina felt her breath freeze in her throat. She couldn't use Sinclair; she didn't have the ability to conceal what she was thinking around the knight. She would fail, and revulsion for such a task was thick enough to choke her. Sinclair was everything noble. She couldn't soil that.

"I shall allow him to think I find his attentions . . . how, my lord?"

"Amusing, for the moment. I am more interested in the

Earl of Hertford. Dress yourself more fashionably and see if you can gain an invitation to join his party for supper."

She had never known so much relief as she did when that door closed behind her guardian.

Except for the day her husband had died.

Her knees felt weak and she pulled in deep breaths while she attempted to steady herself. Despair wrapped its boney grip around her now, threatening to crush her beneath the weight of what Biddeford demanded. Oh, one would think it a simple matter, so much less repulsive than some of the things she had done in the past, but Synclair's face rose up to torment her with how noble he was.

Could she not at least have one memory of a man that was untarnished by the smut and soot that seemed to be her life? If for no other reason than it kept part of her heart alive with the notion that there were men, rare and few, but living, breathing men who spoke the truth and served honor.

She needed that. Needed it so badly she ached with it. Tears burned the corners of her eyes.

"My lady? A letter arrived from your son."

A sob broke through her lips as she turned to take the folded parchment the maid offered her. The woman assumed she cried because she longed for her child so greatly, but the truth was that she wept because she simply could not fend off her unsteady emotions any longer and feared they might consume her, leaving her child at the mercy of Biddeford.

Brandon's writing was neat and clear, his spelling correct even if his sentences lacked the polish that age would bring. The maid fetched her a linen square to keep her tears from marring the letter. Justina read it three times through before forcing herself to fold it and lock it in the small chest that sat on top of the table where she kept all of Brandon's letters, from the very first ones that were naught more than a practice of his letters, with pictures of what he would have rather been doing instead of his studies, to the one that she held today. The neat stacks of parchment gave her the strength to banish her tears and turn around to wash and dress. Brandon was in the country, her efforts gaining what was truly important. Her own feelings did not matter, that was the path that all mothers must follow.

At least the good ones.

The Earl of Hertford enjoyed merry company.

The man had his own large chambers in the palace and that included a large receiving room he must have set his servants to preparing before he left on the hunt. Long trestle tables lined the room, with ornately carved chairs set along their outer edges so that all who sat there would face in at one another. The tables were laid with fine pewter plates and silver-handled dinnerware. There was pepper and nutmeg, their scents casting even more joy to the moment because of the great cost such spices sold for. At the end of each table was placed a salt cellar, its position indicating that the master of the house granted leave to everyone to speak freely while supping this night. He might have kept the salt near his hand, and no one below the salt's position might speak unless they were addressed. Sitting below the salt was never much fun.

Justina heard the minstrels before she entered the room. The sounds of them playing their lutes, mandolins, and even the virginals set the mood for celebration to the delight of the courtiers fortunate enough to be allowed past the Earl's personal retainers. Somewhere, the Queen would be holding her own supper, most likely with the princesses in attendance. Still another gathering would be around the Chancellor Wriothesley and the men who supported him. While the King failed to appear, court would become a separated place, with each person having to make a choice on whom to attend. People were judged by such decisions, the gossips keeping track of who attended whom. Justina approached the Hertford retainers and watched as they cast a look back at their captain for his word on her. A barely noticeable nod from the man granted her liberty to walk into the room with all of its festivities.

A juggler performed at one end of the room, capturing the attention of most of the guests. But Justina discovered herself drawn to a large bird sitting near the head table. As large as a pheasant, the bird's feathers were blue and gold and its beak curved. It was a parrot of some sort; the king kept one that she had heard speak several words. The bird watched her with large eyes, looking for all the world quite intelligent.

"You have a taste for the exotic, as do I."

Francis de Canis wasn't wearing velvet or brocade. The man was more of a rogue and dressed in clothing that was functional. His face bore the proof of his rugged lifestyle, with scars that told of fights in years gone by.

He stood between her and the room because she had stepped up onto the raised dais the bird's perch was sitting on. Behind her lay a hallway, used to connect to the private chambers of the earl.

"I enjoy a good chase, Lady, and you have not disappointed me."

Justina stood her ground, conscious of the hallway behind her and how easy it would be for de Canis to molest her in one of the rooms beyond. No servant would help her and the nobles were all occupied with the juggler.

"I do plan to disappoint you, sir, for I shall have none of this game."

His clothing had warned her that he was a man who enjoyed doing things himself, but that still did not keep her from being shocked when he pushed her down the hallway. His hands delivered a sharp jab to her belly, below her stays where her flesh was soft and unprotected. Her breath went sailing out of her lungs, leaving her gasping for enough to cry out with. Pain filled her body and she stumbled backward out of the need to shield herself from more blows.

"You shall have it, Lady, and the rougher the better will please me well."

The light from the festivities became muted when de Canis reached for her again. This time, he grabbed her upper arms and flung her toward a doorway like a bundle of laundry. Justina stepped on her skirts and fell across the floor in a tangle of fabric. She was torn between the need to cry out and the fear that being rescued might offend the nobles who considered de Canis indispensable.

The bastard knew it well, too. His face was glowing with victory and a smug smile sat on his lips.

"You are no maiden and no man's wife. Your last lover is gone to the borderland to breed his wife, so you, madam, need a new master, and I will be happy to prove my worth to you."

He reached for her, but the word *master* ignited her temper. She was sick unto death of hearing that she must obey.

"You are not my master!"

She launched herself at him, clawing at his face while pushing at the floor with all of her strength. Her nails sunk into his skin, drawing warm blood for a moment before a heavy blow landed across her face. Her body twisted with the strength of the strike and she stumbled away from him, trying to keep her footing while turning to glare at him.

"Step aside, sir, for I will not play your game."

De Canis smiled and chuckled beneath his breath. Gloating sparkled in his eyes while his expression turned mean.

"I'm going to enjoy breaking you."

He stepped toward her and Justina gathered her strength to fight him. She would not yield to him even if it might save her the pain of being beaten. She preferred the bruises of the flesh to ones on her soul.

But a strangled sound came from him and his foot never touched the floor. Instead he was hauled backward and thrown into the hallway. Justina gained only a glance of the man responsible and it was enough to send a shiver down her back.

She had never seen Synclair so angry. His face was darkened by rage and his hands outstretched as though he planned to rip de Canis apart with his bare hands.

De Canis wasn't afraid of him, though. He gained his feet and growled at him. "So you want to fight over the meat? I am your man!"

De Canis lunged at Synclair but the knight met him, and flesh connected with flesh. Both were hardened men who knew the art of fighting well. Justina stumbled to the doorway to see them struggling in the tight confines of the narrow hallway. The harsh sounds of struggle filled the stone-lined walls as the two men tried to kill each other. Their bodies strained but the close confines prevented them from doing more than wrestle. Synclair pushed de Canis back, sliding the man's boots across the floor until they reached the doorway that led to the reception room. With a harsh growl of satisfaction, Synclair threw de Canis into the room, startling the parrot.

The music died abruptly and the assembled guests looked around to discover the cause. De Canis recovered quickly and dove at Synclair with a curse spilling from his lips. The knight drew back his arm and landed a solid punch directly on de Canis's face that sent the man spinning into the men who rushed forward. They grabbed him, struggling with him when the man tried to continue the fight.

"I'll see you rotting in an early grave, Harrow! Baron or not, I'm going to rip your throat out with my own hands!" De Canis struggled violently against the arms holding him, rage glittering in his eyes.

"I am your man, de Canis! This world will be well rid of your brand of filth."

Synclair looked as if he meant to continue the fight, but the Earl of Hertford stepped in front of him, placing a hand flat against his chest. The earl leaned in to whisper something near Synclair's ear and the assembled guests all leaned forward to attempt to hear what it was.

Synclair snarled at the earl but the man lifted his hand and looked at the musicians.

"Play!" He turned his head and looked at a groom. "Bring the meal!"

There was a scurry as everyone tried to please the earl. He swept the nobles nearest to Synclair with a hard look that sent them all back across the room.

"Francis de Canis, I believe it best if you retire for the evening. It appears that my friends do not please you."

De Canis shrugged off the men around him and tugged on his doublet to straighten it. His lips curled into a sneer, without a care for the high position of the earl. Being asked to leave was a public set down, one the assembled guests did not miss. Whispers began to ripple through the crowd instantly.

"No, your lordship, I do not care for that one."

Soft hands cupped her shoulders, startling Justina. An older maid gently pulled her back.

"Come away, ma'am, you have blood upon your lip. It will ruin your gown if we don't tend to it."

Still far enough back in the hallway to avoid being seen, Justina saw the wisdom in the maid's suggestion. She allowed herself to be guided away from where Synclair and the earl spoke in lowered tones. But the stone walls pressed in on her, making her feel as if it were impossible to draw a complete breath. Her lungs burned and she fought against the urge to scream with all of the tension trapped inside her. Every muscle felt tight enough to snap and her blood was rushing so quickly through her veins, keeping to an even pace became impossible.

"I'll see to it myself, thank you."

Justina didn't spare more than a quick glance for the maid. She plucked a piece of cloth that was tucked through the woman's apron tie before she quickened her pace and turned the corner. She didn't know where she was going, only that she couldn't remain inside without going mad.

The corridors were made of thick stone and Justina hurried through them because it felt like they were pressing in on her. She finally made it outside and leaned over a half wall to pull in large breaths to feed her burning lungs. She pressed the fabric to her mouth and felt her eyes widen when it came away stained with crimson. Emotions assaulted her—fear, anger, pain, and too many others to comprehend. The air was bitterly cold and she looked across the yard to see that snow was gently falling. It wasn't melting now that the sun was sinking on the horizon. Patches of it covered the ground and clung to the leafless branches of the trees.

She cursed, muttering the foulest words her overwhelmed mind might recall.

"My thoughts exactly, Justina."

She turned in a swirl of brocade skirts to discover Synclair behind her. His face was still darkened by temper and his eyes were narrow with dissatisfaction. But the cloth in her hands drew his attention.

"That bastard bloodied you."

Justina felt her hand begin shaking and she turned back around to look away from the palace. She felt as if her every muscle was quivering, and was on the verge of either collapsing or running away.

"It shouldn't matter but I find that I cannot stomach these walls." Her voice sounded far too needy but she didn't care; all that mattered was gaining freedom. She saw a reflection of her own desperation in his eyes and she didn't give a damn what anyone else thought. The sound of horses came around the side of the building and Sinclair grinned. It wasn't a kind expression, but it was a relief from the rage that had transformed his features into a stranger.

A groom led his stallion, the animal more than eager to see his owner.

"Then let us escape, at least for the moment." He took the reins from the groom and mounted, his body showing all the tension that she herself was battling. He looked down at her and offered his hand.

"Come with me, Justina. The night will give us the solace we seek."

She didn't think. Her hand lifted and his fingers closed around her wrist. He lifted her off her feet and she landed in front of him, sitting side saddle with his arms going around her to control the animal.

She didn't need to think and she didn't believe that she was capable of it at the moment. All that filled her head was the sound of his voice when he used the word *solace*.

With his arms around her, Justina was sure that she had found exactly what he had promised her.

She needed to feel the warmth of his body, encasing her while they rode away from the palace and all its worries. The snow drifted down on them but she wasn't chilled, didn't shiver with the cold.

CHAPTER THREE

Y et she did shiver.
      Her body began to pulse with excitement in a way
she had never felt. It surged through her blood, rushing to
her head and making her want to giggle like a girl. The air
rushed past her cheeks, turning them cold, but she smiled,
enjoying the contrast between her face and the rest of her
body that was turning hot. In her belly, that excitement
brewed, until it was bubbling with need that rose up to
draw her nipples hard once more. It happened faster this
time, because she seemed to recall the sensation from before and her flesh craved more pleasure from Synclair's
touch.

*She'd known that she'd lose all control if she allowed herself
to lean on him . . .*

He rode into the woods without a care for the fact that
permission was needed to enter the king's forest, or that
the first storm of winter was falling around them. There
was no hesitation in him, only hard strength that drew still
more quivers from her body. She should have worried
that they might freeze but she didn't. The man sitting next
to her was too warm and confident for her to truly worry.

"There."

He leaned low, to make sure his words found her ear.

She felt the warm brush of his breath against her ear and it sent a ripple of delight through her.

"The hunting house."

She had heard rumors of such a place. The house itself was far more appealing to her than the palace with all its grandeur. This was a two-story house with wide stairs that led up to the front doors. Twin panels opened outward, beneath an arched doorframe set with sculpted leaves and grapes. It was refuted to be where Henry Tudor came to consort with his mistresses.

"This is the King's house."

"Yet mine for the time that I am at court."

"Yours?" Her voice trailed off as she took a look at Sinclair's face. Satisfaction shimmered in his eyes now and it sent a shaft of need through her.

He stopped the stallion at the base of those stairs and a groom appeared to hold the reins. Synclair jumped from the saddle, his boots making only a scuff when they hit the ground.

"Indeed, Justina, mine because I have limited tolerance for the palace and the Earl of Hertford is kind enough to indulge me."

"The palace is also full."

Synclair reached up and clasped his hands around her waist. "The King is welcome to his guests. I prefer some privacy."

He lifted her down, but didn't release her immediately. His hands remained around her waist and she was overly aware of the place where he touched her. There was something in his eyes that made her breathless once again, only this time it was because she felt like she was poised on the edge of a cliff, just waiting to topple over the edge.

What was odd was the fact that she was looking forward to falling, anticipation drawing her belly tight with excitement. An urge to behave recklessly began to take control of her and she witnessed something similar in Synclair's eyes. Surrounded by the darkness, there seemed no more perfect time to taste what was forbidden and unwise.

To taste what she desired above all other things . . .

"The King used to come here for privacy, too. Privacy to meet with his mistresses."

She wasn't sure what made her say such a thing. It was a barbed comment, one designed to displease or gain a reaction. But she honestly wanted to provoke him and that was a cowardly thing.

"Exactly what I crave, Justina, privacy to end this chase you have begun."

"I shouldn't have said that."

One of his eyebrows rose. "And why not?"

She took a slow step away from him, more of a nervous motion not truly designed to evade him. But there was part of her that did long for him to chase her and capture her. It was a dark desire but one that refused to be silenced now that they were so very alone. She felt as though she had been waiting forever for such a moment.

"Because I am happy to be here." There was a deep satisfaction in saying the words. Justina felt it burning through the resentment and frustration that Biddeford so often forced her to shoulder.

But there was also something deeper, something that she had been ignoring too long. Synclair closed the space between them, his fingers landing gently on her lower back. Her breath caught and his eyes narrowed when he heard it.

The doors opened and a lantern was held high. The light didn't reach to the bottom of the stairs but shone like a beacon above them. Synclair pushed her gently up the stairs.

He leaned down and she felt his breath on the side of

her neck once more. "If you are happy to be here, meet me on the field, madam, or have your own actions paint you timid."

Justina grabbed a handful of her skirts and lifted them so that she might climb the stairs.

Meet him on the field indeed. The man was every inch the knight and he enjoyed the battles that had earned him that rank.

The servant holding the lantern never looked directly at her. Justina passed the lantern and entered the house to discover that candles had been lit on a table in the front room and at the top of the inside staircase to illuminate the open doors of a bedchamber on the second floor. She froze in her steps, her attention fixed on that second floor and the fact that she knew she did not possess the will to deny her passion for Synclair.

"I will make you no promises." Justina's voice was low but steady.

She turned but Synclair was directly behind her. His hands cupped her waist once again, holding her in place with steely strength.

"Well, Justina, I will make you one promise, and that is that you will never again risk yourself by running away from me."

His words were edged with harsh reprimand and a moment later he swept her off her feet without even a flinch. He cradled her against his chest, taking the stairs with quick motions of his powerful legs and carrying her into the upstairs bedchamber.

"Enough, Synclair, this is insanity."

He put her down but only so that he might turn and close the doors. He shut them with a hard motion that betrayed just how much anger still ruled him. Yet he had controlled all that emotion and never even pinched her. She watched him, astonished at how well he hid his true feelings, admired his control because she was forced to do the same so often. A curious sense of kinship surfaced inside her.

"What is insanity is you riding across the borderland in a pair of boy's britches without even a dagger to protect you."

There was thick reprimand in his tone and she should have backed away from it but her temper rose to the challenge, refusing to be told where her place was when her son's safety was at risk.

"That is not your concern. You didn't have the right to hold me at Amber Hill. Besides, Jemma gifted the mare to me, and I may do what I please with my gifts."

Synclair unbuckled his belt and dropped it on a nearby table. "I pledged my help to you, Justina, there was no reason to place yourself at such risk. My service to Lord Ryppon is finished, and I will keep my word now that I have my leave."

"I never asked for your help."

He growled, low and deep, one finger pointing at her. "You should have."

He closed the distance between them, framing her face with his hands, but in spite of the raging passion flickering in his eyes, his touch was only firm. She shivered, her body begging her to yield because it wanted to feel that passion. A soft sound came from her lips but it was more needy than anything else and his eyes narrowed in response. His hands began to smooth over her cheeks, soft little motions that sent sweet enjoyment through her.

"You made me stalk you, Lady, and what I still do not understand is why, but I do not care. My service is finished, and I swear to you that capturing you is my only goal now."

"You cannot change my guardian's nature."

"I will force him to release you or kill him for the way he abuses his position."

His mouth covered hers, blocking out any further protests. She backed away from his kiss, seeking some distance to maintain her grasp on reality, but Synclair followed her, wrapping one arm around her to bind her body against his own. His lips never relented, demanding that she accept his kiss and open her mouth to allow it to deepen.

She shuddered and her jaw relaxed because she couldn't ignore the sensation flowing from that kiss. It flooded her, drowning every protest inside her. Her hands stopped trying to push him away and began to seek out the skin she could scent beneath his clothing. Desperation made her impatient to discover what she craved, her fingers pushing the buttons of his doublet through their holds to open the front of the garment.

He held her against him, but that didn't allow for her hands to continue working his doublet open. She leaned back and his mouth trailed across her jaw to her neck where he pressed hot kisses to the skin. Sensation rippled down her body in response to each press of his mouth. Deep tremors that traveled impossibly quick to her belly where need was burning white-hot. All of the times that she had avoided him rose up to torment her and push her hands faster. All of the denying that she had forced herself to accept suddenly turned on her, becoming fuel for the raging need.

"We should slow down . . ." His voice was husky and hard, telling her that he was grasping at the last of his control to say what he thought she needed to hear.

"Don't let me think." She pushed at his open doublet, pushing it over his shoulders and down his arms. "I don't want to think. I want to feel!"

"So do I."

His voice was almost raw and his blue eyes shimmered with agreement, but there was also argument there. She watched it battling against his need and once again she felt that sense of kinship with him. They were so alike that she yearned to toss everything aside in favor of seeking out some solace in his embrace. She didn't seem to possess even a shred of discipline to resist now that his hands were upon her.

"We accomplish little with conversation."

His tone should have warned her away but instead it sent a shiver down her back. He shrugged his open doublet off and let it fall on the floor without a care. His eyes were lit with anticipation, but what captivated her was his lack of restraint. Always the knight had been in control. She stared at him, trying to absorb who he was behind that shield of chivalry.

He cupped her face once more, capturing her mouth with his. The kiss was full of everything she had witnessed flickering in his eyes. The demand was firm, his mouth pushing hers open so that his tongue might thrust deeply. A soft moan rose from her chest as the heat inside her body became too much. Her dress was far too heavy and tight. She twisted, trying to escape what felt like endless layers of fabric.

Synclair never lifted his mouth away from hers but his hands slid down to her waist, gripping her and lifting her once more. She gripped his shoulders, kissing him back with every bit of desperation that was bubbling inside her. She felt like a thief, taking what she needed because she simply could not resist what she craved any longer.

Justina pushed her hands into the open collar of his shirt, pushing it away from his skin so that her hands might slide across his warm flesh. Passion flooded her and she willingly let it drag her away, the current pleasing her in a wicked way. Every time that she had watched him and denied herself his company surfaced with the demand that she touch him and be touched in return. There was no building, only the white-hot blaze of need that had been boiling inside her for too long. She thrust her own tongue into his mouth, eager for deep contact between them. Synclair growled and turned with her still in his grasp. A moment later, he pressed her back against the wall, lifting her higher so that his cock was even with her sex. She lifted her thighs, releasing his shoulders to grab her skirts and yank them out of the way.

"I cannot wait, Justina."

His voice was strained almost to the point of being incomprehensible. He pressed his upper body against her, pinning her to the wall while he ripped the opening of his pants apart.

"I don't want you to."

His eyes connected with hers for one slim moment, but it was long enough for her to view the wildness burning there. It was a part of him that he never allowed free, and that satisfied her in a way she had never thought possible.

She twisted her thighs around his hips, reaching for his shoulders to hold herself up.

"Do it, Synclair! Do it now."

He didn't need any further urging. She felt the hard touch of his cock against her slit, the thick staff seeking the opening to her body, sliding easily through the fluid that coated her folds. Her hips tilted toward him and she felt his length touch the mouth of her sheath, sinking in several inches.

She gasped. Her passage was tight and resisting, promising pain when he plunged into her completely. But Synclair held himself steady, sparing her that pain. A muscle on the side of his jaw quivered and she could see his teeth clenching while he stopped, watching her face. Through the blaze of need, she could see him judging her response.

"Thrust deep." Her voice was husky and rich with need. She didn't want to stop, feared that her mind might snap if she didn't gain what she hungered for.

"You're tight." His eyes flickered. "We need to slow down."

"No! I am not a maiden." She cupped the back of his neck, pulling his head down to hers so that she might kiss him. Her passage burned, desperate to feel more of his flesh inside it. She licked his lower lip before thrusting her tongue up into his mouth to slide along his own, teasing it with what both their bodies desired.

His body shuddered, need consuming him. His hands tightened around her hips and his member withdrew before thrusting forward to penetrate her deeper. Pleasure speared through her with the hard flesh and her head fell back, a moan escaping from her lips. Rapture held her in its grip, refusing to be denied or contained inside her. Her fingers dug into his shoulders as her clitoris throbbed.

Synclair growled again, his body moving in short thrusts that drove his cock deeply into her. Satisfaction rippled through her, her passage filling with enjoyment as he impaled her completely.

"Too fast. Yet I cannot stop."

His voice was strained and his words came through clenched teeth, but there was no stopping the need for either of them. He drove his cock into her over and over, his thrusts hard and deep. Justina kept pace with him, working her hips to capture each thrust, groaning when she felt his sac against her bottom. The wall against her back kept her steady for the rapidly increasing pace of his thrusts. Pleasure speared through her with each stroke of hard flesh against her clitoris. There was no controlling it, no tempering how it sent soft cries across her lips. She strained against her lover, equally caught up in the frantic need. Her pleasure crested, rapture bursting through her in a wave as hard as the cock thrusting into her. She cried out, the sound of her own voice strange while her body shivered in the grip of sensation that was so pleasurable she sobbed with it.

Synclair snarled with his. The sound was deep and harsh but satisfying because there was no polish to it, only the raw tone of immense pleasure. He thrust against her hard, his cock feeling bigger, more swollen in those last few moments before she felt his seed erupting inside her. The hands gripping her hips flexed, tightening to pin her in place while his cock emptied its hot load inside her. His chest rose and fell rapidly, harshly, but her own mimicked it.

He cursed softly, still pinning her against the wall with his body. She felt his shoulders quivering and doubted that her own legs would be able to support her. But her knees ached from the tight hold she had used to keep him between her thighs, the muscles complaining now that satisfaction had been gained. Sweat coated her face and her heart beat with hard motions beneath her breasts.

Synclair growled and moved back, allowing her legs to lower.

"I can offer no excuse, Justina."

"I didn't ask you for any." Just as she'd suspected, her legs wobbled when she tried to take her own weight. A hard arm snaked around her waist to bind her against his body. He turned and put his back against the wall while still panting softly. She could feel his heart beating hard against his chest because she was pressed against him.

"You shouldn't have to accept excuses for my behavior. I never intended to treat you roughly."

There was tenderness in his voice, and it sent her seek-

ing enough poise to hide from before she forgot everything except what she craved. There were too many feelings for him inside her, and she dare not allow them to
bask in the moment, else they would grow and threaten
her entire composure. More than one widow had run
away with her lover and turned her back on her guardian,
but both had lost everything when they did so.

"I am not a maiden so discard your concern."

"That has no bearing upon how you should be treated."

He refused to allow her to push away from him. Instead
he cupped her chin and raised her face to meet his.

"But you were tight, very tight, and I know that I
caused you pain by failing to control my lust."

Justina pushed a hand against his chest. "I did not ask
you to show control."

She gained no distance from him, his arm remaining
firm and inescapable yet not hurting her. Disapproval
shone in his eyes now but it was directed at himself.

"You should not have to ask me for such. It is my duty
to control my strength since it is greater."

"Stop it, Synclair." She didn't know how to accept the
tenderness in his words as genuine. Perhaps it was safer not
to accept it, since such kindness so often dissipated the
moment a man was in the mood to bend a woman to his
will.

His lips rose, curving into a satisfied smile. She pushed
against his body again, using more strength.

"And do not become smug because I called you by
name."

He released her, and because of how strongly she had
been straining against his arm, she stumbled back a pace.
He remained against the wall, leaning on it while watching her with piercing eyes.

"I am not allowed to be pleased by the fact that you
mutter my name, Lady?" He clicked his tongue at her in

reprimand. "Now that is most unkind of you, Justina. It is something I have longed to hear on your lips. The sound is as sweet as I hoped it might be."

He reached up and dug his fingers into his shirt. With a swift pull, he drew the garment over his head and off completely. It fluttered to the floor. He straightened up and she stepped back because she had somehow become accustomed to him being so close, forgetting just how large he truly was—the top of her head was even with his shoulders. He walked across the chamber to sit down in a chair that was waiting. He pulled one boot off in a quick motion before she was able to force her mind to function once more.

"What are you doing?"

His smile turned arrogant. "Disrobing. Something I should have done before kissing you." The second boot came free and landed next to its twin. "A quick tumble was not why I brought you here."

"Wasn't it?" She was being coarse but she couldn't afford to think of him as a tender lover. "We both wanted an outlet for our anger."

Synclair frowned and stood up. His pants were still open and they slid down his thighs with only a simple push from his hands. He stepped out of them and she turned away because his cock was still hard. It stood fully erect, the head of it ruby red in spite of the fact that she knew he had spilled his seed inside her.

She had felt it spurting up against the mouth of her womb. A tiny quiver went through her belly as she recalled that moment. It had been more satisfying than any other she had ever experienced during bed sport.

She must never allow Synclair to know that.

"I still want to kill de Canis."

Synclair was directly behind her. She gasped, never hearing even a single scuff against the floor. But he closed his arms around her, pulling her back against his body in a motion that was fluid and impossible to escape.

"But not now." He angled his head so that his words brushed over her ear. The skin on her neck felt the warmth of his breath, and sensation rippled across it. It frustrated her because it was so simple a touch, yet she was keenly aware of it. She strained away from him, struggling when he refused to release her. But his arms were solid bands of inescapable steel about her, keeping her arms pinned against her body, leaving her little to fight with except to squirm.

He leaned down and placed a kiss against her neck. His lips were hot and drew a soft breath from her.

"Does this mean you are not finished resisting me, Justina?" Another press of his lips landed on the sensitive skin of her throat. "Good." He whispered that single word like a judgment, his voice hard and edged with promise. "I believe I am not finished bending you either."

A shiver crossed her skin, rippling down her body in response. There was a promise in his voice, one that was unmistakable.

"You make no sense with such words."

He chuckled, and it was not a pleasant sound, but one that sent anticipation through her. His arms relaxed, allowing her space, and she moved away from the disturbing contact with his body only to be caught on his arm in front of her while she felt his fingers pulling on the lace that held her dress closed.

"I make more sense than you do when you tell me to leave you."

"I told you that because there can be no future in what you seek with me beyond tonight."

Justina gained her freedom as his arms slacked from surprise. At last, it appeared that he was beginning to accept what their reality was. Her victory was short-lived however because she heard him pull the tie free that secured her dress. The bodice sagged and she had to clasp her arms over her chest to keep it in place. Synclair reached down and grasped both sides of the skirt in his large hands and drew the garment up and over her head while she tried to hold onto her dress.

"Then be very sure that I plan to make good use of the entire night, Justina."

He pulled the loosened gown from her grasp with only a slight sound of tearing. With a hard look he threw the dress on the table behind him, remaining between it and her. Justina turned to face him completely, feeling exposed in her stays and chemise. Her shoes had fallen off somewhere near the wall, leaving her in stocking-clad feet. She suddenly worried that he might find her body unattractive. Her husband had told her that childbearing had left its mark on her, and it had been clear that he did not care for the sight of it.

"I must return to the palace." Her voice was low, to conceal her apprehension.

Synclair shook his head, and she discovered it difficult to maintain eye contact with him. Her gaze wanted to slide down his body and soak in all the perfection she knew he'd hidden beneath his clothing. She wanted to be selfish and stay with him. She wanted him to want her to remain even though he had already had her.

Such was a whimsical idea, one only found in sonnets and fables.

She had turned her head away but a soft stroke across her cheek drew her attention back to Synclair.

"Ah sweet lady, I am not nearly finished with proving my worth to you this night. Where you needs go is into that bed where I may take the rest of the night to bend you to my will. I promise you, you will enjoy it well."

Her mouth went dry while her mind whispered dark

temptations about what this man might do if lust wasn't riding him so high. His voice was deep and husky and rich with promise. Many a man thought he knew how to pleasure a woman, but most were naught but arrogant fools, drunk on their own pride.

"You are thinking about it, Justina, I see the passion glittering in your eyes." He reached down and grasped his cock. She failed to keep her attention on his face, her gaze slipping down, over the cut ridges of his chest muscle, across the lean expanse of his belly to the place where his fingers curled around the hard member that had so recently pleasured her.

"Go on and look at me, Justina, I have been waiting a long time to watch you gazing at my flesh and seeing what the sight of my arousal does to you. To see if it raises passion in your eyes as I have so often hoped for."

His hand moved up and down the length of his cock. She trembled, her blood beginning to rush through her veins in excitement. Behind her stays, her nipples drew into hard points that longed for the touch of his hand. There was a practiced motion in the way his fingers moved along his length, the man knew how to handle the more sensitive parts of the human body.

Sweet Christ. She lifted a hand to cover her mouth, overwhelmed by the ideas swarming inside her mind. She couldn't take a lover, not one of her own choosing, and she certainly couldn't allow herself to indulge her whims with Synclair.

She might never be able to leave him.

"Enough, Synclair."

She trembled, need flowing through her like a swollen river. She wrapped her arms around herself, seeking solace while denying herself what she craved.

"You have had what you wanted and now I am going

to return to the palace. You may have your leave from
Ryppon, but I do not have freedom from my guardian."

He released his cock, allowing her to see it clearly. The
staff was thick and long, reminding her of the pinch that
had assaulted her when she took it. It was the largest cock
she'd ever ridden, without doubt.

"You shall have your leave of that bastard viscount, if I
must kill him to gain it."

She gasped, fear cutting through her passion instantly.

"You must not say such things! Biddeford is a noble.
You would be put to death for harming him. You must
dispense with this notion of sheltering me."

She shivered, lament filling her for all of the things that
they could not afford to share with each other. She drew
in a deep breath to steady her nerves and fortify her resolve.

"I must go."

"And so you shall, Lady."

Surprise made her gasp but it turned into a shriek when
Synclair rushed her, capturing her body and raising it far
enough up into the air to be dumped over the footboard
of the large bed. He dropped her and her body bounced
in a jumble of limbs as she tried to push herself up. She
rose onto her knees, only to be knocked backward when
Synclair jumped over the footboard, lunging like a large
predator, stretching out his body and hooking her around
her waist with one large arm. They both landed stretched
out on the surface of the bed, the ropes creaking from the
motion of their landing.

"You shall go to my bed and you shall bend to my will."

Synclair slid one hand beneath her shoulder and rolled
her over onto her belly. He trapped her there with his own
body, lying alongside her and allowing enough of his
weight to rest on her to keep her in place.

"Synclair, you must dispense with this notion of yours."

He pulled the lace on her stays in response, releasing the knot and using his fingers to pull the length of cord free from the eyelets that ran down the back of the garment.

"I have chased you for over two years, Justina. What makes you think that I will dispense with anything now that I have you exactly where I want you?"

"I left you for another. Doesn't your pride have an issue with that?"

He pulled on the lace and she watched it sail over the edge of the bed before another firm hand turned her onto her back. She wished he hadn't turned her when she caught sight of his face. His features were drawn into a tight mask of male frustration. He leaned over her, pressing her to the bed with his wide chest.

"You went to another's bed because that bastard Biddeford ordered you to. That is not leaving me. You had no choice." His eyes narrowed. "He makes you whore for his gain."

"Exactly. Which is why I tell you to set your sights on a more worthy woman."

His fingers gently closed her lips, lightly pressing against them to stop her from speaking further.

"I cannot change the fact that I am drawn to you, Justina, any more than you may alter the fact that you cannot resist my touch. Admit that you are where you have longed to be. I saw it in your eyes, even as you told me to leave you. I saw it."

She wouldn't. Her head began shaking back and forth, denying him and herself.

"I believe I like your resistance more than I would have enjoyed your surrender, for it grants me the challenge of taming you."

There was thick promise in his tone and she witnessed it flickering in his eyes as well. Her belly twisted in response, anticipation beginning to throb in her clitoris. She seemed to have lost all control over her body; it was responding in spite of all her reasons not to.

He rose up onto one elbow and hooked his hand into her stays. In a heartbeat, he pulled the garment away from her body and tossed it over the edge of the bed.

"Ah, undeniable proof."

The thin fabric of her chemise was laying over her body now, the only thing shielding her from his keen stare. But the flimsy fabric molded to her every curve, showing him the hard points of her nipples. He lowered his body again, easing to one side of her body so that he might nuzzle against her breasts. Sensation shot through her so fast she jumped, turning away from him out of pure response.

Synclair trapped her shoulder beneath his own, his fingers threading into her hair and plucking a hairpin from where the maid had secured her curls.

"I am going to taste you, Justina, every last inch of you before I am finished having you."

He lowered his head until she felt his breath against one puckered nipple. Her chemise failed to shield her from it, sensation prickling through the skin and down the sides of her breast. His tongue flicked over it, wetting the fabric and drawing a stiff breath from her. She was acutely aware of the tiniest touch, her skin alive with more sensation then she had ever experienced before.

He licked the top of her nipple once, twice more before closing his lips all the way around the puckered peak. She gasped but her back arched, rising off the bed to offer her nipple to his lips. Need was blistering her, it was so hot. The motion of his mouth, drawing in the nipple, softly sucking on it, made her cry out.

He raised his head and stared at her.

"Tell me you want me to continue."

His fingers took over playing with her nipple, rubbing

the wet spot on her chemise and sending light ripples of sensation through her breast. Yet it wasn't as intense as it had been when his mouth sucked on that same nipple. She bit her lower lip, refusing to send him back to doing what she could not resist.

"Ah, you wish me to seek out more tender parts of you." His voice dripped with promise. "I believe I am up to that challenge."

His hands lowered to her thighs, resting for a moment on top of the tender skin while he allowed her to see the flare of desire that lit his eyes.

"I have spent many a day thinking about touching you, stroking you."

"You shouldn't have wasted your time. There is no future in this."

His lips curved. "I disagree, Lady. There is an entire night at our disposal."

One night. It might be short or impossibly long, depending on how she spent it. Nights in her husband's bed had been horribly endless but the hands smoothing up her thighs didn't breed in her the need to clench her thighs together or fight the urge to retch.

Instead, she resisted the urge to surrender. Synclair was still watching her and his eyebrows lowered.

"Why do you fear enjoying my touch, Justina? I have never raised my hand against you."

"You locked me up."

"For your own well-being."

She shook her head. "Yet that is what you fail to understand. My well-being is not what matters. I strive to provide my son with a decent life, keeping me from that is something I cannot accept. Ever."

"Your guardian is unfit."

She laughed, caught between the urge to cry and beg him for assistance. "There is a court full of women in the same position, Synclair. The king has set a tone of no mercy for women in this kingdom. Have you seen the Queen since your return? She is so docile it sickens me, and I can only think she must think the same of me when she sees me doing Biddeford's bidding. Yet we both continue to obey because we are women."

Justina rolled over, slightly astonished that he allowed her to. She sat up, pulling her legs up beneath her chemise. Synclair watched her, with his head resting on his hand and a bent elbow propped against the bed.

"But more than one man has had to tolerate a cruel master while he trains for knighthood. My struggle is not uncommon."

"You tell yourself that to endure it."

She hugged her legs, taking solace in the embrace. "Tell me you have agreed with every order and task you have been given by your betters."

It was a challenge, her words barbed. Synclair frowned and sat up. "I have not."

"Good, then we understand each other at last. I had to return, no matter the risk; it was my duty and it is my place, and it protects my son."

He flattened his hands on the surface of the bed, caging her between his thick arms. That quickly, she was once more his captive.

"I understand your motives, but what you fail to grasp is the fact that your devotion to your son only draws me to you even more. I understand your need, Justina, and it makes you only more attractive to me."

He pressed his mouth against hers, demanding a kiss that was deep and hard. His lips pressed hers to part, and the tip of his tongue gently licked along her lower lip before thrusting inside to toy with her own. His hands searched through her hair, pulling pins from it until the entire mass came free. Lifting his mouth away from hers, he lifted her up and turned her away from him. Her weight seemed simple for him to move and that knowledge sent a shaft of trust through her because he controlled it so well. She made no choice to trust, it simply began to grow inside her.

"Another thing that I have dwelt on is seeing your hair flowing across my skin."

He combed his fingers through her hair, loosening the braids until the strands lay in soft curls across his open hands. She heard him draw in a stiff breath, and it sent another emotion through her that felt too much like affection. She could not harbor such a feeling. Pushing her feet beneath her, she went to stand but only managed to flatten her feet against the bed. A moment later, Synclair rose above her, pulling her chemise up by the hem as he went. The garment pulled her arms up and slipped over her wrists without pausing.

"Much more to my liking."

Completely bare, Justina couldn't resist the urge to cross her arms in front of her breasts. She had always been told how beautiful she was, but she suddenly feared that Synclair would not find her so pleasing. He cupped her chin once again, raising her eyes to meet his.

"I find you irresistible, Justina."

As she did him. With naught but darkness surrounding them and the chill of winter brushing her skin, stopping herself from leaning against him became impossible.

One night. Was she not allowed a single taste of passion that pleased her and no one else except her partner?

Lover . . .

That was the word, and it felt foreign on her tongue but sweeter than any wine she had ever tasted.

He met her, angling his head so that their lips could fuse. The kiss was deep but slow, the need to hurry gone. Justina lifted her hands and flattened them on his chest, slowly stroking over the firm ridges of flesh and shivering with enjoyment. His arms pulled her closer, until her breasts were pressing against his body. She had never noticed that her curves fit so well against the harder body of a man. His hand slid up her back until he reached her head and her unbound hair. He threaded his fingers into it and grasped it gently.

The kiss changed, becoming more heated. His tongue penetrated her mouth, stroking and thrusting just as his cock had done. The motion awakened a soft throbbing in her clitoris, hunger beginning to heat and churn in her passage once more. Synclair lifted her up and laid her down across the bed. She shivered as she watched him rising up above her. In the dark, he was more shadow than flesh and yet she could sense his warmth, smell his scent. All of her senses were more sensitive, allowing her to hear the sound of his breathing and the way the bed ropes creaked when he lowered his body down to cover hers.

His lips found her neck, placing soft kisses against the tender skin. Delight flowed down her body from each one and she shifted beneath him, unable to decide what she wanted. Her hands roamed over his shoulders and then along his nape and finally into his shoulder-length hair. He kept trailing kisses down her neck until he reached her shoulder, but that did not stop him. He trailed more kisses over her collarbones and across her chest until he reached her breasts. The tender globes were quivering with anticipation. Every second felt as though it were an entire hour while she waited for his lips to begin touching the more sensitive skin.

She realized in that moment that no man had ever taken the time to arouse her. It was a sobering thought and her hands stroked over his shoulders, savoring the moment while she waited for his lips to seek out her nipples once more. When he closed his lips around one puckered peak,

she arched up to offer it to him. Hunger was burning inside her now. The satisfaction from their first encounter
lending heat to a new need that was more intense than the
one that had seen them pressing together against the wall.
She moved her legs, enjoying the way his bare skin felt
against her own. Decadent and rich, the delight flooding
her.

Synclair slid lower, leaving her nipple and pressing kisses
against her ribs and then on the flat of her belly. Her eyes
flew open as she felt his hands cupping her knees and
spreading her thighs.

"Synclair—"

A soft chuckle was his response. His head lifted and the
meager light in the room glittered off his eyes.

"I know the difference between demanding submission
from a woman and seducing a woman, Justina."

"Most men don't." She didn't realize she spoke out loud
until another chuckle passed his lips. His hands smoothed
over the top of her thighs before returning to her knees.

"Have I discovered the means to wooing you, sweet
Justina?" He pushed her knees wide, spreading her legs so
that the night air brushed against her wet folds. She was
keenly aware of the fact that she was wet, too, his soft
kisses having built her passion back up and sent fluid easing down her passage to coat her folds.

"I believe I will exploit that bit of information."

His hands smoothed back up her thighs but along the
inside now. Her skin was sensitive, and her breath caught
as he stroked her. She had never thought her skin might
be so tender or that she would enjoy having it petted. Synclair lowered his gaze to her sex and she felt her cheeks
heat. No one had ever looked at her sex. Justina suddenly
felt unsure, her thighs wanting to close.

Synclair clicked his tongue at her. The sound was warm

and full of wicked promise. "Where is your courage, Lady? Have you not frenched men?"

Her blush deepened and her thighs tried to snap shut again. Synclair looked up her body, and in spite of the darkness, she saw the smile curving his lips. His fingers reached her mons and gently stroked over the wet folds. It was a whisper of a stroke but she jerked because sensation shot through her as quickly as a pistol.

"Have you wrapped your lips around a cock and listened to the way a man is reduced to a quivering mass while you suck him?"

"Of course I have . . ." Her husband had demanded the service often. "But you can not mean to do that . . ."

"To you?" His fingers moved across her folds again, this time making more of a connection. He pushed one fingertip into her slit and stroked her very center until he was hovering over her clitoris, rubbing it gently. She suddenly understood what he meant by being reduced to a quivering mass. Her eyelids closed without hesitation as sensation took complete command of her.

"I assure you, Justina, a lover does indeed return the favor of *frenching,* even if your bastard of a husband was too selfish to give you the pleasure."

She had wondered what it might be like to be pleasured while doing nothing for her partner. To lie back and do nothing except enjoy—part of her wondered if that was where true rapture might be found. She quivered, anticipation beginning to drag her down into a swirling vortex of sensation where there was no need to hold onto her discipline.

"Wait—" She forced her eyes to open and lock with his. She gasped when she saw the determination on his face. He waited until her gaze was locked with his.

"I promised you that I would bend you to my will,

Justina. Women are not the only ones who can drive their partner past reason with a skillfully placed touch."

"I need my ability to reason."

"No, my lady, you do not. At least not for the rest of this night."

His finger pressed a bit harder and she felt her back arching, her hips lifting up to offer her clitoris to his touch. There was a steady command in his touch and hard resolution in his tone. Her entire body shivered but she lost the ability to keep her eyes open, her body demanding that she surrender to the bliss that his finger was inducing. Her heartbeat accelerated and her hands fisted in the bedding. She felt him lean closer, his breath hitting the wet skin of her spread sex. He used two fingers to separate her folds even more and lay her clitoris completely bare. Anticipation twisted through her, pulling her between excitement and desperation.

The first touch of his lips was almost too hot to bear. Her head thrashed on the bedding but it wasn't enough, and she heard a thin cry escape her lips.

"Hmm . . . I believe you enjoyed that."

His fingers moved her folds away from her clitoris even more and he lowered his head to place another kiss against the sensitive bead. But this time he closed his lips around it, sucking gently on it. Delight snapped her like a leather whip, drawing every muscle she had taut, to the point that it felt they might snap, but she didn't care. There was nothing but the pleasure filling her from where his mouth was fashioned around her clitoris. His opposite hand joined in the assault on her flesh, one finger gently teasing the opening of her passage.

She cried out, louder and longer while her hips jerked against that finger. Her passage had never felt so empty, so desperately in need of being filled. The sucking on her clitoris was pushing her toward another explosion of pleasure but denying her that final burst of satisfaction. Instead she twisted on the edge of a cliff, lifting her lower body up, seeking enough pressure to send delight flooding through her.

"Shall I give you pleasure?"

Synclair's voice was strained. "Demand it from me, Justina. Use my name and ask me for what you want."

"Yes, Synclair, yes!"

There was no thought in her mind save gaining release from the twisting knot of need in her belly. He leaned back down, sucking her clitoris back between his lips, harder and faster this time while his fingers thrust smoothly into her passage.

She cried out, her voice echoing off the canopy above the bed, her body contorting and withering while pleasure assaulted her in a storm of white-hot rain. It soaked her from head to foot, so hot, she feared she might be scarred, but she did not care. She clawed at the sheet, hearing it rip where her fingernails punctured it.

"You are mine."

He rose up, rocking the bed with how much strength he used. His face was pulled tight now, desire causing his nostrils to flare. He covered her, lowering his body on top of hers while she gasped and reached for him. Satisfaction was still shaking her but she ached for complete possession, her passage craving the hard presence of his cock deep inside it.

She clasped his hips between her thighs and sighed as the head of his member pushed through the wet folds of her slit. His body shook with the amount of control he was using to mount her gently.

But that wasn't what she craved.

"Take me, Synclair. Now."

He growled and his body flexed, sending his cock into her heated passage. She arched to take him, crying out as his flesh filled her near to bursting once more. His breath was ragged and his skin moist with perspiration. He gathered her hair in his fists while his hips began to move in rapid thrusts. The bed creaked, the canopy jerking and pitching above her head, but all that mattered was the hard flesh filling her over and over.

She felt him begin to give up his seed, the hot spurt hitting the mouth of her womb, and another burst of pleasure clenched her passage around his length. It caught her by surprise and her cry mixed with his deeper one as their bodies rocked through a final few thrusts.

"Sweet Christ in heaven . . ."

Synclair's elbows made deep indentions in the bed beneath her as he supported his weight and kept his wide chest from crushing her breasts.

"I cannot breathe." In spite of his chest not pressing down on hers, her lungs still burned and her heart felt as though it might break through her bones because it was thumping so violently.

He rolled onto his back, lying still while the sound of their rough respiration filled the space between the bed and the canopy. Her mind swam in a mist of satisfaction and exhaustion, her limbs feeling too heavy to move. But she felt Synclair begin to toy with her hair, just a soft motion of his fingers combing through the strands while he continued to draw rough breaths beside her.

"That was delightful, Justina."

There was an arrogance in his tone that had her opening her eyes. Pleasure was still pulsing through her in soft little waves but her mind was beginning to function once more, thoughts forming where there had been none while he touched her. The hand in her hair sent a little bolt of fear through her because his touch had the ability to make her senseless.

She curled away from him, seeking the edge of the bed.

"The snow is falling, Justina, and there is nowhere for you to go while the sun is gone."

A hard arm hooked around her waist, drawing her back against his body. He sat partially up and tugged the bedding free from where it was turned down at the foot of the bed.

"Let us enjoy each other's warmth instead of traveling a frozen path that will be much easier to cover in the light of day."

He covered her with a warm spread and held her tight against his body, even when she wriggled.

"I must go."

"Nay."

Firm and unyielding, his voice was as immovable as his body. Her strength deserted her, bleeding away as her heart slowed and calmed. She was suddenly more at ease than she had ever been. The warm body pressing against her back, more secure than anything she had ever felt. His hands smoothed over her, stroking with a tenderness that sent two tears down her cheeks. He pressed a kiss against her neck before breathing out a long sigh.

"I plan to pray that the storm lasts for a week, for that will give me the excuse to keep you in this bed."

His voice was slow and drowsy and she couldn't even muster enough strength to answer him. Instead she felt the beat of his heart against her back and allowed it to lead her off into sleep. A deep sleep that was free of worry. Warmth and tenderness surrounded her and it was, without doubt, the purest form of perfection she had ever felt.

CHAPTER FOUR

Justina moved, rolling over in her sleep, and the man sharing the bed with her followed her. Her mind instantly roused, refusing to relax back into the deep state she had been in. Her eyes fluttered open and she tried to recall where she was.

And with whom.

Fear spiked through her, making her muscles tense. She never remained in bed with anyone that she was sent to entice.

Memory flooded back into her mind. Synclair was curled around her back, his soft breathing telling her that he was still deep in slumber's grip. She turned her head to see him. His features were completely relaxed, making him look harmless and somewhat like a boy. His hair was tousled and lay swept back away from his face. It wasn't truly golden, but had darker streaks in it. One of his hands was resting on her hip and she looked down at it.

Men did not cling to women after bedding them. To be held was a need that was purely feminine and yet, she could not deny that Synclair was turned toward her several hours after he had gained what he wanted from her.

As you did from him . . .

She frowned and moved slightly away. Even sound asleep she did not doubt that the man would rouse quickly if she was not careful in how she moved. He was a knight and not one dubbed with the title in the middle of a receiving room for the sake of who his parents were. Synclair was battle-hardened, a fact she had learned to respect because he was never easy to slip past. Of course she found that aspect of him hard to resist. There were far too many people in her life who demanded her respect without having earned it. She was drawn to Synclair for too many reasons, and passion was only one.

She had to leave him.

Pain slashed through her so harshly, she expected to feel blood seeping from her chest. It stole her breath both with its intensity and with surprise. Justina stopped, frozen in place while she looked back at the man sleeping in the bed she had shared with him. A longing to return to his side was strong inside her, urging her to discover if he would be happy to find her still in his bed when he awoke.

That was pure nonsense, of course, another feminine idea that men only played lip service to when it suited their purposes. Even if Synclair had meant his words of last night, it would not change the fact that she could not choose to be with him.

Justina moved across the floor with silent steps she had learned and practiced while leaving more than one bed. Her husband had often used her after drinking heavily and his temper was always sour when he awoke after such times. Escaping his chamber had been a pleasure.

Unlike today. She had to force her feet forward while picking up her clothing, making sure that the fabric of her dress did not rustle. Her undergarments were scattered across the floor and some rested on the table. Finding her shoes proved time consuming and she looked back over her shoulder more than once to ensure that Synclair was still sleeping. She allowed herself one long look at him before turning her back on him and their night together.

She eased from the room with all of her clothing hugged tightly against her chest. She didn't stop to put her chemise on either. The house was still silent and dark, the hallway held in the grip of night. She heard every breath she drew and flinched when she gently closed the door because the sound it made seemed loud, though in reality was quite hushed.

Early morning was often that way. She could smell the new snow in the air and feel the pinch of winter chill on her bare skin. No smoke tickled her nose yet, telling her that the servants were still sleeping, too. Justina stopped at the bottom of the stairs, gently placing her bundle of clothing on a table there. She shivered, gooseflesh rippling along her skin. She plucked her chemise out of the jumble and hurried into it to chase away the morning chill. Her nipples still drew into hard points and she shivered again while sitting down in a nearby chair to pull her stockings up her legs. Lacing her shoes on was simple with only the thin fabric of her chemise covering her midsection, but there was no way to lace her stays, so she lifted her dress and allowed it to settle around her without the stiffly boned undergarment. The dress wouldn't conform to her curves without being laced as well but there was no time for that. The fabric covered her and that was enough for the early hour.

She ducked out of the door, taking care to close it gently and leave the house sleeping. Outside, the landscape was glittering with fresh snow, all of it lying pristine and perfect without any tracks. The horizon was only beginning to turn pink, slim fingers of light cutting through the darkness. It was a time of day that she saw too often, but peace settled over her with the solace in knowing that she had made her escape once again.

A smile lifted the corners of her mouth, a sense of victory filling her because she had taken her pleasure where she wished, and for once, at the command of no one.

Well, except for Synclair. The knight had enjoyed telling her what his will was. She crossed the yard toward the stable. Her leather shoes were little protection against the snow that broke beneath her weight, allowing her to sink ankle-deep with each pace.

She was thankful that the hunting house was built for easy access to the horses. Inside, her feet didn't need to suffer the snow, and it was slightly warm from the coals lying beneath the ash in the fireplaces. Two stable boys rolled over when the horses stirred, their ears twitching when she entered. One boy lifted his eyelids and looked at her from where he slept near the fire. Justina lifted a hand and placed a finger against her lips. The boy pulled his blanket closer and closed his eyes once more.

Obviously, a tousled-looking woman leaving at dawn was not an uncommon sight to them. Her cheeks flushed when she considered just how the two boys had become so familiar with seeing women leaving the house with their hair unpinned and clothing unfashioned. Henry Tudor had often kept his mistresses at the lodge, and his nobles followed in the King's footsteps, spending the night hours in bed sport before making appearances at service. None of them were faithful to their wives, many more seeking divorces exactly as the King did. It made being a woman difficult and it also allowed men such as Biddeford to use their female dependents like prostitutes.

Synclair had not made her feel like that . . .

The thought renewed her lament over leaving and she stiffened, because she had to return to the palace before day broke completely. For all the sordid things that happened by night, the court was a vastly different place during the light of day. She would treasure the memory but return to her place without further delay.

She reached for a mare, one of several that were kept in the stable. Saddles were lined up along the railings of one

stall. There was a sense of security in knowing how to saddle a mare with her own hands. She soon had the horse
ready for its early morning ride and led it toward the stable door. She stopped and peeked outside before opening
the door. The yard was empty and still, only her tracks
marring the smooth surface of the snow.

She swung up on top of the horse, gripping the saddle
with her thighs while no one was about to critique her.
Besides, what did it matter if someone declared that she
was sterile because she rode astride? She had no husband
to worry by such news.

The mare cut through the snow with little crunching
sounds. Justina saw her own breath turning white in front
of her while she leaned down low over the neck of the animal. The crisp air flowed through her hair, making her as
giddy as a child who had stolen away from her school-
room tasks.

But all too soon Whitehall came into view. The guards
were diligent at the gates but they allowed her through
without question since the saddle was marked with the
arms of the King. She turned a corner and rode down to
the stables where the King's horses were kept, before slipping from the back of the mare and handing the reins over
to a boy wearing the colors of the Tudor household.

"Feed her well and warm her feet."

"Yes, ma'am."

Justina dug into a tiny pocket on the side of her gown
and pulled a small silver coin from it. The groom's eyes
brightened, and he took the money, pushing it deep into
his doublet.

"Remember me not."

The boy nodded, casting his gaze at the mare. Justina
hurried up the stairs that would take her inside the maze
of hallways that made up the palace. She knew them well,

turning and covering the distance to her chambers through the smaller hallways used by the servants.

But she was not the only lady walking along the corridors this morning. Other women, whose hair flowed down their backs, made their way, too. They didn't look up, did not make eye contact with her, but kept to their side of the hallway when she passed them. There were no words spoken but an undeniable feeling of regret permeated the stone hallways. Justina forced herself to not think of it as hopelessness for she wasn't ready to become so jaded. She resisted thinking about the other women who were but hollow shells of what they had been when they first came to court, drunk on the stories of grandeur and royal majesty. Each of them had learned that marriage was for the gain of the family and their bodies a treat for the men to enjoy. While the horizon continued to brighten, more of her sisters made their way to their chambers and the role of respectable ladies.

She was no different, no worse, but at least she had truly come from a lover this morning. She would hold that thought close to her heart and hopefully keep it from turning to stone.

At least for a little bit longer.

"Did he have you?"

Justina pressed her hands over her mouth to smother a cry of surprise. Biddeford was sitting in the chair again, only this time hidden in the dark. She heard him snap his fingers and then there was a scuff against the floor before sparks flew out from a flint stone being struck. The groom had to strike it several times before the candle's wick caught fire and light illuminated the viscount.

Justina preferred the darkness, for his expression chilled her. Displeasure was showing clearly on his face and there was a warning in his eyes that she had suffered only a few times in the past.

"The maid claimed that you rode off with Baron Harrow last night after he fought with Francis de Canis."

Of course the maid had told him. For a bit of silver any servant might be encouraged to recall where nobles went and with whom, even if those same servants had been paid to remain silent. One never knew; the only thing certain was that if one failed to bribe, the servant would most definitely talk.

The viscount's eyes narrowed as he raked her from head to toe. "You look well and truly tumbled."

Justina forced her enjoyment of the night down deep inside her, into a place that only she knew of. Reality had arrived, just as she knew that it would.

"What else would he have taken me with him for?" She turned to hide her distaste for how her words sounded. Synclair did not deserve to be talked about in such derogatory tones; however, it was better than allowing Biddeford to know that she admired Synclair. The viscount might decide to make an example of him, just to prove his power over her. She would not take the chance. "But I am returned and no one the wiser."

The viscount slapped the table, the sound drawing her back around to watch him. The man didn't have any qualms about striking women so it would be wise to keep him in sight.

"Francis de Canis knows and he is most displeased with you, madam." The hand on the table began to tap against the hard surface. "De Canis has powerful friends who enjoy his work enough to want to see the man happy."

A shiver crossed her face. She failed to suppress it and Biddeford noticed it.

"Letting de Canis use you might have been advantageous." He tapped the table again. "Then again, he is the sort of man who likes what he is told he cannot have best of all."

Justina watched the way the viscount contemplated her. He was weighing the amount of gain to be had, peddling her like a moor did a slave girl.

"Continue to tell de Canis no. Let him nurse a swollen cock when you walk by him. Dance with him if he asks and tease him, but refuse him anything further."

Justina felt like a weight had been lifted off her chest. She drew in a deep breath but knew that it was far too soon to celebrate anything. The viscount was merely attempting to drive up the price before he made a bargain.

"We'll see how much he desires your sweet flesh and more importantly how much he will give me to take you away from Baron Harrow."

"The Baron Harrow is on close terms with the Earl of Hertford."

The viscount made a soft sound of reprimand beneath his breath. He stood up and closed the distance between them. He raised one hand and stroked a single fingertip across her cheek.

"Be very glad that your worth is in your beauty, else I would strike that insolence from you." His hand trailed down to her arm. "A pity that I cannot even mark you where your clothing will hide it but I will not lament it very much. There are many who will give me a great deal to possess your body."

He twisted his fingers in her unbound hair, pulling the strands cruelly. She bent, leaning over while he watched her suffering, his hand never easing its hold.

"You may fuck only when I give you direction to, my dear Baroness. Do not forget that again. Harrow hasn't paid for your sweet flesh, so make sure he doesn't sample it against my will or I shall be very displeased."

He released her hair and walked to the door while his

groom scurried to arrive there before his master and open it for him.

"Make sure you do not conceive."

The door shut with a whisper but still she flinched.

Conceive? She would never make that mistake again, hadn't allowed it to happen twice in spite of her husband's rage over the lack of more sons to brag about to his friends. He'd beaten her for the lack of more children but she refused to allow herself to be caged with any more souls that she loved. It wasn't hard to keep her womb empty. There were women who knew the way and they sold their herbs, which when seeped in hot water would keep a man's seed from taking root.

Justina turned and pushed the kettle over the fire. It was kept in her private chambers just so that she might brew her own remedy for the passions of the nighttime. But today, tears stung her eyes while she dug out the small, cloth-wrapped bundle that she would need. Synclair needed children, just not hers.

But she couldn't dispel the feeling that it was a pity she couldn't allow nature to take its course. Maybe fate would bless her with a babe. At least then she would be returned to the country. But her child would be bastard born and subject to Biddeford's will even more so than Brandon, because someday Brandon would inherit his title. Any child she conceived out of wedlock would have only her to champion it and the world was controlled by men. Synclair would not wed her; she wasn't worthy of that.

She pulled the kettle out of the hearth and carefully poured a measure of water into the wooden mug holding the little bundle of herbs. Steam rose into the air, tickling her nose with the scent of bitterness. She waited just a few moments before lifting it to her lips and draining every last drop. She would not hesitate or give herself time to fail.

Tears wet her cheeks when she sat the cup aside and she lowered herself into the chair while feeling the hot liquid warming her insides.

Lament? It was not harsh enough a word for how she felt.

"His lordship, the Earl of Hertford, requires your presence."

Synclair snarled at the page but the boy didn't flinch. Instead the youngster looked somewhat bored, his attention straying to the window and the winter landscape visible through it.

"Tell your master I will be there shortly."

At least the earl was at Whitehall. Synclair looked back at the bed and growled. Oh yes, he was interested in going to the palace, but not to seek out Edward Seymour. The earl and his power were not what Synclair was interested in, but he was not a fool either. Justina was tangled in a sticky web and pulling her free would not be a simple task. Legend and lore liked to suggest that knights could be noble and win the day but that was rarely so. Honor might be present on the battlefield but a wise man didn't expect it from his enemy. You had to be ready to fight, any way that the moment demanded. Let the minstrels sing their tunes of chivalry, but as for claiming his lady, he would need men such as Edward Seymour to make it happen.

Synclair refused to think of the fact that he might fail. The memory of the night was so fresh in his mind, it felt like he might return to the bed and be once again in her embrace. He hadn't slept so deeply in months, didn't think he'd awoken so refreshed in years. All of it had dissipated when he had realized his bed was empty.

He turned away from the rumpled sheets to begin

dressing. Justina didn't know him very well because the lady seemed to think that dismissing him was enough to gain her way.

He was going to enjoy showing her the error of her ways.

The Earl of Hertford received him like a prince.

Synclair had to wait outside the receiving chamber while the doors were guarded by royal yeomen. They kept to their stations while Synclair scanned the room and discovered that he was not alone in wanting to see the earl. Ambassadors spoke to one another in low tones, the sounds of foreign languages such as Italian, French, and German touched his ears. The fact that these ambassadors waited outside Edward Seymour's door spoke much of the attitude of the rest of the crowned heads of Europe.

They would be looking at the earl as the man controlling England. There was no other reason for the attendance of so many outside his chambers.

The doors opened and the room went silent instantly as everyone waited to hear what name would be called.

"Baron Harrow."

There was a mutter of frustration from more than one party. Synclair stepped forward. The earl spoke in the same instant that the doors banged shut, confirming that they were in privacy. Synclair offered the man a quick reverence and controlled the urge to grin. Seymour was a bit too eager. Henry would have made him wait before voicing what was on his mind.

"Francis de Canis is a man many consider a friend of the King. Fighting with him was not in your best interest."

Synclair stared straight at the Earl of Hertford. "Is he Henry's friend? Maybe I shall ask His Majesty about that."

Seymour's eyebrow rose. "You have business with the King? What manner of business?"

"Private correspondence from the Baron Ryppon. Lord Ryppon considers the King a friend I believe."

The earl relaxed, although it was only a slight change that most would have missed. Synclair didn't. He'd remained alive riding across France only because he knew how to read a man's face for the things that he didn't want you to know. More than one young knight had been ordered into a hopeless battle for the better good of the army. He had learned not to be one of those pitiful men sacrificed by his better-blooded commanders so that they might live. The earl flicked his hand toward a chair.

"I will be happy to see the correspondence to his majesty."

Synclair sat down and smiled. "You know me better than that, Edward. What duty is mine, shall be finished by my hand."

"Edward, is it?" The earl's eyes narrowed. "Are we friends then?"

"It has been said by some, even you as I recall." Synclair didn't allow his emotions to color his tone. "Unless you're too tempered by these palace walls to recall what it was like to have me riding at your side in France while half of those fine nobles hid behind the army for fear of their lives."

The Earl of Hertford frowned. "My memory is sound, even if your judgment is as astute as ever. These walls do change a man. Yet I summoned you here to make sure that those who would take issue with you over your fight with de Canis know that I consider you someone I do call friend."

There was a warning in the earl's tone, one Synclair knew he'd be wise to heed. The Earl of Hertford was a very powerful man and one who didn't have to suffer any man insinuating that he was less than honorable, but there was always more than one way to win against those who felt they should never be argued with because of their high position. Synclair shrugged.

"So what if I took Justina away last night? She is a widow and I snatched her fairly away from de Canis, so who should care? I doubt the man remained lonely for long. At least that is what rumor says about him."

Seymour's lips twitched up. "I concede that point in your favor. Just have a care for her guardian. Biddeford likes to keep her close and her favors in his hand to dispense to those that he chooses."

Synclair ground his teeth together, holding his emotions behind a face that told the earl nothing except what he wanted the man to know. It was not the first time he had listened to men discussing women like they were mares for the buying but today, he discovered that it irritated him almost beyond his endurance to hear such talk centering on Justina. He found that he was taking it personally.

"I plan to make an offer for her."

The earl choked on the wine he'd just swallowed. "Offer? Are you mad? She's been known by a few too many."

"Not that many, not more than I have known. I want her."

"You're a man, you wench and enjoy it but you don't have to marry Lady Wincott to gain that. Enjoy her, while you investigate some of the pretty little heiresses here for the winter." Seymour waved his hand to dismiss the topic.

"I've had enough girls. I want a woman in my bed."

The earl shrugged. "And so you have one. I hear she's more fair under her gown than in it and knows her way around a man's member very well."

Synclair felt his fingers curl into fists. The earl suddenly sat forward.

"Be careful, so newly lord Harrow, your face tells me that you're actually jealous. That isn't a wise position to take in this time of shifting alliances. Don't make any enemies, especially for the sake of a woman. They are replaceable."

"I'll remember that you said that."

"Good." But Seymour frowned, clearly noticing that Synclair did not agree with him, but what made the earl frown was the fact that Synclair wasn't very concerned about the fact that he did know. Most men at court feared him and did everything in their power to appear as though they agreed with everything he said.

Synclair offered the earl a slight smirk. "Come now my lord, don't you grow weary of having your ego buffed? Every man has his own ideas."

The conversation wasn't satisfying him. Synclair sipped the fine French wine Seymour offered and allowed the man to turn the conversation away from Justina. But there was warning in the earl's eyes that he stared back at with unrelenting determination. The earl finally sighed.

"I believe you have gone mad up on that borderland, Synclair. Marriage is for gain."

"Her late husband's estates are profitable, and I believe they can become more so with the right steward. Unlike the late Lord Wincott, I plan to run my lands and those under my jurisdiction, not through a secretary while I am at court."

"That might gain you a better yield on your crops and income but the lady has a son who will inherit those lands." The earl sat his goblet down and stroked his beard while he contemplated the matter. "Still, it will be many years before that happens, which could allow you to make quite a sizable sum on something that you will owe no inheritance tax upon. A clever idea actually, I can see the appeal of it."

"Exactly, and I will have the lady herself, a proven

breeder of sons. Virgins do not bring that sort of promise. One of those heiresses might be naught but a yoke around my neck if she proves barren."

The earl snorted. "Or gives you a daughter." He shook his head and scratched at his beard. "You won't hold onto any coin if you have a wife that births naught but girls, but one that is barren, her, you might divorce."

"As if I want anything to do with that spoilt kettle of fish." Synclair grumbled. "I've done enough deeds alongside the King to find myself in need of the blessing and goodwill of the Church."

The earl sobered, something flickering in his eyes that Synclair understood. They had both sinned plenty in their campaigns, one might call it duty but that did not change how the memories struck a man when he was sipping his wine and no one was around to praise him for things that he found regrettable.

"Divorce is messy, I will grant you that. But the Viscount Biddeford enjoys the income from her son's properties now and he will not release those easily." The earl slapped his leg. "So wed her, if and when she conceives. Wait until her belly rounds, so that you know she is not deceiving you." The earl smiled. "I will support you, if you need to wed in a hurry."

"Will you witness the ceremony?"

That was asking for a great deal from a man such as the earl. It would place his name on the matter and make it impossible for him to whisper that he had not supported it all along. Such favors did not come easily and Synclair's intention to leave court didn't offer Seymour much opportunity to call upon him when he was in the mood to have the favor returned. The realities of court intensified his need to pry Justina away from it. This was an example of what had seen her leaving his bed before sunrise. The calculating look in Seymour's eyes renewed Synclair's need to free her from this life where there was nothing genuine. He longed to leave it behind himself and share his future with a woman that would cherish a country life every bit as much as he would.

Justina would, he was certain of it.

The earl drew in a stiff breath.

"If she is breeding, yes."

Synclair nodded but the earl held up one finger.

"But only if she is carrying, Harrow. Beyond that, the times do not permit me to upset the men who consider de Canis indispensable. You'd be wise to remember that he has many nobles who would not cross him because of the things he knows them guilty of having a hand in. If you plan to make Lady Wincott's lands profitable, you will need other men to do business with. Make an enemy of de Canis and that might never happen."

Synclair stopped outside the Earl of Hertford's chambers and drew in a deep breath. It was not the first time he had kept his true feelings hidden, but it felt as though it had been the hardest. His temper was still hot in spite of the fact that he'd gained what he wanted from the earl. Even that promise to witness his wedding didn't cool the anger that had flashed through him while listening to the man talk about Justina as though she were a commodity to be weighed and judged. He forced another deep breath into his chest and focused his mind on the outcome of the meeting. He had the man's word and that was all he needed from the Earl of Hertford. With luck and good planning, he would be away from court with his lady and not have to suffer the arrogance of the man again.

That was what mattered and still, the urge to smash his fist into Seymour's face persisted.

"You took a piece of meat from me last night."

Francis de Canis stuck true to his nature, speaking out

from around the corner when Synclair made his way out of the Earl of Hertfort's private chambers. De Canis was leaning against the wall but Synclair didn't make the mistake of thinking the man was at ease. There was a subtle tension in his body that betrayed just how quickly he might strike.

"If a man isn't quick enough, he tends to go hungry." Synclair walked out far enough to be able to face the man completely. His temper relished the idea of a fight and he didn't give a damn if de Canis saw it in his eyes.

"Missing one meal only tends to make it taste better when I finally sink my teeth into what I truly desire." De Canis finished his thought with a smirk.

"She is sweet but you'll never know from personal experience, de Canis."

De Canis stood up, closing the gap between them. "So says you, Harrow, but you don't have as many friends as I do in this court."

Synclair stepped up until they were nose to nose. Every muscle strained, begging for a chance to release some of his frustration by tearing into the son of a bitch in front of him.

"I didn't need my friends to take that meat out of your hands, and I don't need anyone to keep her."

"Yes, you do." De Canis sneered, confidence radiating from him. He leaned closer and dropped his voice. "I'm going to have her and when I do, I promise, you will hear every sordid detail."

CHAPTER FIVE

S ynclair found her before evening.
Justina had to bite her lip and force her happiness
down at the sight of Synclair. He sent her a hard look, one
that sent a tingle down her back because there was a warning in it.

But staring at her was all he might do because she was
once more sitting with the Queen and her ladies. No men
were allowed near them, not even old ones. The snow had
trapped them all inside and the first true day of winter was
passing slowly.

Of course it was mostly due to her mind dwelling on
memories best left in the night that had gone. But she remained with the ladies, pretending to enjoy the reading
from Chaucer's *Canterbury Tales*. Justina worked her needle in and out of a shirt for Brandon, hoping it would fit
him once it was finished and sent to him.

"Lady Wincott."

Justina looked up, almost doubting that anyone had spoken because the tone had been so soft. But the Queen's
eyes were upon her.

"Yes, Your Majesty?"

Catherine Parr offered her a sympathetic look before
tightening her hands. "I cannot shoulder gossip. Not for

anyone. You must send that knight away or go, so that he will leave."

Justina felt her stomach tighten. All of the Queen's ladies offered her no mercy.

"As you will, Your Majesty."

She stood up and felt Synclair's eyes move with her. Forcing her steps to be even and polished taxed her almost beyond her strength because her temper had begun to flare. He waited for her, his eyes watching her while a small, victorious grin curved his lips.

Why did the man have to be so handsome? It was grossly unfair of fate to craft him with such a face that she could not ignore him. Of course, there was more than his face that she found appealing. There were the wide shoulders she had clung to last night that drew her interest. Indeed, she found his body very difficult to dismiss from her thoughts.

"You must stop watching me."

His lips curved even more, while one of his eyebrows rose. "If you wished to be in a position to tell me what pleases you, Justina, you should have remained in bed this morning."

"I couldn't do that."

His eyes darkened. "The hell you could not, woman. You stole away while it was still dark, like a thief."

Each word was hard as stone, transmitting his displeasure perfectly. She walked out of the room the Queen was in and Synclair followed her, but he reached out and caught her arm the moment they were no longer in sight of the women.

Justina stiffened, quelling the urge to push him. She had no idea where such thoughts came from but they bubbled up from the temper blazing through her.

"I would think you would be happy to have me gone and expecting nothing from you."

He drew in a stiff breath. "Think again, Lady, and look into my eyes to see just how far from the truth your words are."

Justina shook her head. "It doesn't matter what either of us wants. My guardian has warned me to stay away from you, and I must obey his dictates."

"Wed with me."

Her eyes rounded and he used the grip on her arm to pull her down another hallway. He looked in all directions before tugging her into a small workroom.

"Are you insane? If we are discovered here, Biddeford will be very displeased with me. I must consider my son, Synclair."

"Wed me, and I will be the boy's guardian."

"That is not assured. Viscount Biddeford is a compatriot of Chancellor Wriothesley. If I wed without my guardian's permission, my son might remain in the man's custody."

She shuddered, her temper dying in a sputter of longing. She reached out for the man she could not have, her hands on his chest, absorbing his strength. Just her fingertips brushed against him, but she couldn't resist the need to touch him; it was likely for the last time. Tears burned her eyes but she forbid them to fall.

"I will treasure your offer."

"You will do more than that, Justina. You will be my wife, and you will give me children."

She shook her head, the memory of the brew she had swallowed making her insides burn. Synclair suddenly cursed. Her eyes widened in surprise. Most men would have been pleased to know she was not planning to snare him into marriage with a child conceived through lust.

"You will cease taking anything to prevent my seed from ripening your belly."

She shook her head, incredulous to hear him making such a demand from her.

"To what end, Synclair? We have no permission to wed. It would be selfish indeed to bring a child into this world as a bastard."

He cupped her chin, his touch gentle. His tenderness made her shudder. "Edward will witness our marriage if your belly is round. I have his word upon the matter."

She gasped, time freezing for a moment while her heart filled with joy. She felt it burn through her, warming her in spite of the winter chill. Synclair slid a hard arm around her body, bringing her against him in a solid embrace that completed the moment perfectly.

Yet, life was not perfect.

"That will not ensure that you will gain guardianship of Brandon. I must think of my child before myself."

"Trust me to shelter him, Justina."

She felt her eyes widen and her hands left his chest to cross over in front of her own. Trust? She couldn't. It was a fact that she wasn't even sure that she knew how to trust any man. There had not been one man in her life who hadn't used her. She began shaking her head, the denial rising up from inside her too thick to hide. Synclair cursed, low and deep, before he pushed her farther into the room.

"It is a good thing your father and husband are dead because I would like to crush the life out of them with my bare hands for not treating you with the respect you deserve."

"You must not say such things. My situation is not unique. Most daughters marry to please their father and then they kneel in front of their husband. England is full of women who do what they must, not what they want."

His hand covered her lips, gently but firmly. A warning flashed through his eyes, making her gasp. Inside him was a warrior and not the gentle one that she had somehow convinced herself he was.

"Take a long look, Justina, and witness the fact that I am not so different from yourself. I have carried out orders that I despised because they were handed down by my king, actions for which I still feel guilt."

His voice was razor sharp and his face tight. She reached up, pulling his hand away from her mouth but she pressed a soft kiss against it.

"Then you truly must understand, Synclair. I cannot wed with you. The viscount controls my future."

He pulled his hand out of her grasp, while a small smile appeared for a moment on his lips. She shivered because it was not a kind smile. The warrior inside him was seeking victory, and he allowed her to see it.

"What I think, Justina, is that you and I are going to dance."

He stepped away from her, his expression becoming pensive. "But not here. When I come for you, Lady, believe me, you may expect to see me coming."

He turned and began to cover the space to the doorway. Her lips were suddenly sorry that he had not kissed her.

"What are you talking about?" Justina couldn't help asking the question; she felt her heart accelerating while she waited to hear his reply.

He turned and smiled at her once more. She had actually begun to follow him and his keen gaze noticed it. A soft chuckle crossed his lips.

"You see, Justina? You are as drawn to me as I am to you."

A moment later, her wish was granted. He swept her up against him, securing her to his body with a firm arm around her waist. The skirts of her gown billowed backward while his head lowered and tilted slightly so that he could capture her lips. It was a hard kiss, one that punished her for fleeing from his bed. She could feel his wounded pride in the way his mouth mastered hers, pressing against her lips until she surrendered and opened her mouth. His tongue thrust deep inside, stroking along the length of her own and sending a sensation down her back. Her heart began beating faster and her rapid breathing drew his scent deep inside her. It was suddenly not enough to be kissed by him. She reached for him, her hands stroking over the sides of his firm jaw and into his shoulder-length hair. A sense of urgency filled her, a desperation to kiss him back with every ounce of need that was boiling deep inside her belly.

But he put her away from him. A tiny sound of misery escaped her open mouth before she pressed her own hand over her lips to seal them.

Victory and determination shone in Synclair's eyes.

"I shall have you, exactly as I want you, Justina." A warning flashed in his eyes. "And you shall be glad of it."

"But—"

Her protest fell on an empty room. Synclair was gone before she moved her hand to allow the single word out. She shivered once and then several times more as a deep hunger nipped at her body. It was not confined to her clitoris or even her passage but far more widespread. Need bit into her along her limbs and across her breasts to the nipples that had so enjoyed his hot mouth around them last night. The skin on her neck was sensitive, clamoring for the gentle touches that had built her passion to such an unbelievable height.

It defied reasoning.

The hand she held over her lips was shaking and every bit of her flesh argued against the harsh realities of her life. There was nothing logical about her longings; there had never been a time when she could not ignore the cravings of her flesh.

Except for now.

She wanted to lie with him again, but more than just lie, she wanted to reach out and touch him until he shivered. It was shocking, but she realized that she wanted to take him. Touch him in every way that she had ever been forced to learn about when it came to pleasing a man, except that this time, she wanted to do it for nothing but the pleasure it would give him.

She wanted to be Synclair's lover.

Henry Tudor, King of England, Ireland, and Wales, knew how to receive those who wanted his attention, in such a manner that left no question that he ruled with absolute authority. Synclair waited on the King for half a day and knew there were men who had been listening for the chamberlain to call their names for days, sometimes weeks if the King was not in the mood to listen to their cause.

The chamberlain held a large white staff that was capped on the bottom with a brass fitting. When the man made ready to announce a name that the King would honor with an audience, he lifted the staff and struck the floor three times. The men waiting all quieted, their attention turning to the ornately carved double doors that would open to reveal the King. Henry sat on a large throne that was placed on a raised dais. There were costly Persian rugs beneath his feet and intricate tapestries hung behind his back. Every time the doors opened, trumpeters sounded off from some unseen point inside the receiving room.

"The Baron Harrow."

The staff struck the floor and the guards opened the doors, allowing Synclair to enter the King's presence. He barely crossed the threshold before those doors were firmly shut behind him.

"So you remember the way down from the north, Synclair. Some men up there become drunk on their power and forget there is a King in England."

Synclair offered Henry Tudor an appropriate reverence but he didn't draw it out, and that gained him a short bark of amusement from his monarch.

"At least you recall that behind closed doors I have no taste for pompous behavior."

"I could never forget your preferences, sire." Synclair straightened. "Or your tastes. You do have a way of expressing them to those who take the time to notice, and a wise man remembers details like those."

"I see that you are still as boldly spoken as Lord Ryppon."

Synclair offered his king no apology and stood firmly in place while Henry considered him from hard, glittering eyes. The King chuckled and pointed one thick finger at him.

"It's one of the reasons I approved your inheritance of title and land. I need men in the north whose loyalty I don't have to question. At least I have no trouble discovering what you are thinking."

Henry Tudor was aging quickly. Synclair gritted his teeth while his gaze took in the changes that had befallen him. The man who had once led men across France was now too large to sit on a horse. He wasn't wearing a doublet but a garment that had wide skirting beginning at his mid-chest. The fabric allowed for his increased girth, and it was quite a large increase, too.

"My leg continues to heal, making clothing a bother at best."

Synclair felt a prickle of worry cross him. Henry Tudor snorted at him.

"And I have enough people looking at me in that manner, man. Don't test my patience by becoming one of them."

Synclair tilted his head to one side and offered his king a grin. "Well, my liege, that would leave me the option of looking like one of the men who is anticipating hearing of your demise . . ."

Henry choked on his laughter. "I plan to make them wait a good long time." The King pointed to a chair. It was considered an honor for a man to be invited to sit while in the presence of his king.

Synclair offered Henry a slight incline of his head in gratitude before taking the seat. The King flicked his fingers and a servant appeared with a silver tray that held a decanter and goblet.

"Venetian glass, it makes the wine taste divine."

Synclair picked up the goblet. "It feels too delicate for a man's grip."

"They are surprisingly resilient."

Henry lifted a matching glass to his lips, pulling a deep swallow from the dark-colored wine. A look of disgust twisted his lips for a moment.

"I spend too much time these days nursing my pains." The King spoke quietly and there was the unmistakable hint of worry in his tone. Anyone who knew Henry Tudor wouldn't make the mistake of calling it fear; he always had possessed more bravery than was often wise, but it was what made him the king he was.

"I bring a message from Lord Ryppon." Synclair offered the rolled parchment to a servant.

"Ah, my friend Curan. Tell me, how is that pretty wife of his? I envy him her, that girl has fire in her."

"Now she carries a child."

The King nodded and sipped his wine again. A servant refilled the goblet the moment it was placed back down. The King considered him with narrowed eyes for a moment.

"So now you have your leave and your title." Henry sat

forward, his hands curling around the armrests of his chair. "What do you seek among my court?"

Synclair slowly smiled. "I find it hard to believe that Your Majesty has not heard what I have been about."

Henry laughed. The sound was deep and full, echoing off the closed doors behind Synclair. The King slapped the armrest before he finished.

"So I have heard about your rather indelicate dealings." The King sobered. "Francis de Canis is a dangerous man to cross."

"So am I."

Silence settled between them while the King drank more of his wine. His face became pensive and the ghost of something from years past crossed his eyes.

"I remember feeling so passionate."

The King frowned, a pinched look taking control of his expression.

"Thank you for delivering the message, Baron Harrow. It is good to receive good letters from friends."

It was a dismissal. Synclair rose and offered the king a curtsy but he did not lower his eyes. He aimed a hard look at Henry Tudor.

The King drew in a stiff breath. "I have no answer for you, Synclair. There is a balance that must be maintained in this country, and I will not upset it for one woman. You will have to find a way to pry her out of Biddeford's control if you want her."

"I want her."

The King smiled, an arrogant curving of his lips that spoke of times when he had been just as determined to have the lady of his choice.

"Then I will look forward to hearing something amusing from the gossips for a change, for I have wagered my money on you over de Canis."

★ ★ ★

Synclair moved through the men waiting to see the King with a stride that sent them out of his way. It was also possible that the look on his face cleared the path in front of him.

Whatever the cause, he took advantage of it, moving quickly away from the King's receiving chambers. Henry's confidence in him was little compared to the help that he might have granted. Synclair didn't stop until he reached a door that led to the gardens. Snow covered the plants now, the stalks frozen beneath the white blanket. He continued to move quickly until he heard the ice crunching beneath his boots.

Fine. Henry's help would have made things very simple, but Synclair confessed that there was part of him that would not have been truly satisfied with that sort of victory. What he craved was surrender from Justina. It was suddenly not so hard to understand what had driven Henry to break with the traditions of his ancestors in order to have Anne Boleyn.

He would have Justina, there was no other thought in his mind. He'd spent two long years dreaming of her. He drew in a deep breath, savoring the chill in the air while he forced his mind to move away from how much he yearned for Justina. What he needed was sound strategy and the formulation of a plan.

His lips began to curl upward as he recalled exactly what Edward Seymour had promised him. Now there was something that he would not mind accomplishing or making sure that Justina enjoyed full well.

The conception of a child, yes, they would both enjoy that. He'd given his word on the matter. All that remained was to trap his vixen, so that he might spend time teaching her to trust him. His temper burned hotter as he considered the fact that Justina did not trust him. That fact stung his pride but it also made his heart ache. Most men didn't value trust in their daughters or wives; they expected obedience and never took the time to notice that trust was far more satisfying.

He was going to have that from Justina but he did not expect it to come easily. His lips suddenly split into a grin.

What it was going to be was his pleasure to prove.

He stepped out into the yard, ignoring the grooms who might have fetched his horse for him. Let men like Biddeford stand and waste time while servants rushed to please them.

He had a plan to place in motion, and he could feel anticipation coursing through his muscles.

Action, that was what he craved, and he would have what he wanted by the sweat of his own brow.

He would have Justina for his wife.

Even if he had to take her.

CHAPTER SIX

Winter closed in tighter, trapping everyone still with the court inside the palace. Embroidery and shirt-making became the main amusements while the food was plainer and less plentiful. The river froze, stopping the barges from coming to the water gates with their loads of goods. But what made the palace even quieter was that the King was seen only briefly. He received only a few hours a day and on some days, not at all. His children, Edward, Mary, and Elizabeth, had been removed from Whitehall. The young Prince Edward was residing at Hertford with his tutors while the Princess Elizabeth lived at Enfield.

With the children gone, Whitehall became hushed, a deadly sort of silence that seemed magnified by the snow growing deeper around its stone walls every day. Tension drew everyone into its web as the privy council met behind closed doors. The Queen was careful to measure her words and actions to the point that Justina could almost not stomach being near her, as she felt such pity for her.

She understood the Queen's situation, the trapped sensation of knowing that your husband might kill you if you displeased him or if you simply happened to be in his sights when something else set his temper ablaze.

But that was not what made Justina feel so desolate. It was the lack of feeling Synclair's gaze upon her. She had told him to go. She reminded herself that it was best that the knight was missing from the palace, and yet she ached to see him. She had watched him for so long, every day at Amber Hill, and before that too when he had been at court with Lord Ryppon.

The man Biddeford had ordered her to take as her lover.

That had been a cruel twist of the knife. It was a wound that still ached. Curan Ryppon was not like her husband. He had been a considerate lover, but she had still dreaded each time she had gone to his bed. The reason was Synclair. She had passed the knight on her way to his lord's bed because it was his duty to stand guard over his lord. She'd felt his eyes on her, felt guilt raining down on her because she had gone to Curan over him.

But she had not chosen . . .

Her temper burned bright, chasing away the chill of the day. She had only ever wanted Synclair and now he was gone. She felt her fury building, burning away the wise reasons that kept her on Biddeford's leash. Why did it have to cost her so much? Where was the reward for her devotion to family? The Church would condemn her for such thoughts but she could not prevent them from boiling up inside her. She was angry, so very furious at the lack of justice in her life.

Justina found herself looking toward the stables, wishing to be gone.

"Longing for a country home?"

Justina stiffened and turned to see Francis de Canis standing far too close to her for her taste. He pulled a pair of leather riding gauntlets from his hands and offered her a cocksure grin.

"Or have you missed me, sweet Lady Wincott? I will be happy to keep you from looking so longing since it appears that Baron Harrow has failed to keep you entertained."

"I have no need for your attention."

He laughed at her reply, a soft sound that reminded her of a cat when it played with a weak creature before killing it. Justina stared straight at him, refusing to cower before him. Heat flickered in his eyes and it turned her stomach. He had more in common with an animal than a man.

"Francis de Canis, you're a welcome sight."

The Viscount Biddeford waited for de Canis to give him deference. Justina watched the way the man tightened his lips before reverencing. That pride would cost the man his life someday. She might hope so, anyway, and never mind the fact that such a thought was unchristian. The man was a beast, one that needed to be put down before it killed again.

"I see you have found my ward."

"Yes. We were just discussing how much we have in common."

Justina stiffened but Biddeford chuckled.

"Indeed? I have always found that men and women have very little in common. Lady Wincott, attend me."

Justina heard de Canis mutter something beneath his breath while she joined the viscount and followed him down the hallway.

"That sound coming from our friend is very reassuring." Biddeford looked at her for a short moment. "The man is too proud by far; his blood is not blue, and I believe he forgets that." A soft sound of amusement passed the viscount's lips. "Besides, we cannot make it too simple for him to claim you. The man has yet to offer me anything of value."

"We could not have that." She wasn't sure what prompted her to speak; she knew it was unwise and still her spirit refused to remain silent.

"No, we shall not."

Biddeford stopped and stared at her. Displeasure flickered in his eyes but there was something else, too, something that he wanted.

"Synclair departed immediately after being received by the King."

She knew that, thought about it far too often. "Doesn't that please you?"

The viscount snickered. "My dear lady, my only argument against you being in his bed was the fact that I gained nothing from it. You are my whore, and I expect payment when you conduct business."

Her cheeks colored at his blunt words. If his men found them harsh, they didn't show it, but Justina doubted that they did. Being always with the man would surely dull the edge off any sensibilities. She knew that feeling herself, except for some reason she was now refusing to be trampled. Rebellion was growing inside her.

"I do not know where Baron Harrow has gone." Her tone was too sharp, and it gained her a narrow look.

"I want to know if the King sent him on some personal matter. They rode together in France, and His Majesty might use that friendship to secret away some important business."

"You are assuming that the Baron Harrow will return to court. He may have ridden for his lands to spend the winter."

"The reports I have say the man emerged from an audience with the King looking determined and that he went directly to the stables, wasting no time at all. His men had to ride after him with his belongings."

Could it be? Justina shifted her eyes to look out a window that was behind the viscount. Her heart filled with dread and the harsh truth that Synclair had indeed left now that he'd had her.

"When he returns, join him for the night and see what information you can gather."

Justina jerked her attention back to the viscount only to discover that he wasn't even looking at her. The man cared so little for what he ordered her to do that it was not even worthy of his full attention.

"But . . . why would you think that he might return?"

The viscount scoffed at her. "Do not sound so despondent, my dear. The man will return; I have faith in that."

But the viscount wasn't planning on sharing his reasons for believing that Synclair would return. She chewed on her lower lip for a moment.

"Going to him would only see Synclair pressing to have me remain with him."

"Excellent." Biddeford turned to look at her. He reached out and lifted her chin with a single finger. "Make sure he enjoys himself enough to come looking for me."

She shook off his touch, and he frowned at her. She could see him contemplating how to deal with her defiance.

"The privy council is sitting today. I believe you should attend, my dear ward. My men will escort you."

He said nothing else, but the look in his eyes sent a shiver down her back. Still, it was not enough to completely drown the courage that had seen her speaking her mind.

"If you like, I will go and listen to His Majesty's privy council. An escort is not necessary."

The viscount touched his fingertips together while his smile brightened.

"Oh, it does please me. I believe you will gain a new understanding of your place after hearing the cases being judged today."

He snapped his fingers to send her on her way. Justina couldn't quite bring herself to offer him a curtsy. The idea of it stuck in her throat, because he deserved no respect from her. The viscount was no better than a tavern owner along the waterfront. He peddled her flesh just as those men did their whores. Synclair's proposal surfaced from her thoughts, pricking her with more fuel for her rising need to rebel.

But her son remained and his plight shackled her to Biddeford. So she made her way to where the council was sitting. But that did not mean that she would spy upon Synclair. She refused and maybe one noble deed was but a small silver penny compared to how many times she had sinned, but she would not pass one word on to the viscount.

It was a small thing, yet it was the one way she might give something virtuous to Synclair.

The privy council was sitting in open court for a rare change. It was also a reason for hushed voices and careful steps, lest any scuff draw their attention. They were powerful men, and many of them enjoyed using that authority for whatever pleased them or placed the highest profit in their hands. Sixteen of them sat at a pair of great tables, in fur-lined half coats and hats that twinkled with jewels. Ink wells were opened and quills sharpened by the secretaries who sat behind their masters. There was a rustle of parchment as the Earl of Hertford and Chancellor Wriothesley leaned their heads close together, discussing what case would be heard. They lifted different parchments, scanning their ink-stained surface for bricf moments before continuing to whisper.

Several women fingered the skirts of their gowns, waiting for their petitions to be judged. Many of them returned each month when the lords were meeting outside their sealed council chambers, and many of them would not be gaining the attentions of the privy councilors today either.

There were others who waited with dread on their faces. These were the ones summoned to appear, and being summoned rarely resulted in any good news. The grand room filled with more nobles as the time for court came and went without the King showing himself.

Edward Seymour tapped the top of the solid table and the chamberlain called the session to order.

"Oyee, oyee, oyee. All give deference and heed to His Majesty's most high councilors."

He lifted his staff and struck the floor three times before the bishop rose and began a prayer. The assembled courtiers all bowed their heads, obedient to the will of the King, that he was head of the Church. The bishop made the sign of the cross with his hand before sitting back down.

Edward Seymour looked to the Chancellor and the man cleared his throat.

"Lady Tows, daughter of the Baron Loewen. You shall appear before this noble court."

There was a soft step as a young woman glided forward. She was dressed very somberly, with an over-partlet covering the swells of her breasts. Her gown was made of modest black wool, a strand of pearls and silver beads her only vanity. Still, her appearance did not gain her any approval from the lords waiting to speak to her. She moved forward and lowered herself, remaining down for a long moment before rising and waiting for the Chancellor to address her.

"Lady Tows, you wed without permission."

Justina watched the woman in question. Her lips were tight but she stood sure and straight before the Chancellor.

"I am wed by my father's command, my lord. I did not think to question if he had the right to direct me to go to the altar; no daughter should. I obeyed without question as I have been taught to do by the Church. My father stood at my side while I took my vows."

It was a polished response, one that half the women in the room might have given. Chancellor Wriothesley slapped the table in front of him.

"You are a brazen jade, madam! That is what you are. Your groom was a Frenchman. As a noble, your father needed permission for you to wed, especially to a foreigner."

"My husband is dead, my lord Chancellor."

A ripple of whispers went through the men sitting at the tables. The Earl of Hertford leaned closer to the Chancellor and the man tilted his head to listen. His face turned red and his fingers looked as if they might carve grooves in the wooden top of the table.

"Your father is indeed fortunate to be beyond the justice of this council. We understand there is issue from this union."

"Yes, my lords, I have a daughter."

More whispers crossed the assembled courtiers. More than one lord of the privy council frowned. A first-born daughter was indeed something that would be held against Mary Tows.

"And your husband's family, madam? Where are they?"

Mary stiffened, her hands clasping one another in a hard grip.

"Dead as well. It was the plague that took both my father and husband and many others. It is a blessing that I and my babe survived."

"I find it no such thing, considering your husband betrothed your daughter to a Scot, madam. In fact, he promised a good piece of English-held property to the man as well, a Laird McQuade I believe."

"Yes, my husband claimed the man was his friend."

A few of the lords struck the tabletop with their displeasure but the Chancellor held up a hand for silence.

"Your father's will is binding, but do not think that we
shall yet find a means to undo this match your husband has
drawn up for your daughter. For the time being, your
daughter and you shall reside within this court with the
Earl of Bridgewater as your guardian. You shall not have
leave to depart, and mark my words well, madam, I expect that you will obey me since you claim to be an obedient daughter of the Church's teachings."

Justina flinched as the chamberlain stamped the floor
with his large white staff. As quickly as that, the fate of the
woman and her daughter were sealed. The others waiting
for their turn became ghastlier shades of gray. The Earl of
Bridgewater was a newly created earl and the rumors surrounding him were dark. He watched his new ward with
an expression that showed nothing of his personal feelings.

Mary lowered herself before leaving the middle of the
room and returning to her nurse and child. The baby
reached for her mother, betraying the fact that Mary took
care of her own child instead of leaving it to the nurse.

"Oh, my sweet daughter. What will become of you?"

Justina felt her temper burning hot once more. It was
clear what Biddeford had wanted her to witness, another
woman being denied any justice from the council. Her
nurse patted her on the shoulder, attempting to comfort
her.

"They can't break the will, my lady, and by the time she
is old enough to wed, it might not be important any
longer."

Mary turned bright eyes on her nurse. "England has
forever loathed Scotland. I do not see that changing. Why
could my husband not take his displeasure out upon me
for giving him a daughter?" Tears began spilling down her
cheeks. "To betroth our daughter to a Scot, that was more

cruel than if he had killed me. I can never allow my sweet child to marry this Laird McQuade's son."

Mary hugged her child tight and left the hall with her nurse trailing her. Justina watched them go and realized that she was not the only one who did so. Near the doorway, several other women watched the unfortunate girl with looks in their eyes of compassion. One of them reached out, capturing Justina's hands within the folds of her skirts where no one might see. She offered a quick squeeze before releasing it.

"At least she did not get Biddeford for a guardian."

Justina felt her eyes widen with shock. The woman was Bessie Portshire, a high-ranking woman in her own right. She had never spoken to her before. The girl was the daughter of the Duke of Portshire. As such, she was practically royalty, and her friendship was very coveted.

Bessie leaned closer. "I know that your guardian is the monster who makes a mockery of his position to steward your estate. We all know because he is too arrogant not to brag about it."

Bessie reached out once more and captured her hand, tugging her to the hallway and away from the council.

"My father likes the Baron Harrow well."

Bessie said no more but she looked both ways before continuing. "My father wants you to tell Lord Harrow that."

"That is welcome news, Lady Portshire."

"And you must call me Bessie henceforth. I don't care what that toad of a guardian thinks to do with it, either. The men running this country are drunk on their own power. It sickens me."

"I know the sensation well."

Bessie smiled, displaying even teeth that were white and polished.

"Good, and you may help me learn to be beautiful."

"Do not ask that, Bessie; beauty is a curse."

Bessie tilted her head and her dark hair shifted. "Being plain is not such a delight either. It makes it pathetically simple to know that the men courting you are interested only in your father and dowry."

"I never considered that."

"Come, we shall spend the afternoon together and go to the masquerade tonight. I hear there is to be some fine entertainment." Bessie laughed. "Anything would be better than watching the snow grow deeper. Besides, you can help me by telling me which of my suitors are lying about how devoted they are to me."

It was an outlandish thing to say and Justina laughed. She clamped a hand over her mouth but not before her laughter echoed between the hallway walls.

Bessie smiled brightly. "See what fun we shall have? And I suspect it will annoy Biddeford as well."

"Why would you want to do that?"

Her new friend frowned. "Because he is so often at my father's table trying to gain a contract with me. He thinks I am a blind woman who does not see what he does to his own ward. As his wife, I'd fare no better, I think. I never talked to you because everyone whispers about you, but now I know better and I refuse to be anyone's puppet. So let us go enjoy the party tonight. It will be so much better than waiting for another suitor to come calling."

Or waiting for Synclair to return. Justina looked out at the blanket of white laying over where the gardens had been. There was no trace of springtime left anywhere and she felt just as frozen. Bessie wouldn't allow her to wallow in longings. The girl reached out and grabbed her hand before pulling her down the hallway.

The Earl of Bridgewater was hosting the entertainment that evening but the man didn't even make an appearance.

That didn't keep his guests from enjoying what his money paid for. Mary Tows greeted everyone in the place of her guardian. Music drifted down from the alcoves above the main floor. The air was filled with the scent of good food and wine. There were meat pies, made with dried fruit and costly spices. Small sweets decorated trays, each of them a miniature work of art. But there were no places set at the tables. Instead there were plump pillows, strewn on Persian carpets. There were low couches and chairs, but they were set in small groups. Candles cast their yellow glow around the room but there were not too many of them, giving the gathering an intimate feeling. Many of the corners were in shadow, allowing suitors to try their hand at wooing in hushed tones. The party was somewhat in defiance of the strict teaching of the Church but not quite so far removed from propriety to keep the better names from attending. There were flushed cheeks and a few gasps as ladies arrived, but they all remained.

Bessie Portshire was true to her word. She walked in with Justina and remained by her side, even when that meant that the girl was pulling Justina to wherever she wanted to go.

Justina didn't argue; it had been too long since she had allowed her cares to slip off her shoulders. She smiled and sipped at the French wine while allowing her new friend to drag her along.

"I wasn't sure you knew how to smile, Justina."

She gasped and turned, only to have to tip her head up in order to set eyes on Synclair's face. She had somehow forgotten just how much larger than herself the man was. Sensation rippled across her skin beneath her clothing. A soft recognition of him that seemed to be rooted deeply in her belly. His eyes settled on her lips, approval flickering in them.

"But I say that a smile suits you very well."

"Thank you." It was the expected response, the polite one, but the words were more sincere than any she had spoken that evening.

"You are returned."

He took a step away from her but captured her hand and performed a low reverence before bending over to touch his lips to the back of her hand. She shivered, feeling that connection between their flesh all the way to her toes. Her breath was suddenly difficult to draw, and she heard her own heartbeat inside her ears.

"You noticed, Lady. I shall enjoy knowing that."

Bessie turned to see who she was talking to and the girl giggled. She sank into a curtsy that made her silk skirts rustle. "Welcome back to court, Baron Harrow. Lady Justina missed you."

"Did she?"

Justina turned wide eyes to Bessie but the girl only fluttered her eyelashes.

"Yes, she never stopped talking about you."

"Bessie—"

"Oh look, there is Lucy. I must go and ask her how her sister is." With a rustle from her skirts, the girl went skipping across the room.

Synclair waited until Bessie was far enough away before laughing. He pressed his lips together but she still heard him choking on his amusement.

"Oh, stop it, Synclair. You know she was toying with you."

His eyes narrowed and his lips became more sensuous. "I would enjoy being toyed with by you, madam."

She had permission . . .

Her teeth bit into her lower lip while she contemplated the man in front of her. That thing she had longed for was hers, well, at least in part. She could choose to lie with him but only because she had Biddeford's permission.

Did it matter?

Was there anything that truly mattered beyond gaining what she desired?

Synclair reached out and used his thumb to pull her lip away from her teeth. He leaned close so that his voice reminded her of how it felt to lie next to him in bed.

"So I shall ask you directly, Justina; did you miss me?"

"I did." Her voice caught in her throat and her cheeks burned in response. She gasped because it had been years since she had blushed. She hadn't considered herself capable of such anymore.

"Ah, there is the sweetest of testimonies." He reached up and stroked one fingertip across her cheek. His eyes closed and she heard a sound that was almost a growl, but one born from enjoyment.

"It's warm in here."

"It is rather cold, and you are blushing for me." He leaned closer, so that his lips were next to her ear and she felt his breath on her skin. "Pray have some mercy and do not offer me false pretenses for the moment. Your guardian is not here. Be honest with me, Justina, while we may."

"I have been truthful with you, in all things, and Biddeford has no need of being here. There are many who will tell him every detail of this evening." She stepped away, so that she might see his face once again. A tremor was working its way along her limbs and she could not deny that he was the cause. Excitement was flowing through her veins like too much French wine.

"No one will know what words you speak so close to me, so why not be honest?"

She bit her lower lip once more but there was a flicker of expectation in his eyes that she wanted to be worthy of. That rebellion that her spirit had begun rose up proudly in the face of the way Synclair looked at her. He craved boldness from her because the warrior in him had not been forged in anything less than fire.

"You are correct, Synclair."

"And you are blushing . . . for me." His tone became sharper. She could see the flare of his nostrils and smell the scent of his skin. All of her senses were suddenly aware of him.

"If you must hear me say it, yes I am."

His lips curved up in victory. "I enjoyed hearing you admit it."

Her temper began to heat again. "You enjoy hearing me voice my admissions? Well, sir, here is one for you . . ." She leaned forward so that her words were whispered against his ear. "The Viscount Biddeford has instructed me to lie with you upon your return to hear where you went and why."

Dread went through her, in a short and harsh motion, because she expected him to be repulsed by her words. Instead his hand wrapped around her wrist, his thumb slipping over the delicate skin in slow circles.

"I find it difficult to believe that the man has said anything that I like hearing, and yet it is so."

Shock held her tongue frozen. Synclair drew his head back so that their gazes might meet and there was nothing teasing about his expression. His eyes were full of heat and determination.

"But, I just told you that the man wants me to spy upon you."

"I heard you." He leaned closer and she saw more than one courtier notice. But he had captured her other hand and held it firmly, making it impossible to move away without struggling with him.

"If Biddeford is fool enough to send you to my bed, I will be smart enough to take what is offered, even if I deplore him sending you to anyone's bed. I find I am too weak to reject you for honor's sake alone, even knowing that I should."

She was weak, too, her body beginning to warm with her rising excitement. The night seemed to stretch out endlessly in front of them but the look of distaste in his eyes was a sort of compliment. She didn't know another man who would have cared how she came to his bed, only that she was there to please him.

"Synclair, you know he only seeks to use me against you."

He lifted his head, showing her a smile that was cold and calculating. "Leave that to me. Walk with me, or I swear I will go and ask Biddeford for you since that is the man's game."

It was a true threat, one that pulled her into a battle between Biddeford and Synclair. Yet her surprise came from the fact that it was Synclair threatening her now. Beneath his noble exterior was a hardened fighter who would do what was needed to win. If he asked for her, the viscount would know that she had been disobedient to his instructions. She had never thought to have Synclair bending her with Biddeford's words.

"Make your choice, Justina. Come now or watch me go and negotiate with your guardian for you."

He was sincere, she heard that in his tone and witnessed it in his eyes. He didn't allow her any further time to debate her decision; he took one long step away from her, preparing to make good on his threat.

Justina jumped, reaching for him, needing to pull him away from an action that would surely lead to trouble for them both. She felt trapped, her throat tightening. He turned instantly, her hand barely connecting with his before he captured her fingers and kept them inside his own hand.

"I'm not sure if I like your choice or not, Justina. It

might have been satisfying to face him. It is far past time to have this matter between us settled."

Justina shook her head. "My son would remain his ward. He will never give that up."

"Not without persuasion, I'll grant you my agreement to that fact, but it can be done."

Something hard appeared in his eyes, a look that she had seen only a few times, but it drew a shiver from her. His teasing nature was a façade tonight. Synclair had come looking to claim her and now he even had her consent.

"What are you about, Synclair?"

"I am here for you, just as I told you before."

"And you shall take me by any means available?" There was a tartness to her tone and she didn't bother to soften it. He was tarnishing her image of him but her cheeks heated once again because she found that streak of ruthlessness far too attractive.

"Yes." Curt and blunt, his voice offered her no relenting.

He began crossing the room with her hand clasped in his. Synclair didn't cut around the people watching the entertainers, he walked in front of them, maintaining his grasp on her hand when she would have tugged free. He didn't ease his pace or his hold until they were near the stables and she saw his groom waiting with his stallion. More of his men waited there as well, proving that he had planned exactly what he would be about this night. The hair on the back of her neck stood up.

"You did that most purposefully."

"I find it interesting that you are surprised to see that I do not act without considering every detail."

A groom came forward and placed a thick cape over her shoulders. It had a wide hood that the man raised and placed over her head. Her breath came out in white puffs and she pulled the heavy fabric around her gratefully. Another man led a mare forward that was fitted with a side saddle.

Synclair grasped her waist and lifted her onto the back of the mare before his man handed her the reins. Moonlight cast silver light over his face, showing her his satisfied smile.

He fitted his foot into the stirrup of his saddle and mounted his stallion. The animal tossed its head, eager to be off. The knowledge that he had planned to take her to his bed tonight sent need through her veins. It was as potent as French wine, undermining her ability to reason. It should have annoyed her but she could not deceive herself by saying that she was not happy to see his men waiting with a cloak for her.

Synclair kicked his horse into action, sitting firmly in the saddle and moving with the stallion in perfect harmony. Her mare followed and his men closed around her. A ripple of some emotion went through her, but she wasn't sure exactly what it was. Perhaps it was fear, or pride in seeing him act as a lord, rather than as a knight serving his master. He deserved it, she felt that firmly in her heart. No matter what his position with Curan Ramsden, Lord Ryppon, it had never eluded her notice that Synclair would one day take his place alongside the man as an equal. He was a true knight, one who had been hardened on the field of battle. At court, there were many who proudly displayed their golden knights' chains, but they never did without their comforts.

For the moment, that included her.

CHAPTER SEVEN

Synclair was at home in the night with nothing more than his stallion and men. He would ride with those men, every bit as capable as they with the sword that hung from his belt.

The landscape had changed much since their last ride together. Snow blanketed everything. Ice was collecting on the bare limbs of the trees and the wind howled with a mournful sound, as though it was crying for the loss of life now that winter was here.

She shivered and pulled the hood of her cloak further down to shield her face. The animal she rode was eager to make its way to a warm stable but the hunting house did not come into view. Instead, Synclair rode past the road that would lead to the King's forest. His men kept her mare following, even when she tried to pull up on the reins. The mare wasn't interested in standing still with her hooves in the snow.

They rode on, her muscles tightening as the distance between the palace and them increased.

"Where are we going?"

The wind ripped her words away but she noticed a slight tensing of Synclair's shoulders in response to her question. He turned his head, only part way so that he might look back at her. His lips were still formed into a smug grin and he offered her no reply. He turned around and continued to ride. There was no light except for the moon, and the only sound was the horses' hooves followed by the wind. Every fireside story she had ever heard whispered began to rise from her memory. Tales of human-eating beasts and witches who preyed upon those foolish enough to venture out into the woods after darkness fell. Justina found herself grinning for she believed none of it and in fact, enjoyed the night.

Synclair had no fear of them either, it appeared. He rode forward, never easing their pace or turning to look back at her again. He seemed to be confident in his direction, and she gasped when a faint light twinkled through the black, ice-covered branches of the trees. She stared at the light, like a starving person might a meal laid out on a table, her eyes remaining on it as they rode closer. A house materialized out of the shadows, its stone walls looking dark and cold in the moonlight. A single lantern was hanging from the foot of the stairs that led up to the front doors. A lone candle flickered inside the glass panes that kept it from being extinguished by the night wind. It hung from a large metal ring fitted onto a large hook, and as the wind knocked the lantern back and forth, an eerie sound rose from it.

One of the front doors opened as they gained the steps. Another lantern was held high as a woman peered out into the night. She nodded and opened both doors wide in welcome.

Synclair was already off his horse and he made a straight path toward her. His hands were warm against her waist, making her aware of how chilled the ride had made her. He lifted her down and her knees felt stiff. He gripped her hand and guided her up the stairs while she struggled to control her skirts and the heavy cloak. The thick fabric was pushing down on her skirts, collapsing her boned slip and making it a chore to avoid stepping on her hem. She heard a soft grunt that sounded suspiciously like amusement before Synclair bent and swept her off her feet.

"I can walk."

His chest rumbled and she heard him chuckle clearly.

"Not with so much fabric wrapped around you, you cannot, and the steps are icy." He angled his head to look down at her. "And more importantly, I am enjoying carrying you."

He made quick work of gaining the inside of the house. The woman was still standing there, an apron pinned carefully over her bodice and falling down to protect her skirts. She wore a linen cap, too, and a set of keys that marked her as the housekeeper and not simply a maid. Those keys would open locks on cabinets that held silver dinnerware and linens and spices. All of the expensive items that she would be expected to keep an accounting of for her mistress.

"Bring Lady Wincott some mulled wine to cut the chill."

Justina felt her eyes widen but there was no hint of repentance on Synclair's face for the fact that he had so boldly used her name. Instead, his expression was set into a mask of determination, far harder than she had seen aimed at her in a long time.

Since the day he'd dragged her to the chamber at Amber Hill he had locked her into.

"What is your game, Synclair?" She kicked her feet but he only clamped his arm around her knees tighter to control her.

"I am merely playing the game that you are shackled to, Lady." He aimed a hard look into her eyes. "But be very sure that I play to win the prize."

He carried her up the stairs, through the open doors of a chamber that was grander than the one they had shared before. In spite of his odd manner, she couldn't suppress a ripple of passion from moving through her body. They had shared a scorching night once before, and her flesh was eager to do so again.

The doors closed and he lowered her feet before lifting the cloak off her shoulders. Removal of the heavy garment allowed her gown to be supported by her boned slip once again. Her gown was made for evening wear and the bodice was cut in a wide square neck that allowed a great deal of her cleavage to be seen. His gaze settled on the swells of her breasts as he tossed the cloak onto a nearby chair.

"I'm glad I thought to bring the cloak. We couldn't have those lovelies frostbitten."

Justina moved away from him, going further into the chamber. A fire was warming the air and there were a few candles lit on a table, but not enough to make the room bright. Synclair grinned at her while pulling his riding gloves off.

"And now to enjoy the prize I have managed to bring home."

"Home?"

One of his eyebrows rose. "Aye, this house belongs to me now. The housekeeper is good, but I will leave her direction to you."

"Stop it, Synclair, I am not wedding you."

But she wanted to, yearned to. How was it to marry a man that you enjoyed being with? Her soul cried out for her to experience it.

"I shall always treasure knowing you thought to honor me in such a way, Synclair, which is why I did not want to accompany you here. Biddeford will destroy you if he can and I refuse to aid him in that quest." She shivered with the dark possibilities, her heart aching.

He walked forward, closing the distance between them

with slow steps. He reached out and cupped her chin in his warm hand, raising her face for a kiss that was both soft and simple. It pierced her heart with tenderness.

"I understand your thinking, Justina, but I told you clearly that I came to court for you, and I have no intention of leaving without you. Defeating your guardian has always been my goal. If he was fool enough to order you to my bed and think he will regain you, I shall happily show him the error of his ways."

His eyes darkened, and as he stepped back, his expression lost every trace of softness.

"Now, we shall not have you worried about lying to the viscount should he gain the opportunity to ask you about this evening."

His gaze traveled over her, slipping over the curves he knew so well and that she had enjoyed him learning.

"What do you mean?"

One light eyebrow rose. "I mean, sweet lover, that I intend to ensure that you have plenty of details to report."

He worked the buttons loose on his doublet and shock held her silent while he finished opening the garment. He shrugged it off, revealing a linen shirt. He opened the cuffs before raising his hands to the collar.

A rap sounded on the door. "Enter."

Her face heated with another blush because she had forgotten about the mulled wine he'd requested. The housekeeper appeared with a tray held securely in both hands. Synclair turned to make sure that the woman saw the state of undress he was in. She did not blink nor did her expression alter even a tiny amount.

"Ah, some mulled wine should warm my lady quickly."

There were twin goblets and a pitcher on that tray. The housekeeper lowered herself before placing the tray on the table and retreating from the room.

"You are entirely too sure of yourself."

He chuckled, his lips rising into a smug grin.

"Admit it, Justina; you are enjoying the fact that I have stopped waiting for you like a gallant knight."

"You are misbehaving." He grinned instantly at her words. "I will not reward you with praise."

His smile faded into a hard line. "Not yet anyway. I will maintain hope to hear many things that praise my efforts from your lips later tonight."

"You should not say such things; it is a sin to speak so."

"Why? It is the truth. I have brought you here to tumble, and I plan to do a very good job of it."

Synclair moved to the table, lifting one goblet and taking a sip from it.

"Come and drink with me, Justina."

A shiver moved across her skin, and she shook her head before thinking. It was pure response, from deep inside her. A sort of recognition of his ability to do exactly what he proposed, even if she decided to resist.

He watched her over the rim of the goblet, sending a bolt of anticipation through her. The man was planning her seduction. She could see it glittering in his eyes. Part of her was tempted to make him work harder at it just because she needed to feel like her consent was something worth striving for.

Such a pitiful thought, and yet, Justina realized that it was very true.

There was a soft clink as he sat the goblet back on the tray. "Maybe you are correct, the only intoxicating influence needed is our reaction to each other."

Indeed it was almost too much to control. Justina felt heat rising from inside her. Passion was beginning to twist deep in her belly.

Synclair sat down and stretched out one leg toward her.

"Come, Justina, show me how well you can cater to my needs."

His voice was mocking but there was also a hint of need, and that was what drew her forward. He sent so much passion through her, and she needed to know that she affected him the same way.

"As you will, my lord."

She muttered the meek words with enough heat to raise one of his fair eyebrows. Leaning over, she wrapped her hands around his boot, watching the way his gaze lowered to the swells of her breasts. She took her time removing the boot, and she could tell that Synclair enjoyed the view while she lingered over her task. By the time his second boot was removed, his lips were thinning, and she recognized his straining control. But he stood up, branching his feet wide.

"Now the britches."

Her heart accelerated, pumping faster behind her stays. Sensation rippled across her skin, going down her back and over her belly. She knew that so much dwelling on him would lead her to trouble. Now, her hands shook as she reached for his waistband and opened it. She craved another taste of that hard flesh but his silence promised her that he was not going to grant her what she wished unless she asked him for it.

Just as she had before.

She pulled his pants down, and his cock pushed against the fabric of his shirt, but she was prevented from seeing it completely, even when she knelt to pull the pants away from each foot when he lifted them.

But being on her knees did not belittle her. Smoothing her hands along the outside of his legs, she gently stroked her way to his knees where the top of his socks were. She rolled the thin fabric down to expose his skin. Now her hands began to move up again, her skin against his. She did it slowly, lingering over his calves and up further to his thighs. His breathing increased and in the silence of the chamber she heard a log shift in the fireplace. That didn't matter; her senses were alert and soaking up all the tiny details of touch and scent. It seemed as if it had been years since she had filled her nose with the scent of his skin. Far too long since she had touched him and listened to his breathing to see if he enjoyed her hands upon him.

His breath caught when her hands made it to the curve of his backside.

"French me."

His voice was strained but she heard the desire. He was attempting to play a game but in truth, he was as much caught in it as she was. That drew her to him, toward surrendering to the passion once more because she had never felt so close to any other man. Nor had she ever suspected that any of her partners had cared whether she enjoyed their attention.

"Ah, and do you think you have the strength to stand in place while I do such? A man should stand firm, if he wants that particular kiss."

He chuckled, the sound dark and promising. He reached down and caught the back of her head. "I assure you, I would rather die than move away from your sweet lips."

She slid her hand down and over the warm skin of his inner thigh, stopping only when she felt the sac that hung beneath his cock. He flinched, just a tiny motion but she witnessed it.

"So sure, are you?" She stroked the wrinkled skin of that sac, gently touching it while her passage began to warm and heat.

The hand in her hair tightened. "I am sure that I can re-ciprocate well; the question, will you be able to impress me with your firm stance when it is your turn? Two may play the game of teasing, Justina."

She drew in a stiff breath and his hand gently rubbed at the tense muscles of her neck. Her clitoris began to throb between the folds of her slit. She trembled while her fingers gently toyed with a man's flesh. It had been a very long time since she had been affected so deeply while being intimate.

"Come, Justina, pleasure me, and while you are doing it, think upon the fact that I plan to repay you touch for touch and rapture for rapture."

He pulled his shirt off, allowing her to see his length clearly. The head of his cock was flared and red. The slit glistened with a drop of fluid that she leaned forward and licked away. She had done it before, but tonight she heard his swift intake of breath and shivered with enjoyment because she had caused him to respond to her. That knowledge was like dry tinder, cast down onto the gentle flames building inside her. It caught instantly, making her hungry for far more.

Her hands moved up, stroking along his member, gently gliding over the satin-smooth skin. A man's cock was every bit as sensitive as her own slit, and the memory of the last time they had lain together made her eager to take her time teasing him. The French court was even more traitorous for women than England's. But it seemed that French women had learned to beguile their men with more than the parting of their thighs. The technique of frenching had come back from campaigns and the King was rumored to enjoy it most well.

Justina smiled. She planned to make sure Synclair enjoyed more than any man ever had.

She leaned forward, allowing her jaw to relax and open to take his girth. His skin smelled of soap, and the head of his cock entered her mouth completely.

"Holy Christ."

His hand returned to her hair, but this time he cupped the back of her head, gently guiding her toward what he craved. She heard his breathing become rough and hurried, a tiny indication that he was being pressed closer to the point where his control would fail and his body would take command.

That was what she wanted. She needed to be the one who drew a climax from him, while she remained in control. It was an insane desire, many might claim an unnatural one in a woman, but she pulled her head back and then returned to take more of his length. His hips began to thrust against her and she took more of his member. She fingered his sac, teasing the wrinkled skin as she felt his cock swelling harder against her tongue. She closed her lips around his girth, making them tight as he pulled out of her mouth.

He trembled, and she didn't wait for him to thrust back against her but wrapped her fingers around the base of his cock and pushed her mouth down to where her fingers held him.

"Justina—"

Her name was nothing but a ragged moan. He was fighting the urge to hold his seed back. She could feel it in the way his cock continued to harden, to the point that it seemed too rigid to not cause him pain. She worked her mouth back and forth in quick motions while his hand tightened on the back of her head. His hips drove toward her, moving faster and faster until he groaned. A warm burst of seed filled her mouth, followed by several more. Justina continued to move, drawing a strangled sound from Synclair as his member pumped out the last few spurts of his seed.

She sat back on her knees, gently stroking his cock with her fingers. She kept her touch delicate because she knew his flesh was extremely sensitive now.

Synclair suddenly cursed. It was a nasty grouping of words that drew a small giggle from her.

"That wasn't exactly the sort of comment I might hope for after frenching a man."

She rose to her feet and walked to the table to lift one of the goblets up to her lips. She was suddenly nervous, wondering what sort of treatment he might give her now that he had been pleasured. Most men lay down and slept, completely ignoring the woman who had pleasured them.

The wine had cooled but it was not yet cold. Two hands cupped her shoulders and she felt him against her back.

"Are you accustomed to being ignored after servicing a man on your knees?"

He whispered the words but she felt them in her soul.

"Yes."

One tortured word that represented years of frustration as she had tried to come to terms with the place her husband had told her was for women. It was the same thing that Biddeford forced her to submit to. She would please and expect to be left wanting.

Synclair turned her, plucking the goblet from her fingers and setting it aside. His eyes were brilliant, shimmering with emotion that touched her heart.

"Do not expect such from me."

There was a subtle warning in his voice that sent a shaft of tenderness through her. The word *lover* surfaced once more from her thoughts but she did not have time to dwell on it. Synclair plucked the pins from her hair until it fell down to cover her shoulders and back. She heard them hitting the tabletop in tiny tapping motions before he combed her freed locks with his fingers. The motion pulled the strands, just a small amount, and she tipped her head back, her eyes closing as sensation took control of her mind.

"I do not know what to expect from you, beyond the

fact that you are not like any other man I have ever
known."

It was the most that she had ever shared of her tender
feelings with any man. She opened her eyes and found
him still watching her with those blue eyes that both un-
nerved her and soothed her. Tonight, they were full of
promise.

"That is something I have longed to hear from your
lips, Justina. More than you could possibly know."

"Why?" The question crossed her lips before she thought
about the wisdom in asking. She couldn't be disappointed
if she did not voice the question. Nervousness invaded her,
making her feel vulnerable. She walked past him, keenly
aware of the fact that she was still fully clothed while he
was completely bare.

"You mean because you think you bring me nothing?"
She turned to peek at him over her shoulder. "Exactly."

His expression was hard and he shook his head. "I agree
with you on one thing you said before, Justina." His tone
deepened. "That the poison that took your husband to hell
took him there too gently for the sins he was guilty of."

He closed the space between them and pulled her against
his body. "For he was a selfish bastard that your father
should be whipped for wedding you to."

He pressed his lips down onto hers in a kiss that was full
of the passion she heard in his voice. Justina reached for
him, her hands tangling in his hair while his tongue swept
over her lower lip. Sweet sensation shot down her frame.
She trembled with growing anticipation and opened her
mouth to allow him a deeper kiss. The bold thrust of his
tongue made her gasp. The walls of her passage felt empty
and in need of his hard flesh. She felt him working the
laces along the back of her dress, letting out a frustrated
sound when the ties knotted and refused to slide from
their eyelets.

Justina laughed and allowed him to turn her so that he might see the laces.

"I am going to keep you in a chemise."

The bodice of her gown sagged down her front and she moved away from him, peeking back at him through the curtain of her unbound hair.

"But I do not belong to you, Synclair. I am your lover and not bound to obey you." She moved farther away and turned in a full circle so that her skirts flared up to give him a glimpse of her ankles and calves. "I believe I like being your lover very much."

He grinned, bright and menacing. "I plan to ensure that you cannot live without being my lover."

He took a step toward her and she shook her head. One of his eyebrows rose in question.

"Stay there."

"Why?"

Justina smiled and allowed the bodice of her gown to slip down her chest. His attention dropped to it instantly.

"Because I am your lover and I may give you instructions, too."

He folded his arms over his chest, the action making his arms look thicker with muscle. "I await your command."

She was playing. Justina had to suppress the urge to giggle like a girl because it had been so long since she had simply given herself over to imagination. Of course, it was not quite the same as when she was a child, her gaze drifted over the man in front of her. His body amazed her; it was so different from her own and yet she craved to be in contact with it. The hard expanse of his chest was covered in light hair that her breasts longed to be pressed against.

Her attention sank lower, until she was looking at his cock. It stood erect, the flesh still hard. He suddenly chuckled.

"You seem to have become distracted, my lady, so perhaps I should take command." He moved closer but stopped before reaching her. "Release the gown."

There was the ring of firm authority in his voice and she recalled it well from her time at Amber Hill. She had listened to him ordering the men to their posts and duties, but her cheeks turned scarlet in response to hearing him command her.

"Do it now, Justina. Release that dress so that I might watch it fall to the floor."

She did so, and the bodice draped down to expose her long stays, but the skirts were still resting on her hooped slip. He frowned, clearly disappointed.

"You seem rather ill-prepared to give commands in this subject." Justina teased him gently.

One of his light eyebrows rose. "I adapt quickly."

He reached out and gripped the waistband of her hoop slip between both of his hands. He snapped it quickly, and she felt the small button that held it closed pop off, the threads broken.

"You mustn't ruin my clothing. It costs a fortune to attend court."

Synclair wasn't interested in her concern. His hands found the band of her hip roll and snapped it exactly as he had the slip. A moment later, it all slithered down her body to puddle around her legs. He reached forward and lifted her right out of the mess and carried her to the bed.

"All the more reason for us to wed and retire to the country where you may wear more practical dresses that are easier for me to remove."

She reached up and sealed his lips with her fingers. He snorted at her and laid her down on the bed. The blankets had been pulled back to the foot, prepared for them. The bed ropes creaked as he joined her, hugging her tightly against him while he rolled over so that they were further into the huge bed.

He stopped with her on top of him and her knees settled on the surface of the bed on either side of his hips. His cock was pressed against his belly and her slit, making her shiver. She drew in a stiff breath, her clitoris throbbing for attention.

"I hear some men worry about women getting the notion that they might rise above their male counterparts in this life, but I must say, I see advantages."

He reached up and cupped her breasts, his thumbs teasing her hard nipples.

"You are part boy."

He smiled at her, looking exactly like a boy plotting mischief.

"And I enjoy sneaking treats between meals."

He sat up and rolled her onto her back. He did it so quickly she didn't have time to react. In a moment, he had slid down her body and parted her thighs. He spread her wide, pushing her knees up to the level of her waist while hovering over her sex.

"Ah, the sweetest flesh any man ever had the privilege to dine upon."

He separated her folds even further, and she felt the brush of the winter air against her clitoris. Only for a moment before he lowered his head and his tongue lapped through the center of her slit. She jerked and twisted, her body responding instantly. She heard his chuckle.

"You did challenge me, Lady." His eyes glittered with determination. "I do not lose challenges."

"I still broke your control."

His face tightened. "So you did, but let us see what I can entice from your sweet body."

Synclair did not tease her. He lowered his head and boldly sucked her clitoris. He closed his lips around the small button, pulling on it while his tongue flicked over it. His fingers drove into her passage, two thick ones penetrating her deeply. She gasped and bucked beneath him, her body held in the grip of a need so intense, she couldn't draw breath. Her lungs were frozen while her body twisted beneath his lips. Her heart began thumping so hard, she heard nothing except for her own heartbeat.

He removed his fingers and her hips lifted up, begging for more. When he granted that, she felt her body tumbling into a climax that she hadn't anticipated. It consumed her, hitting her hard and shaking her with its force. Pleasure surged through her, leaving her twisting beneath him while she clawed at the sheet.

"Now that was a very enjoyable victory. I shall have to make a habit of meeting you on the field regularly."

She growled at him, still struggling to draw enough breath into her lungs to supply her racing heart. All of her thoughts were in a jumble, her emotions mixed with them, making it impossible to sort them out.

"That was unfair." She sat up and sent her hand out to strike him.

He snorted with amusement before catching her hand and pushing it to the opposite side of her body. Her arm was crossed over her chest, and he leaned down over her face, his eyes filled with satisfaction.

"I never promised to be fair, Justina, only that I would prevail."

He slid his hand beneath her shoulder and flipped her over onto her belly. But he didn't leave her there; he gripped her hips, lifting them and pulling her back so that her knees bent to raise her bottom into the air.

"I told you that I would have you and I will." His cock pressed against the opening of her sheath, the flared head stretching her body as it tunneled deeper inside her. The walls of her passage resisted slightly but her climax had left her wet, making it easy for him to thrust deep inside her.

"And you will enjoy being had."

His hands gripped her hips while he snarled his last few words. She offered him only a half sound that was part moan and part whine. There were no more thoughts in her mind; there was nothing but his hard flesh filling her. It unleashed another round of need, but this time she needed his cock to feed it.

"Yes! I want to enjoy it."

"Then you shall!"

He held her hips in a grip that might have normally hurt her, but at the moment it felt perfect. His hips began to flex forward and back, driving his hard length deep inside her. Her clitoris was still sensitive from her climax and the position allowed it only the lightest of touches. That was the only part of their bedding that was delicate. Synclair rode her hard, penetrating her passage with quick thrusts that did not slow down. The bed rocked and the canopy swayed but she didn't care, she pushed her hands against the sheet and braced herself for his pace, enjoying the slap of his body against her own.

She felt his cock hardening, the head swelling once again.

"Yes."

"No!" He suddenly pulled out of her and turned her onto her back. His hands captured her wrists, pinning them to the surface of the bed above her head.

"You will climax with me this time."

He slid back into her and their new position allowed his cock to slide across her clitoris completely. She whimpered, needing to release the tension building up inside her.

"And you will take my seed."

He growled and she opened her eyes to see a muscle on the side of his jaw twitching. His eyes glowed with need so intense, she became hypnotized by it. Drawn toward it just like the only light in a dark forest. Her body moved with his, arching up to take each thrust, and a moment later pleasure burst deep inside her belly. She had felt it before but this was harder, and she released a sob with the intensity of it. Every one of her muscles strained up toward her partner, and she heard him groan as his seed began to flood her. He pressed deep, lodging his length tight inside her while their cries mingled and she lost the ability to tell whose was whose. In that moment they were one, joined so completely, there was no possibility of separation.

"Oh Christ, I cannot breathe!"

She struggled against him, her heart racing so fast she felt it might burst. Her wrists were suddenly free, and he lifted his chest away from hers, but remained deep inside her while they both struggled to regain enough breath.

Justina was too hot, her skin covered in perspiration. She wiggled away from her lover, and he rolled onto his back, jolting the bed yet again when he allowed his weight to drop on it. But he reached for her hand, locking his fingers around her wrist while they both panted. Delight was still rippling through her, carrying away every concern. Her eyelids closed, and she sighed as her heart regained a normal rhythm. She felt the winter chill again but Synclair pulled the covers up to shield her from it. Once the thick blankets were over her body, she felt him curl along her back, his arms embracing her while his legs tangled with her.

Tenderness filled the spot where yearning had been. His member was spent against her bottom and yet he clung to her. She tried to savor the moment but slumber took her away before she had much of a chance to.

Lovers truly were worth risking everything for.

Justina smiled as she awoke. She had not slept so deeply nor so soundly in too many nights to count. She nuzzled against the bedding, convinced that it was by far finer than any she had ever laid upon before. Her mind began to form thoughts again, in spite of how comfortable she was.

Synclair was curled around her, his breathing even and deep. The chamber was dark, but the sort of darkness that hinted at dawn approaching. The bed curtains were not drawn and the fire had died down to nothing but ash. The candles were no longer burning either, but her gown was still crumpled on the floor where it had dropped.

She sighed, a silent little lament for the fact that time waited for no one. She moved slowly, drawing her feet away from Synclair's and freezing to make sure he continued to sleep. She turned her head and listened to his breathing; it was still slow and even, so she moved further away from him, making sure that the bedding was tucked against him so that the cold winter air didn't rouse him.

"Do you truly believe you can find your way back to the palace in the dark?"

Justina jumped, turning over to face Synclair like a child caught stealing a tart from the kitchen between meals. His eyes were focused and clear, no hint of sleep clouding them.

"I must return to Whitehall, you know that."

His expression betrayed none of his thoughts, even his eyes narrowed.

"I do not wish to fight about it, please understand."

He inclined his head. "I understand why you think you must return, but I disagree with you, Lady."

Tears burned her eyes because she did not want to leave him and there seemed to be no way to avoid it.

"I'm sorry, Synclair, but I will not abandon my son to Biddeford's whims."

"Even when he sets you to prostitution?"

She stiffened. "Better I suffer than my son."

Synclair let out a disgusted sound. "I agree that your child would come to no good in the hands of your guardian."

Justina should have been relieved to hear him agree with her but instead pain filled her chest because she knew without a doubt that they were destined to part. Sorrow carved a deep path down the center of her chest. "I am sorry, Synclair, but at least you understand why I must go."

She offered him a last look that was full of longing before she gathered her courage and slid out of the bedding. Her feet touched the floor and she stood up, intent on hurrying to her clothing. Something jerked her wrist when she gained three paces from the bed. She heard the metallic sound of links hitting one another before she turned to look at the chain that bound her to the bed. A small manacle was locked around her left wrist and a length of chain ran from it to the bedpost.

"I am sorry, too, Justina, but I have no intention of allowing you to return to that bastard."

Her mind was in shock, her gaze locked on the chain and what it meant. Justina pulled on it, certain she had to be somehow imagining the moment, but the chain held and the manacle bruised her wrist. "This is barbaric. Release me at once!"

Synclair sat up and swung his legs over the opposite side of the bed, giving her his back. In spite of seeing that the chain was solid, she couldn't help jerking against it another time.

It held true, binding her without mercy to the huge bed. "Synclair!"

He walked past her and stepped into his britches. There was a hard set to his face that sent dread through her.

"You cannot mean to lock me up here."

But the look in his eyes was familiar and she recognized it from when he had approached her last night. He shrugged into his shirt and carried her chemise in one hand. There was nothing in his eyes but ruthless determination.

He held out the chemise. "I must go see to a few things." His attention dropped to her wrist with its manacle. "You will be here when I return."

"You brute!"

She aimed a slap at his face and the sound was loud in the predawn stillness. Synclair turned his head with the blow but beyond that, he did nothing to avoid her strike. He dropped her chemise on the bed before turning and walking to the door.

"You cannot do this."

"I have, Justina, and I will keep you." He turned to look at her. "So get back into bed before you catch a chill."

"But my son—"

"You shall have to trust me with the well-being of your child, Justina. I will not allow Biddeford to harm him."

The door shut behind him and her jaw actually dropped with astonishment. Her temper flared up, threatening to light her hair on fire, it was so hot.

Oh men!

Power hungry, every last one of them. She tugged on her bound wrist but only managed to bruise the skin on her hand. She tried to make her hand into different shapes to allow the manacle to slide over the bones, but none of her efforts gained her anything but more pain. She cursed as she began to shiver, her body chilled.

It would serve him right if she did take ill.

She sighed, disgusted by her own childish thinking. Reaching for her chemise, she pulled it over her head only to discover that it was impossible to put her left arm through the sleeve. Her right arm was in the sleeve but that left half the garment resting on her shoulder and baring the entire left side of her body.

So she was chained to the man's bed . . . nude.

She began to shiver, her teeth chattering. With a snort she tossed the chemise aside and climbed back into bed. The covers had lost their warmth and she pulled them close to have them hold her body heat against her. Justina curled onto her side, with her eyes upon the door. Sinclair was in for a surprise if he thought she would submit meekly to his plan to keep her.

Except that he had already imprisoned her. The long months at Amber Hill flooded her with their endless hours of worrying over Brandon's fate. It sickened her to think that the man she'd embraced as her lover would force her to endure such a betrayal.

Yet wasn't that the fate of most lovers? Bitter betrayals that often led to misery. Tears slid from her eyes and she failed to control them. It was foolish to cry, a waste of energy and emotions, but she could not seem to talk herself into stopping. The pillow beneath her cheek became wet while she huddled beneath the bedding, her heart torn.

That was the truth of what taking a lover did to a woman. It separated her from her family. It was a torment indeed. Brandon or Sinclair, she would have to live without one of them being happy.

A soft knock woke her. Justina blinked, wondering how she could have fallen asleep with so much turmoil inside her. The burning in her eyes reminded her that she had wept, and that gained a disgusted mutter from her as she sat up. Crying always wasted energy and she had fallen asleep like a child after allowing her emotions such freedom.

"Excuse me, mistress, I did not mean to wake you." It was the housekeeper who stood in the doorway. The woman was a credit to her position for she did not poke her head around a partially opened door, instead the woman stood firmly in the doorframe, ready to face any displeasure without cringing.

"It's too late to be sleeping. I am glad you woke me."

Light was spilling in through the open door. Justina looked at the windows. There were floor-to-ceiling draperies covering them. The fabric was thick and they were designed in such long lengths to keep the morning light from disturbing the master of the house if he should choose to lie abed after dawn.

"The master suggested a bath before he departed."

A bath, of course! She had to think of any reason to be unlocked. Her gaze flew to the ring of keys hanging from the housekeeper's belt.

"I should adore a bath." Justina pushed her hand into view, so that the housekeeper might fit one of those black keys into the lock, but the woman only turned to address someone in the hallway.

"Bring the tub."

The double doors were both opened wide and two burly women carried a slipper tub into the chamber. One end was higher than the other, making it a comfortable tub for bathing. It was a newer design and this one was made of silver, so that it would not rust.

"I have only women with me, since the master told me you are unclothed."

Justina snorted. The unladylike sound gained her looks from the women bringing the tub in.

"Surely you have a bathroom below stairs. I do not need such service, simply unlock me and I shall bathe below."

The housekeeper looked nervous for the first time. "Begging your pardon, mistress, but the master did not leave me a key. I cannot unlock you."

Justina growled and didn't care what looks were cast her way. She jerked against the chain. "I cannot dress in anything with sleeves unless this foul thing is removed."

The two women had set down the tub, and they stepped closer to look at the chain and manacle. They stared at it intently, clearly trying to think of a solution.

One of them turned to look at the housekeeper. "I'll fetch the sewing box up here. We'll likely have to stitch her into a dressing gown."

"Yes, there's an idea that may work well. Bring young Amy along. She's quick with a needle."

The woman bobbed her head before hurrying off into the hallway to do as she suggested. A line of maids began filing through the doorway with yokes across their shoulders. A bucket of water hung from either side of those yokes, and they dumped them into the tub with a practiced hand.

"It is ridiculous to waste so much effort on one bath when I can walk very well."

The housekeeper was pulling the drapes back, using a careful hand when touching the fabric. Thick curtains such as the ones hanging in the windows were worth a fortune and the under maids in any house wouldn't be allowed to handle them until they had proven their skill.

"Not so, mistress, the staff are paid well and having someone to perform our duties for is a welcome thing. This house has been empty for too long." The housekeeper finished and snapped her fingers at two younger maids who were standing shoulder to shoulder awaiting direction. They nodded simultaneously before moving to the bed and rolling the covers down toward the footboard.

"I am named Arlene." She lowered herself before bending down to pick up the chain so that it would be easier for Justina to walk to the tub. The two maids finished with the bedding and went to pour the last two buckets of water into the tub. Steam rose from the water, and Justina had to admit that the bath looked inviting.

She stepped away from the bed, refusing to worry about the fact that she was nude. Modesty was something she had learned to live without the day she married. She stepped over the edge of the tub and found the water delightful.

"I'm sorry you cannot bathe closer to the hearth, but the cook has more water on the fire and will send it soon."

"This is not your doing."

The two maids looked at each other with quick glances but they kept their lips sealed. Justina took a cloth from Arlene and a small piece of soap. It was scented with gilly flowers and she inhaled the scent deeply before dunking it beneath the surface of the water. She rubbed it across the cloth before beginning to wash her arms and chest. More hot water arrived as well as more cold water. Arlene directed those beneath her authority with a practiced hand. It took little time to complete her bath, the housekeeper even helping her to wash her hair.

"Begging your pardon, mistress, but I'd suggest not lingering in the water with that iron about your wrist."

"I believe you are correct." The manacle would likely stain her skin orange, especially since it was winter and the air so cold. The water that ended up beneath it would likely take a long time to dry.

She stood up and Arlene took up the weight of the chain once again. Amy had arrived and stood near the table looking at several garments. She would glance back at Justina from time to time while she pondered the task given to her.

Arlene brought toweling forward and dried every drop of water from her skin.

"Amy?"

There was a soft note of apprehension in the housekeeper's voice. Justina had to admit to feeling the same. Being chained to the bed could only be made worse by having to spend the day wrapped in toweling like some Greek statue.

"I believe we might simply stitch a few seams while on the mistress." Amy fingered the point of her scissors. "But I fear that there is truly no way to dress you back into your gown, mistress."

There was a good wool dress lying on the table, one that looked inviting in the cold weather, but she would have to do without it.

"It would take the entire day." There were a few quick smiles in response and Justina returned them with one of her own. Making friends with the staff might gain her freedom at some point, if not today. "I would be grateful for a chemise and maybe a dressing gown with wide sleeves."

"Yes, excellent idea." Arlene sent one of the maids off with a flick of her fingers. "The master had some garments purchased for your arrival last week."

"He did?" Justina had to bite back her temper.

Arlene turned and offered her a smile. "Yes, the baron did. He is a man who sees to the details and planning. Why, he even consulted with me upon what items a lady might need for her personal comfort. I shall show it to you later to see if it meets with your approval."

Comfort indeed.

Amy came forward with a chemise that had the left sleeve detached. The side of the garment was also open to allow for it to go over her head and fall down to cover her body. The girl already had a needle threaded and began sewing up the side seam. Since the edges of the fabric had been rolled and hemmed before being seamed together, it was a simple enough task to sew the side of the chemise back together.

The sleeve itself was also opened beneath the arm. A maid laid it over her left arm and Amy began to sew the center seam shut before she fit it into the body of the garment and reattached it to the chemise.

Justina felt her temper simmering the entire time. At least her long stays had ties on the shoulder straps making it simple to get into them. The dressing gown the maids brought had to be opened exactly as the chemise had been, and Amy had help with the sewing, one girl working on the bottom of the dressing gown, while Amy worked on the sleeve.

"There." Arlene looked at the finished work and nodded. "At least there is a good length of chain and you are on the window side of the bed, so you'll be able to look out."

The maids had begun moving a small table and chair across the chamber to the corner by the bed. More staff members entered the chamber, and they all stopped to offer her a curtsy before delivering whatever they had in their hands. Several books were placed on the table, along with a small travel desk. A sewing basket came next and then several carefully folded lengths of cloth. Still another woman brought a box that she opened to reveal face powder and other makeup. The last thing that arrived was a mirror, set in a silver frame. It was set down with great care, in the center of the table, where a careless bump might not knock it to the floor. The polished-looking glass was a rare item and one that must have cost a small fortune.

"As you can see, the master was most thoughtful in making sure there was plenty for you to do."

"Yes, it does appear so."

Arlene was raising her voice, just a small amount, but every maid in the room lifted her eyes from the task she was doing. Justina felt them all looking at her and the housekeeper while they listened to the true meaning of what Arlene was saying. The master of the house had given an order that she be chained. Anyone who went against the master could expect to be turned out. Snow was thick upon the ground, the trees bare and frozen beyond the window. Anyone who decided to condemn Synclair for his treatment of her would find the world very unforgiving. One by one, they all looked back down at their tasks, not a single one looking at her.

She understood well what it was to bend to the will of the man who had charge of you. Her hope of gaining help in escaping dwindled until there was only a mere whisper left. The firm look on the housekeeper's face as she directed a newly arrived girl to place her tray on the table confirmed what Justina felt. There would be no help from Arlene or anyone taking orders from her. The consequences were simply too grave.

"Thank you, Arlene, I shall be well upon my own."

"Yes, of course."

There was a hint of pity in her voice, but the housekeeper lowered herself and left the room with her staff following. Justina turned to look at the view from the windows. She could smell the breakfast that was hidden beneath silver dome plate covers. Her eyes scanned the tabletop again, noticing the expense that went into everything there. She lifted the lid of the travel desk and found parchment, silver-tipped quills, and ink. In the sewing box were needles, thread, scissors, and pins. All of it new and shiny. The makeup box held everything a court lady might ask her father for and the books were bound in fine leather.

"Well, Synclair, it seems that I am awaiting you, sir."

She spoke quietly, not truly caring if someone might consider her odd for conversing with a man who was not in the room.

For there was nothing sane about her relationship with Synclair. It was insanity at its best. The sort that the

Church warned against because it would lead good souls from the path of narrow and straight.

She was longing for his return, the chain binding her to his bed causing her to feel wanted instead of captured. Her temper might be irritated over his means but her heart was dwelling on the table full of amusements he had planned to leave her with.

She began pacing, as far as the chain would allow her, walking to and from the wall.

Her emotions were in a jumble and refusing to be controlled. She had mastered them so often in the past that it was shocking to have them rise up and over the barricades she had thought her heart was hidden so completely behind. There seemed to be no sense left in her, for she failed to hate herself for sharing the night with him.

She was such a fool. The only other person she loved was Brandon, and that drew enough of a toll from her, but one that might be expected because he was her child. To love Synclair was a vastly different matter.

Love?

She froze and felt a jolt of emotion shake her. Her knees threatened to buckle under the weight of her own thoughts.

To love any man was foolish. It was bound to bring her grief and yet, her heart felt fuller than it had in many years, possibly her entire life. She sat down. She dreaded the future, because loving Synclair did not mean he would love her in return. Her gaze wandered over the table once more, and she could not overlook the care that the items represented.

Gifts. They were true treasures, ones that most women waited until they married to own. Such things as scissors and pins and needles were passed down through generations because the metal was so expensive. Some of the needles were bright gold, ensuring that they would glide smoothly through even the finest fabric.

Synclair cared for her, there was no denying it, but even a mistress often collected expensive gifts from her lover.

Yet Synclair had offered her more. She longed to wed him, and that was the truth. It was hard to admit it, but surrounded by his gifts, evidence of his caring, she lost the will to deny what her heart truly longed for.

A husband whom she loved. Was that such a terrible thing? To love one's own spouse? There wasn't a person she might ask that question of because she knew what the reaction would be.

Love was considered an insanity, and it had surely brought England great grief as Henry the Eighth loved and then fell out of love.

But in her case, it would be her child who suffered for her decisions.

She sighed. She could never wed Synclair, no matter how much she might long to.

The day stretched out into hours that felt longer than they were. The table held ample things for her to do but she discovered herself restless and pacing more times than she could count. The chain was long enough that she might make it to the water closet, telling her that Synclair had thought about it and tested it.

No wonder the man had been missing for so many days from court. He had been busy setting his plan into motion.

A maid brought her meals, but with little activity, she did not eat much. Arlene appeared after sunset with Amy, and they split the seam of the dressing robe so that it might be removed for the night.

"The cook would like to know if you have any instructions for her, mistress."

"It's rather odd to hear you calling me mistress, when I am chained by your master."

Arlene twisted her apron between her fingers. "The master said you were the mistress."

Justina lay back in the bed and sighed. "I see. Please tell the cook that her skill is great and appreciated, I simply do not require much when I am sitting the day through."

Arlene's eyes widened with understanding. "Yes . . . yes, that makes good sense. Good night, mistress."

Mistress . . .

Justina couldn't deny that she was indeed being treated like the mistress of the house, with the very notable exception of having the freedom to survey her domain. The bedding that surrounded her was fine. There were plump pillows behind her head and the mattress was thick and wide. The bed itself was huge, with thick posts at each corner that were carved at the tops to look like falcons. Curtains were hung along the sides of the bed to keep the heat inside during the cold months of winter. She didn't see the chamber door close tonight because Arlene drew the last length of fabric closed before she left. Justina discovered herself grateful for the privacy because she found the bed very lonely. It was far more of a challenge to attempt sleeping in it than she had thought it would be. The winter chill forced her to snuggle down beneath the thick comforter but even that did not seem to warm her.

That was because the cold was coming from inside her heart. She frowned and turned over only to hear the chain clinking when she moved. Frustration made her grumpy, but even having her temper aroused failed to banish her longing for the man who had shared the bed with her last night.

If he was going to chain her to the bed, couldn't he at least share it with her?

It was an audacious question, one sure to gain her the displeasure of the Church if they ever discovered the direction of her thinking, but for the moment, she was quite alone with herself.

She did long for Synclair, and that was a fact. Her body was softly yearning for his, the memory of how much she enjoyed his touch sending heat along her skin. The sheets were smooth and soft but her mind was centered on the way his body felt when they had shared the bed. Never had she suspected that she might enjoy sharing a bed so much, but she had with Synclair. Some doctors warned against couples sleeping too long next to one another, claiming that each heart had its own unique rhythm and that being too close to another might cause each heart to lose its beat.

Justina doubted it. Being locked in the tower at Amber Hill and separated from him by stone walls had failed to keep her from dwelling upon him and affection growing inside her heart. The truth of the matter was, she was too weak to resist him and he too foolish to listen to her reasoning.

Her sleep was anything but peaceful and the bedding proved it when dawn finally arrived. She had tossed and turned and kicked until the coverlet and sheets were pulled from the corners of the bed. Arlene and her staff put it to rights while Amy stitched her into a fresh chemise and the dressing gown after her bath. A morning bath was much wiser given the cold weather; her wet hair was less likely to cause her to catch a chill during the day than in the evening.

But all too soon she was sitting at the table, waiting for time to pass while her mind ran in circles.

Where was Synclair?

"Right fine day for riding."

Synclair couldn't help but snort at his captain in reply. The sky was growing darker and the wind had turned sharp, the icy claw of winter present. His armor breastplate was a welcome weight now because it kept that wind from slicing through his clothing. In the summer the thing was a torment that trapped heat against his body.

However, no sane man took to the road without breastplate and helmet. An archer could put an arrow through a man from two hundred yards away. With the King in his last days, foreign assassins were a far too real possibility. Synclair kept a sharp eye on the area ahead of him because it would be simple to murder them on the road and bury them. With the beginning of winter upon the country, no one would notice him missing for months, and by the time anyone thought to ask after him, there would be nothing left to point the way to the shallow graves their bodies were tossed into.

Henry had been a brutal king in many ways, but he had united a country on the brink of disintegration. His father, Henry the Seventh, had married Elizabeth of York to end the war of the roses. That had been a bloody time, two thirds of the nobles in England died during the battle to see who would finally sit upon the throne. Henry the Eighth only kept the crown by killing off those relatives who made the mistake of challenging him. It was absolute rule or a return to the war between noble houses. That was the knowledge that drove Henry in his quest for a son, a quest that had claimed the lives of three of his wives and seen him divorcing two more.

It was also the thing that convinced men such as Viscount Biddeford that he might treat his ward in any manner he decided fit. Synclair felt his temper heating to a dangerous level. He knew his own limits, had seen them tested in France, and he felt his tolerance stretching thin. Chaining Justina to his bed was the only way to prevent him from challenging Biddeford and the consequences be damned.

He wanted to kill the bastard. It was that simple. The urge was growing stronger and more uncontrollable with every day.

The road in front of him offered him a diversion from his rising intolerance for Justina's guardian. Killing Biddeford might still be his pleasure but he would make sure that there were no innocents left to suffer for his actions.

There was also the lady herself. His lady. He planned to teach her that, in a manner that no man had ever tried to teach her before. Through earning her trust. She had passion for him, even affection that he'd witnessed in her eyes, but there was no trust in his ability to protect her and her child from Biddeford. That was what he craved, because love could not live without trust, and he needed her love.

It was the thing he had dreamed of for two years. The single thing that he craved as his reward for persevering through years of training and service.

Love. That rare thing that blossomed between only a few couples. He wanted it and he would do anything to keep it.

Even chain up the woman who held his heart in her hands. He loved her and he planned to prove that he was worthy of her trust. Synclair leaned down over his stallion's neck and gritted his teeth against the chill.

Nothing was going to stop him.

Nothing.

A storm began gathering around the house two days later. Justina watched the sky darken with black clouds. They pressed lower and lower, until the tops of the trees were difficult to see. Arlene brought candles to the chamber and their light was welcome, but it also made Justina more aware of the chill. She felt drawn to the circle of light the flames gave off. The fireplace was too far away from the bed and what little warmth there was in the chamber was seeping out of the glass panes. She had enjoyed having the curtains open, after all, glass-paned windows were quite expensive. Her chambers at Whitehall did not have glass but iron-work screens that allowed fresh air inside. At night or when the weather wasn't fair, wooden shutters closed over the screens. She was fortunate to have even those; many at court made do with rooms that had no windows at all because the palace had once belonged to the Church and monks had been expected to live in humble accommodations.

So she sighed in lament as Arlene began to pull the curtains over the glass. It was nearing supper time, and she was not tired enough to seek her bed even if the thick coverlet looked inviting. Arlene had found the cape that she had used to ride to the house, but the weight of it over her shoulders made it difficult to sew or move her arms at all. She had it draped across her legs but the dressing gown was too thin for the winter. She still resisted having the windows covered. It would make the corner dark and too much like a prison cell for her taste. Every time she moved too much, the chain would give off sounds of the links hitting one another. Her left wrist was sore from lifting the weight of it.

"Leave one open, Arlene."

The housekeeper turned to look at her in question. "But, mistress, you are shivering."

"Why is your mistress cold?"

Two shrieks filled the chamber as Synclair spoke. Arlene's was far louder, earning her a scowl from her lord. Justina lifted her right hand up to cover her lips because the sight of Synclair in the chamber again startled her a second time. It felt as though she had conjured him from her longings.

"Oh my, you frightened me something terrible, my

lord." The housekeeper was still flustered, with one hand pressed over her heart, and she forgot to lower herself, too.

"So I heard." Synclair sounded exhausted, more so than Justina had ever heard him.

Footsteps sounded in the hallway, hurried heavy-booted footfalls of men running. The door burst in, drawing a disgusted sound from Synclair.

"There is nothing amiss, Captain Repel, the women were not paying attention and my appearance startled them."

Captain Repel was just as dedicated to his post as Synclair had been when Justina first crossed paths with him. The captain scanned the chamber, his keen stare missing nothing before he aimed his attention at his lord and offered him a bow. Synclair placed his riding gauntlets on the table near the door and waited for his men to quit the room.

The moment they did, he aimed his attention at her. He was still wearing his spurs, and they tapped against the floor when he moved closer so that his eyes might inspect her.

"Why isn't your mistress dressed in this chill, Arlene?"

Arlene gasped and began sputtering. "Well . . . you see . . . my lord . . . 'Tis—"

Justina stood up and the chain filled the chamber with noise. "Because it is impossible to put my arm through a sleeve, and everything that I am wearing must be sewn onto me each time I bathe, *my lord.*"

Arlene snapped her lips shut with a small click of her teeth. Justina refused to speak in a smooth, respectful tone when talking about that chain. The man deserved to hear the frustration in her voice.

"Arlene, fetch a gown for your mistress. She needs to dress, and I will unlock her now that I am returned."

The housekeeper lost no time quitting the room, ducking her head in a show of respect even while she was moving toward the doorway. The moment she was gone, Justina heard the unmistakable sound of male amusement.

Synclair was watching her from eyes that were ringed with dark circles, but his lips were set into a grin.

"You have always had a great deal of spirit. Something that I find irresistible in you." His gaze traveled down her length and back up. "My apologies for not considering that you would be unable to dress in the clothing I had purchased for you."

"You should not have bought so many things for me." She found herself struggling against the feeling of being cherished. She couldn't help that she loved him but it would never do for her to allow him to know her feelings.

"I plan to wed you, Justina."

She lifted her left hand and a soft growl came from her. "Is this designed to soften my heart toward you?"

His smile brightened. "No, that was necessary to keep you from performing your duty, as you see it, by returning to your guardian."

He moved closer and she felt her breath freeze in her chest. All of the annoyance with the chain didn't stop her belly from fluttering now that he was so close once more. She couldn't keep herself from locking stares with him or halt the joy that flooded her.

"Did you miss me, Justina?" He reached out and captured her left arm, raising it and fitting a small key into the lock. With a turn of his wrist, the thick iron opened and fell to the floor.

Justina couldn't help but sigh, and Synclair rubbed her skin where it had begun to discolor beneath the band of iron.

"I missed you, very much."

His voice was dangerously low and dark. It reminded her too much of the way he spoke to her while they were locked together.

"I missed being able to wear clothing."

One of his fair eyebrows rose. "You shouldn't. It is a sin to cover your body with so many layers. I suggest you reform your ways and wear naught but a chemise inside this chamber."

He was playing with her, the boy hidden inside the body of the man who towered over her and winked at her. Heat surfaced in her cheeks, annoying her with the fact that he would see the blush staining her face.

"Ah, the most perfect welcome . . ." Synclair reached out to touch her face, gently stroking his fingertips along the sensitive skin.

"It isn't a welcome when you used a chain to keep me here, Synclair."

His eyes darkened. "I will do anything necessary to secure you, Justina."

"That is not chivalrous." Her attention lowered to the gold knight's chain he wore around his neck. For once, it was dusty, surprising her because he customarily kept it so pristine. It was his most treasured possession because he had earned it.

A warm hand cupped her chin and raised her face so that their eyes met once again. Emotion blazed in his eyes, fierce and unrelenting.

"I disagree, Lady. I spent many years following my king, and what I learned at his side of the arts of Knighthood makes that chain look soft."

His tone had sharpened until she winced.

"That was war."

"It was an attempt at conquest, Justina, and I was trained to do anything necessary to bring home victory to my monarch. As far as I see, the court is very similar, so I will use whatever tactics necessary. I will have you for my wife. How long you wear that chain is your choice."

Arlene knocked on the door and Synclair called out to her instantly.

"Enter!"

There was a scurry of footfalls on the floor as several maids followed the housekeeper. Synclair stepped back but remained in the chamber with his attention fixed on her. The level of attention irritated her and she aimed a hot look at him while his staff began to dress her.

First they removed the dressing gown that had been sewn onto her each morning. Her stays had to be unlaced and taken off so that a small hip roll might be secured about her hips to hold up the cartridge pleats of the skirts, keeping the weight of the fabric from giving her a backache. Over that went an under skirt, secured around her waist. There were no steel hoops in this one, pleasing her. The dress would be a more practical one and much easier to move in. The maids relaced her stays and then lifted the dress up and over her head. Justina lifted her hands to allow the dress to be slid down into place around her body. The maids made quick work of closing the back with a lace threaded through the eyelets. They brought her the sleeves and slid them up her arms before using silver-tipped ribbons to tie the sleeves to the bodice of the dress.

She sighed as the chill she had tried to ignore for the last few days finally left her skin. The dress was made of good wool, finely spun and woven into a fabric thick enough to keep her warm, yet soft enough to not bind at her elbows.

Arlene finished her duty by placing a French hood on her head. It was made of wool but lined with fine linen to keep it from irritating the skin of her ears and neck. The hood curved around her head to keep her warm. At court, such a hat might be decorated with gold and jewels; this one was simple with only a bit of knitted lace. She liked it full well.

"Leave us."

Justina folded her hands together, dreading the possibility that Synclair meant to lock the manacle around her wrist once more. The maids all lowered themselves before leaving on quick steps.

"I enjoy seeing you free of those court dresses."

A smile tugged at the corners of her lips. "I agree; I have no love for the necessity of fashion that court seems to deem so important."

Synclair moved toward her, and she pressed her lips into a firm line to conceal the sickening twist moving through her belly. But she refused to act the coward. She kept her chin level and her gaze on the man approaching her.

"I wonder, Justina, would you tell me what you do harbor affection for?"

The question shocked her, distracting her from her fears. "My son, you know that well."

He nodded and something flickered in his eyes that drew her attention. He lifted his hand and she flinched, her hands going behind her back, making a mockery of her intention to stand firm in her stance.

He frowned but his hand remained between them with the palm facing up.

"Come with me, my lady, I have something for you."

She stared at his face for a long moment, trying to read his thoughts, but his expression offered her no hints. Her curiosity needled her until she moved, placing her hand in his.

Synclair curled his fingers around hers and turned to the door. His grip was firm and his pace quick. He opened the heavy door with one hand and joined her in the hallway before it closed under its own weight. Feeling the fabric of her skirts about her legs was a welcome sensation. Synclair took her through several hallways and she tried to memorize them. The house appeared to be built in a block, with two wings stretching back from the front of it. Sinclair took her around a corner and down the length of one wing until they reached a set of double doors. The framing was decorated with carvings in the wood announcing a room that was reserved for an honored guest.

Synclair reached out and pulled the door open.

"Go on, Justina, and see what I have brought you."

His voice was deep and sincere and full of tenderness. She was torn between the need to remain near him and discover what he meant, or enter the chamber and see what his newest gift was.

"Look, Nan, it is beginning to snow now, just as Sir Synclair said it would, and he was most correct; it waited until we arrived."

The young voice drew a gasp from her. Justina ran through the open door and skidded to a stop only a few steps across the threshold. She felt the blood drain from her face as every muscle she had drew tight enough to snap. Her lungs refused to fill but she didn't care. Brandon was kneeling on a chair near the windows, his nose pressed against the glass while he watched the snow falling in the evening light. She knew him more by the older woman sitting near him, for she had chosen Nan carefully to be her son's nurse when she was forced to return to court. The middle-aged woman nodded to her while she reached out to gently tap her young charge on the shoulder.

"Brandon, your mother is here to greet you."

Synclair pressed an open hand against her back, gently urging her forward. Her son turned and smiled.

"Good evening, Mother. I am very happy to see you." He offered her a polished bow that Nan smiled proudly at.

Justina sobbed before running across the room and sweeping him off his feet.

CHAPTER EIGHT

Justina twirled around and around until her balance failed and she had to stop or tumble to the floor. Brandon wrapped his thin arms around her neck and placed a wet kiss against her lips. But he wiggled out of her embrace the moment his feet touched the ground.

"The snow is falling, Mother! In great white waves, like the tide coming in." He ran back to the window with a scamper that belonged only to a carefree child.

Tears fell down her cheeks as she watched him rise up on his toes and press his hands against the glass. She raised her hand and pressed it against her lips to smother the sobs that rose from her chest. Every hour of anguish that had tortured her began pouring out of her in a flood of emotion so thick it threatened to choke her.

Two thick arms closed around her from behind. Synclair stepped up and she gratefully turned to him.

"Thank you, thank you, thank you . . . I have not seen him in so long . . ." She reached up and cupped his face between her hands, placing kisses against his chin and mouth between her words of gratitude.

Synclair cupped the back of her neck, easing her head up so that their eyes met. "You should never have been kept from your son, Justina. I swear I will never allow it to happen again."

"But how—"

"Hush. For now, trust me. At least until it is time to put Brandon to bed for the night."

He placed a firm kiss against her mouth, sealing any reply beneath his lips. It was a hot kiss but one that lasted only a moment before he turned her around to see her child once more. Brandon gestured her forward to watch the snow falling.

It was the best invitation she had ever received.

Justina watched her son sleeping, unwilling to leave him even after his breathing deepened and she knew he was deep in slumber. Nan stood nearby, her chin sinking lower and lower while she waited for her mistress to be finished for the night. Justina finally left the chamber because she knew that Nan would wait the entire night and go without sleep if she did not leave.

That unfaltering loyalty was the reason she had selected Nan to look after her son.

It was still difficult to leave the chamber, her heart feeling as though she was tearing something off it. The hallway was quiet and chilly, the storm wrapping the house in a freeze that made Justina hurry along because fires would be set only in the hearths that were being used. Wood was a resource that would have to be carefully used if the inhabitants of the house were to have enough to last through the season. Waste made for suffering.

The house was quiet, all of the servants no doubt huddling near a hearth somewhere in the kitchens. Justina turned the corner and made her way to Synclair's chamber.

A single candle was burning on the table near the door. Its light was welcoming, as was the heat coming from the hearth. The fire had died down but the embers glowed red as air moved with the closing of the door. The bed curtains were partially closed, only the side facing the door still open. It allowed her to see Synclair, lying among the plump pillows and coverlet. He was completely bare, the yellow candlelight dancing off his skin. She stared at him for a long moment, enjoying the fact that he was there. The last few nights had been endless, and she suddenly felt very weary, the bed beckoning to her as the most comfortable bed she had ever seen.

"Is he finally asleep?"

Synclair sounded groggy but his eyes opened, and he stretched his arms up and over his head before sitting up. He blinked and looked at her, one eyebrow rising because she had failed to answer. In fact, she was staring at him with her mouth slightly open, the sight of his body fascinating her.

"Um . . . yes. He is."

"Good, then I may claim what remains of your time." He flipped the covers aside and stood up. Words deserted her once more as he walked, completely nude, across the floor.

A soft chuckle filled the room while he covered the space between them.

"Come, sweet lady, you have seen me without clothing." He reached her and gently lifted the French hood off her head.

"Why so shy this evening?"

He sat the hat down on the table.

"I am not certain shy is the correct word." She felt him move behind her and begin unlacing her dress. The chamber was so quiet, she heard the cord sliding against each eyelet when he pulled on it. The bodice loosened and then drooped down. She tugged on the cuffs of her sleeves, not bothering to untie the ribbons that held the sleeve to the bodice. Instead, she slid them down her arms and reached beneath the front of the dress for the tie that held her slip and hip roll closed.

"I believe it is." He lifted her up the moment her dress hit the floor, his arms cradling her against his chest while he carried her to the bed. He laid her down and joined her while the bed ropes groaned.

"I rather like to think you are shy about our current situation because you are unaccustomed to enjoying a relationship, Justina."

"Is that why you brought Brandon to me? So that I would enjoy being with you?" Justina reached up and pulled one of her hairpins free. Synclair laid back down, stretching out and blocking her exit from the bed with his body. He was lying on the side of the bed closest to the chamber doors, and she realized that his sword was leaning up against the wall near within reach.

"I brought him here so that you might begin to trust me."

Trust?

Justina looked down at the surface of the bed, her hands frozen in the act of pulling another hairpin. She heard him exhale stiffly before the bed moved and he plucked the pin from her distracted fingers.

"When I asked you to wed me, Justina, I offered my name to both you and your son. I brought Brandon here so that you might see that."

She lifted her head and stared at him. She wanted to trust him but Biddeford's face rose up in her mind to prevent her from yielding to the man lying next to her.

"We would not be the first couple who discovered their union dissolved when the privy council voted against it. You are a peer, you need permission to wed. So do I."

"Edward Seymour promised to witness our wedding."

"What?"

Synclair's eyes were no longer sleepy, now glittering with purpose. "Does that change your answer, Justina?"

There was something flickering in his eyes that warned her he was plotting again. Suspicion needled her, making her think.

"You are not telling me everything."

Synclair's face instantly drew tight, his expression becoming stone hard and unreadable.

"And you speak of trust, but I am correct, there is more to what the Earl of Hertford said." There was a note of triumph in her voice even if it was a hollow victory. Reality was always far too complicated for simple happiness to flourish.

A muscle on the side of his jaw twitched. "If you truly want to know, Edward claimed he would witness us wedding if you were with child. My child."

Of course, she was a proven breeder of sons. That was something a man such as Edward Seymour would consider valuable. She suddenly snarled.

"Is that why you chained me to this bed? So that your seed might have time to take root in me?"

Her temper sizzled and she rose up onto her knees, intent on climbing over him. One solid arm wrapped around her middle and he pushed her down onto the surface of the bed. She was still struggling against having her back pressed to the bed when he rolled on top of her to pin her there.

"There is nothing back at Whitehall except danger for you, Justina. I will not willingly allow you to return there."

She pushed against him, grinding her teeth when she found him immovable.

"That is what you fail to understand, Synclair. I have always known the dangers, but if I am not there, Biddeford has sworn to send for Brandon, and allow him to be used by those men who prefer boys."

Synclair spat out a word she had never heard spoken. His face was a mask of rage and the emotion went deep into his eyes. Synclair rolled onto his back but he maintained a grip on one of her wrists, his fingers tight.

"He told you that? In plain words?" His tone was quiet. The sort of quiet that warned of true rage.

"Yes. Do you think I would continue as I am, if it were a matter of silver that the man thought to deny me? I should rather be a scullery maid than a whore in silk skirts. Besides, he could never take my widow's thirds from me, and that would be plenty to live on."

Synclair turned his head to look at her.

"I thought he placed Brandon under guard to keep you separated. That was monstrous enough, which is why I took him away."

"But for how long, Synclair?" Her voice quivered and she pulled her hand away from him to hug herself. "How long before that man challenges you in front of the privy council? They will side with him, because he is noble. No one will believe that he might be guilty of threatening my son, even though we all know there are men at court who prefer boy lovers."

"You will have to trust me, Justina." He slid his arm beneath her and pulled her into his embrace. She struggled against it, frightened of the way she could feel her will surrendering to his.

He tucked her against him, his legs tangling with hers, and she heard him sigh against her head.

"Be at ease, Justina. For the moment, the storm will keep all of us where we are."

"But—"

She raised her head to make her argument and his mouth

captured hers. The kiss was firm, but tender, too. The joy that had flooded her when she held her son combined with the longing she had nursed the entire time that Synclair was gone. She clasped her arms around him, returning his kiss until he tucked her back against his side and sleep claimed them both.

It was by far the most peaceful sleep she had experienced since leaving her son.

Whitehall Palace

"You are playing a game with me."

The Viscount Biddeford allowed his lips to curve, and he didn't bother to alter the expression when he turned to look at Francis de Canis. The hallways were darker than normal, the storm keeping the candles flickering and even blowing several out. It made for more dark corners, and those were always inhabited by men such as Francis de Canis. He was obviously waiting on him and that pleased the viscount well.

"Am I, Francis?"

"You are, my lord, and I admit that I find it difficult to resist. So name your price and allow Justina back out where I can catch her."

"Ah, so simple, but why would I do such a thing?"

De Canis shrugged. "Your reputation precedes you, my lord. You are a man who makes clean bargains and keeps them. I am the same sort. So tell me what you want to step out of my way, or shall I tell you what I can give you?"

"By all means, my good man. I would like to hear if you know anything about what I like."

Francis de Canis smiled. He moved closer and glanced down both hallways before returning his attention to Biddeford. There was a flicker of arrogance in his eyes that the viscount found rather misplaced, but he admitted that he wanted to know what a man such as Francis de Canis might offer him. It would not be common or boring and that was what kept his lips sealed and him waiting on a man of common birth.

"You want Bessie Portshire, not that I blame you any. She has a nice pair of tits and her bloodline is impressive."

Biddeford snorted. "That is no secret and you cannot get her for me."

De Canis continued to smirk at him. "So little faith in me, my lord. Now that is almost enough incentive for me to prove my worth to you, but not quite. I want Justina, and in return I will show you how to neatly trap Bessie into agreeing to marry you."

The viscount frowned. "Of her own free will? Her father is insistent upon it."

"There is more than one way to force a woman to kneel." De Canis dug inside his doublet and pulled out a small bundle that was wrapped in cloth. "This little sack will rob the lady of her wits once it is steeped in warmed wine. Toss her skirts and spill her virgin's blood. I will burst upon the scene, suitably shocked, and she will wed you before I make it public knowledge, ruining her."

"But how would I get her into my private apartments?"

"Simple enough, she has befriended your ward Lady Wincott. Have the lady invite her."

The viscount snarled but de Canis chuckled.

"So it is true, the lady has slipped away from your leash."

"I am still her guardian. She will return and suffer my displeasure so that she recalls her position quicker the next time I send her out upon an errand. Have no doubt that the lady is still very much beneath my heel."

De Canis shrugged once more and pushed the little cloth sack back into his doublet.

"We don't need her to trap Bessie, since everyone thinks your ward is here. All we need to do is send out a message to Bessie. The girl is naive enough to come if she believes her friend is ill and in need of company."

Biddeford knew for certain that de Canis was a man who lived up to his reputation. He was offering him Bessie like fresh meat waved in front of a hunting hound, and the man had learned enough about him to know it was something he couldn't resist. He did want Bessie as his wife; her dowry was a fortune and her father a duke. She was plain-faced enough to keep men such as de Canis from trying their hand at seducing her, too. When he wanted a pretty face attached to his bed partner, he would go to his mistress. He could breed Bessie Portshire and gain powerful relatives in the doing of it.

"Then arrange it, tonight."

De Canis held up one finger. "I do not work for free, my lord. This little bundle comes from the heart of the Moors' empire. It is no easy thing for a Christian to purchase. Those Persians like to keep the secret of their harems, but I wanted to know how they managed to catch so many rare and beautiful women and keep them."

De Canis watched Biddeford carefully. The man's eyes were glittering, and he looked as if he might begin drooling. De Canis patted the top of his doublet again.

"But I've seen it at work, it's very potent. A few swallows and even a virgin will suck your cock without a single whimper. All you have to do is instruct her with a soft voice, like a child."

"I am a nobleman, you may count on me to keep my end of the bargain."

That earned him a soft snort from Francis de Canis. The sound sent his temper to raging.

"You may be a nobleman, my lord, but I am a well traveled common man and I tell you truthfully. You shall never find another with this same formula, and I do assure you, I have seen it put to the test. The Moors have men who know how to bend the wills of their females."

"It is truly from the East?" Biddeford licked his lower lip. Anticipation made him almost giddy because he had heard tales of the sultans in the East who kept harems full of women, every one of them devoted to pleasuring their masters. Completely devoted.

"It is and you are not the only man I can trade it with."

"I will fetch Lady Wincott back to Whitehall. I sent her along with Synclair Harrow to see what the man was about after his meeting with the King."

"Excellent. I will look forward to doing business with you, my lord. As soon as I hear that Lady Wincott is returned to court, you may count on me to arrange your evening with Bessie."

Biddeford clenched his fingers into fists and snarled, but there was nothing he could do but suffer his frustration.

The stupid bitch. He was going to enjoy watching her suffer for placing him in such an awkward position. His rage transformed into lust as he considered what dragging Justina back to court would get him. He'd wasted hours and hours on courting Bessie, only to have the girl respond with little interest to his efforts. When she was his wife, he was going to enjoy having her try and appease his temper. She would serve him, on her knees like a wife should. It would be his pleasure to teach her all of the delights that her female body might provide, from using her mouth to ease his cock, to filling her passage with his seed. All of it would be his.

Soon.

Her nose was chilled.

Justina snuggled down, humming when she discovered

it warm and toasty beneath the bedding. Another body was there and she pressed against it, uttering another little sound of delight when that body moved, the hands sliding along her limbs to send sweet enjoyment through her.

"I can become accustomed to waking up with you in my bed, madam."

Synclair's voice was husky and still edged with sleep. He lay behind her and her chemise had risen up during the night to bare her bottom. His hips pressed against her, warming her and also allowing her to feel the thick presence of his erection.

He placed a warm kiss against her neck, while his hands smoothed up her belly until he cupped her breasts.

"Very accustomed to it."

So could she.

Her clitoris began to throb, gently demanding attention from the hard flesh pressing against her bottom. Her back arched slightly, without any thought on her part. It was pure reaction to the warm, male hands cupping her breasts. He toyed with her nipples, making a soft sound as they drew into hard points while he fingered them.

"Shall I take that as encouragement?" He gently pressed her nipples between his thumbs and fingers. Pleasure went through her, shooting down her body to her clitoris.

"Or shall I seek out further proof of your willingness?"

She couldn't help but laugh. A soft, little feminine sound that drew an answering rumble from the chest behind her.

"Perhaps I should gather my own information about your state of arousal." Justina made sure her voice was sultry.

"An idea I adore, madam."

She rubbed her bottom against his cock, swiveling her hips from side to side so that her cheeks moved over the surface of that hard flesh. He gently pinched her nipples again, slightly harder this time, sending heat snaking through her belly. She could feel her passage warming, becoming moist with need. Her back arched again, wanting nothing more than a gentle climb toward passion's peak this morning.

"Mother! You must come and see how high the snow is!"

Synclair jumped and Justina found herself flung onto the far side of the bed as Brandon scampered across the floor, his small boots tapping against the stone.

"Brandon . . . you must not push in doors. . . ." Nan was out of breath and only half dressed.

Brandon was too excited to heed his nurse's instructions. His face was lit with a smile that warmed her heart because it spoke of his longing to be with her, too. He climbed right up into the bed, and she had to smother a giggle when she watched Synclair pull the coverlet up to hide his aroused state.

Brandon didn't stop until he was sitting on her lap, his small hands reaching for her cheeks to turn her attention completely onto him.

"It looks like heaven fell onto the ground because everything is sparkling."

"I cannot wait to see it."

His eyes lit with anticipation, but he turned his head to look at Synclair.

"Did my mother agree to marry you, Sir Synclair?"

Synclair reached out and plucked the boy off her lap. "Not yet, you scamp, but I plan to attempt to soften her resolve today."

Synclair ruffled Brandon's hair before setting him down beside the bed. Nan came forward with her hand outstretched.

"Come, Master Brandon, and allow your mother time to dress."

Brandon went back to his nurse with a lighthearted step but he turned at the door and performed a perfect reverence before leaving.

The gesture melted her heart.

"Isn't he the most wonderful child?"

"His timing could use a little refining." Synclair sounded grumpy, and he pushed his lower lip out in a pout to complete the moment.

Justina lifted her chin. "Now I simply cannot have such behavior. My son is at an impressionable age, you understand. I will not reward surliness."

Synclair laughed. He tilted his head back and roared with amusement. A moment later, a pillow hit her square in the face. The bed bounced and she fell backward onto the jumbled comforter while Synclair chased her with his weapon, hitting her several more times with it.

"How is my behavior now, madam?" There was wicked enjoyment in his voice and he hovered over her on all fours. While covering her face with her hands, she looked down his length and spied his erection. Reaching out, she grasped it, tightening her hand enough to freeze Synclair in the midst of his attack.

"I seem to have found the means to controlling you."

A soft rumble of male amusement shook his chest.

"That has yet to be proven, but I am willing to explore the idea with you, madam."

He rolled over and landed on his back, sending the pillows near the headboard flying onto the floor as his feet landed where they had been. He reached over and gripped her waist. He lifted her up and over him, bringing her down with her thighs straddling him.

"I cannot wait to see how you plan to master me."

Now he was toying with her like a man, and she found it equally charming. Leaning forward, she combed her fingers through his sleep-tousled hair.

"Is that so, my lord?" She lifted her bottom and felt his cock spring up from where it had been trapped against his belly. His hands slipped up her thighs, beneath her chemise, to grip her hips.

"It is, Justina."

He pushed her down, slowly guiding her onto his length. Her passage was wet and welcoming, the head of his cock burrowing between the folds of her slit to the opening of her sheath.

"Ride me."

His eyes glittered with passion and need. She allowed more of her weight to drop and his cock began to penetrate her body. The walls of her passage stretched around the flared head while his hands guided her down further, until his length was completely inside her.

With his length clasped inside her passage, Justina sat up and grasped the sides of her chemise, pulling the fabric up, baring her body completely. The cold morning air didn't bother her now. Her heart was beating fast enough to warm her and the feeling of his hard cock inside her sent more heat across her skin.

"Perfection." Synclair growled the word, his gaze on her breasts.

Justina rose, lifting herself off his length, and then allowed her body to sink back onto his erection. Her breasts bounced, just a tiny amount, and his jaw tightened, the fingers gripping her hips flexing at the same time.

"It that what you craved, my lord?"

Justina purred, lowering her voice and drawing her fingernails down his chest in gentle scratches.

"It is a good place to begin, but I fancy a brisker pace, my beauty."

One of his hands lifted and delivered a short smack on the side of her bottom.

She yelped, more in surprise than in pain. The spot

stung but it somehow intensified the heat inside her. She rose up and pressed back down faster, his cock sliding smoothly in and out of her passage.

"Ah, so obedient to your master."

"I am the one riding you, sir." She increased her pace, intending to show him that she could be the leader, but another smack landed on the opposite side of her bottom and it drew a moan from her.

"And I say, faster, my beauty!"

Her breasts began to jiggle with her motions and his gaze became fixed on them, but his hips also lifted to meet her on every downward plunge. She could hear his breath rasping between his clenched teeth and he lifted one hand off her hip, making her gasp.

But he didn't deliver another smack to her bottom; instead he moved his thumb between the folds of her slit to find her clitoris. He rubbed it, sending sharp need through her passage. Her thighs quivered but she tightened her muscles and kept her pace, riding him with quick motions, lowering herself all the way so that his cock was buried completely inside her. Pleasure began to tighten beneath his thumb, the hard flesh stretching the walls of her passage, carrying it deep into her belly. She could see his cheek twitching as he held off his own pleasure until hers peaked.

"Ride me to the finish, my beauty."

"I shall!"

She kept her pace by sheer force of will, and pleasure exploded beneath his thumb a moment later. It raced into her passage, where the walls of her sheath tried to grasp his cock tighter.

"Christ in heaven."

Synclair grabbed her hips and held them in place while he bucked beneath her, driving his cock in a series of hard thrusts while his seed spurted inside her. She felt it hitting the mouth of her womb, hot and smooth. Pleasure shook her, moving in waves through her body until she slumped down onto his chest, unable to maintain her position above him. For a long moment there was only the sound of his heart beneath her ear and the brush of the morning air felt refreshing against the skin of her back.

"We should ride every morning."

He rolled her over, gently smoothing her hair away from her face before tapping a fingertip against her lips.

"Just as soon as you wed me."

Synclair didn't remain in the bed long enough for her to protest. He rolled over and stood up. He reached for a tassel that hung from an iron hook near the bed and gave it a pull.

"It is not my permission to wed that we need, Synclair."

He turned to look at her and the expression on his face stunned her. Raw, unrelenting determination shone from his eyes, and there was not a hint of yielding. Instead, she saw only his challenge, daring her to try him.

He walked back to her. "I ask your consent, Lady, because that is the correct thing to do, but I assure you, I will not be so soft when it comes to the men who run this country. I have bled for England, and her nobles will give me the woman of my choosing for wife." He reached out and cupped her cheek in one hand. "If I must take you from them, so be it."

A knock on the door announced the arrival of Arlene and her staff. Synclair leaned over to place a kiss against her lips before striding from the room with his sword in hand. The man didn't have anything on except for a dressing gown, but the pommel of his sword rose above his shoulder because he cradled it across one bent arm like a babe. He was every inch the hardened knight she had struggled to avoid and escape at Amber Hill, and yet, her cheek was still warm from his hand, a touch so tender it warmed her heart.

For the first time, she wished him success in his quest, even knowing that she would be his prize.

Let the arrogant lords sitting on the King's privy council think she was being awarded to him. All that mattered was the fact that she knew he had asked her.

She stopped wishing and began praying because it was far too probable that his quest would fail.

Far too much so.

CHAPTER NINE

"Not too far from the house, Brandon."
Her son smiled with glee and plunged into the new blanket of snow, just beyond where it had been swept off the steps in front of the house. It was drifted up to his waist but that did not stop him from running full speed toward it and jumping to land in it. White powder flew up in a little cloud all around him while the sound of his laughter made Justina smile.

"Come, Mother! Jump and see how far you fly!"

A husky chuckle was her only warning before a hard, male body captured hers. Justina squealed but it was more from excitement than fear. She recognized Synclair's scent as he wrapped his arms around her and swept her off her feet.

"You want to see your mother fly?"

Justina felt her eyes round with horror. "Don't you dare, Synclair."

He offered her a smug grin. "You should know by now that I dare quite often, Lady."

He tossed her toward the snow drift and she squealed again, the sound intensifying when she landed in the frozen powder.

"Synclair . . . you toad!"

The snow chilled her skin everywhere it wasn't covered, and her body heat melted it where there was fabric. Her dress began to turn wet as she struggled to crawl out of the snow bank Synclair had tossed her into. He stood grinning at her with his hands propped on his hips. Justina grabbed a handful of the frozen snow and hurled it at his mocking face. Her aim proved true and snow exploded all over Synclair's face and chest. She jumped, his body instantly bracing for battle, but it was the surprised look on his face that made her laugh, in spite of the way her bottom was turning numb.

Brandon howled with approval and threw two more balls of snow at Synclair.

"So you want to battle, do you?"

Synclair began tossing large handfuls of snow at Brandon. Justina gasped and tried to fight her way clear of the snow, but heard a mock growl before she was scooped up and tossed further into what had been the yard a week ago. Now it was deep drifts of snow and she sank into it while balls of snow continued to fly.

"I shall never surrender!" Brandon sent out a war cry while continuing to throw snow at Synclair. Justina tried to fight the fabric of her skirts and gain some sort of footing.

"Then you shall be defeated!"

Synclair drove Brandon back but at the last moment, her son threw a final handful of snow at the looming knight and he stopped, pretended to stagger a few paces before falling backward as though he were mortally wounded. Snow flew up in a white mist as his large body collapsed onto its surface.

Her son howled with glee.

"I am victorious!"

Brandon flung his small body at his victim and she heard Synclair laughing as the child landed on top of him.

"And I am growing wet, lying on this snow."

Synclair stood up, taking Brandon with him. He set the boy down on his feet and dusted what snow he could from his clothing. Justina made her way out of the snow bank and kicked her skirts with a disgruntled sound.

"Women's clothing is so cumbersome."

"But what else would you wear, Mother? A kilt like a Scotsman or robes like the Greek statues?"

Synclair winked at the boy. "I think your mother would look interesting in britches."

Her son's eyes widened.

"Sir Synclair is jesting, my lamb," Justina informed her son gently, while she tried to hide the blush beginning to stain her cheeks with guilt.

Brandon frowned and his little nose wrinkled. "I know I shouldn't correct you, Mother, but I am no longer a little lamb. I just defeated my first knight."

"Ah yes, well you are correct, my lion."

Her son roared and ran inside the open front doors, his voice echoing off the walls.

"You are a good mother, Justina."

It was true praise, she turned to see it shimmering in Synclair's eyes. Large wet splotches marked his britches and doublet and snow still clung to his knight's chain, but he was interested only in looking at her.

"And you will make a very fine father some day." Her eyes narrowed. "Unless you chain me to your bed again, in which case you may not live to see the new year."

One corner of his mouth twitched up. "Is that a fact, Lady?"

"Quite a solid one."

He pulled her against him, nuzzled against her neck. "Does that mean I am forgiven this once?"

Justina squealed and pushed against him. "Your face is cold!"

"And I want you to warm it for me with words of peace

between us." His arms didn't release her, but molded her against him.

Justina lifted her face to lock gazes with him. "How could I refuse you that? I have not seen my child in far too long, but it does not change the fact that I will have to return to the viscount at some point. The law is on his side of this matter."

He frowned, his arms tightening around her.

"Which is why I chained you. The thought of you not being here when I returned was too harsh to bear."

Justina reached up and placed her hands against his jaw. The skin was warming up quickly and she smoothed her hands up to his cheeks and then behind his neck.

"I cannot bear the thought of you in chains over this, Synclair. You know the law as well as I do."

"Trust me to find a way to negate the law, Justina." He made a sound beneath his breath that was blissful while her hands drew the chill from his nape. But his eyes suddenly became serious.

"We will begin with Brandon; he will not stay here for very long."

There was a light in his eyes that hinted at the intelligence that must have been responsible for seeing Synclair through the hostile territory he had traveled at the King's side. Justina could see him formulating a plan and it sparked hope inside her. It had been a very long time since she had felt that emotion.

"What do you mean?"

She pushed against his chest and he frowned but released her. Justina took several paces away from him before turning to face him again. It amazed her how completely he could change from being playful to embodying knighthood. She wasn't finding it so simple to remain logical while pressed against his body. While they were discussing Brandon, she needed her wits clear.

"We are far too close to Whitehall. It will not take very long for Biddeford to discover that this house belongs to me now."

"It is a private residence."

"One that I recently paid the inheritance taxes on."

Justina drew in a deep breath. "I see." It would be very simple for Biddeford to consult with the court records.

"Good. That will make it simpler for me to tell you that it may be necessary to send Brandon to Scotland."

"Scotland—"

"Laird Barras owes you a personal debt of gratitude."

Justina bit back her first words because they were nothing but an emotional response, one born from her resistance at allowing Brandon to leave her side. Of course he had to go. If he remained, every one of her nightmares would become reality. Her failing to return to Whitehall had no doubt sent the viscount into a rage. One that might so easily be turned upon her child. The man had threatened to do it often enough, so she had no reason to think he wouldn't make good on his threats. Especially if he discovered Brandon so easily within his reach.

"Laird Barras is a good man . . ."

One who had married Curan Ramsden's sister. It had been Jemma who had gifted her with the mare she rode back to court and away from Synclair. Someone had poisoned Jemma, and there was one thing Justina had learned about living at court, and that was how to deal with poison. She had helped to expose the culprit and that would surely earn her favor with Jemma's new husband, Laird Gordon Barras. Even Biddeford would not find it simple to take her son away from the Scot.

Synclair captured one of her hands, freeing it from her skirts where she had begun twisting the fabric.

"I will try to send him north to Curan to begin with,

but it must be done on the morrow. Curan will send him across the border if it becomes necessary."

Justina nodded her head, keeping her lips sealed because she feared that her voice might quiver. She had to remain strong; it was her duty as a mother.

Synclair pulled her back into his embrace, his arms wrapping around her while he placed a soft kiss against the top of her head. His strength was her undoing. Her resistance strained beneath the weight of Biddeford's threats and threatened to buckle now that Synclair was sheltering her. Sobs shook her body and tears began wetting his doublet. She pressed her face against the wool to muffle her weakness.

Synclair held her, his hands attempting to soothe her, and when she finally ran out of tears, he framed her face between his hands and wiped away the drops still clinging to her cheeks.

"I swear, Justina, I will not rest until your guardian is no longer able to meddle in your life."

It was like hearing something out of her dreams. Words that she had so often longed for but knew had little hope of ever becoming reality.

"But I have given you nothing but struggle, Synclair. Wedding me will bring you only more conflicts and none of the benefits that a marriage should yield to a man of your position."

"I disagree, Lady."

She laughed, caught between the urge to smile and the need to cry even more.

"You and I are forever disagreeing."

He made a soft sound beneath his breath. "Something I enjoy."

He leaned down and sealed her reply with his lips. The kiss began softly but increased in pressure until she opened her mouth and yielded to him. His hand cradled the back of her head, while his tongue penetrated her mouth, taking it, just as he had taken her.

The Viscount Biddeford had been raised at court. His father had taught him well how to cultivate relationships among those in positions of power. He would not call them friends, for a wise man never allowed himself to fall to the weakness of having friends. Court was for gaining power and wealth. It was not for fostering emotional ties. Men who hadn't been taught that so often ended up losers to men such as he.

Many nobles departed from court during the winter but that was their mistake. Now, while the weather forced them all to remain indoors, was the time for arranging details to suit his needs. Besides, the King was not improving. His wound was being tended every day now, sometimes twice. That doubled his own need to see things settled before there was a change in power. He would have Bessie Portshire as his wife and thereby gain a powerful connection to her father, the duke.

But that meant retrieving Justina. The viscount made his way down another length of hallway and into a chamber that quieted when he appeared.

"Good day, my lords. Thank you for coming."

Half of the privy council was present, men he often did business with. He owed some of them favors and knew secrets about the other half that they didn't want repeated. What they all shared was a love of power and knowing that they held it.

"I need to introduce a petition tomorrow and I am hoping for your support." Biddeford watched eyes narrow in response but he did not allow that to affect his confidence.

"My ward, the Lady Wincott, has gone missing, and I want her returned to me."

There were a few dry chuckles but the viscount silenced them with a raised eyebrow.

"As I am sure that every one of you would show the same devotion to your own wards, I am hoping you will agree with me that the Baron Harrow must be held accountable for his actions."

"The Baron Harrow is well respected, enough so that the King received him almost immediately." Lord Faulkner spoke up and there were too many heads nodding in agreement with him to suit Biddeford's taste.

"Is that so? And how is His Majesty feeling today?"

The lords all fell silent. Being on good terms with Henry Tudor would soon benefit no one. It was an unspoken thing but one that every man in the room understood.

"As I was saying, I believe the Baron Harrow should be arrested and placed under house arrest until the matter of how my ward has come to be detained by him is investigated." The viscount spread out his hands. "I simply cannot fail to do my duty as her guardian."

No one truly believed that he was sincere about sheltering Justina, but the men in front of him were silent as they considered the risks of failing to side with him. He had often raised his own hand to vote for them when they called upon him, and it was time for them to repay him.

"May I count upon you, my lords?"

Bessie Portshire plucked a gold needle from the cuff of a shirt she was making for her father and tried not to appear as pitiful as she felt.

She was surrounded by daughters of other nobles, many of them feigning an interest in sewing just so that they might sit with her. She pushed the needle back into the linen and smiled while looking at the cuff so that Elizabeth Faulkner might not notice that she had seen the mess she was making of the project in her hands. Elizabeth had no love of sewing because it was clear that she spent little time with a needle and thread. The shirt in her hands was bunched and pulled in all the wrong places. It truly was a pity because the cloth was very fine and had no doubt cost Lord Faulkner a good measure of silver.

"Did you see Lord Harrow with Lady Wincott?" Elizabeth was watching her with wide eyes that didn't look very innocent on the girl. There was a sly twist to her lips that betrayed the fact that she was fishing for information.

"Yes, I believe them a most handsome couple."

More of the girls angled their heads, so as to hear every word clearly.

All that much better for gossiping later . . .

"But there is no understanding between them. I heard that Lord Harrow has not even spoken to the Viscount Biddeford."

Bessie lifted her face and stared at Elizabeth. "Lady Wincott is a widow, so I suspect that courting is done a bit differently the second time."

Elizabeth narrowed her eyes. "Yes, I believe the man is trying her out to see how she rides."

Several of the girls giggled but Bessie dropped the shirt into her sewing basket and stood up.

"Lady Wincott is my friend."

Elizabeth lifted her pert nose. "You would be wise to rethink that position. There are many rumors about her."

"Well I shall have none of the business of concocting new ones. I find Lady Wincott honest and truthful. She is a woman with honor."

Elizabeth drew in a sharp breath as Bessie left the room. She felt the weight of the other girls staring at her and sweat trickled down her back beneath her corset.

"Well, she has some pride." Elizabeth kept her nose in the air and aimed her hardest stare at the other girls. She had to swim or sink now. "As if she is any better than we are. She is a woman, dependent on a good match and then upon her ability to produce a living son quickly. That temper of hers will not see her gaining any favor, mark my words. If her reputation is spoilt, she will come to no good end, high-born or not."

There were quick glances between many of the girls, and Elizabeth watched to see who looked to whom. Such information would please her father as well as be useful when seeking out who spoke ill about her. Several of the girls nodded, agreeing with her publicly, if not truly. Elizabeth didn't care what they really felt, only that once a few heads began moving, the rest followed. She smiled, enjoying the moment of being the one that the other girls looked to for direction.

And her father had claimed that girls were of little use. She would show him the error of his thinking.

"Francis de Canis, my lord."

The Viscount Biddeford watched his manservant reverence after announcing his guest.

"Yes, yes, show him in."

The servant withdrew before he heard a step on the stone floor that told him de Canis had arrived. The viscount didn't rise. He continued to finish writing until the ink ran dry on the quill he was using. He set it carefully in the small wooden holder made to cradle the expensive silver writing implement before raising his attention to the man waiting on him.

"Francis, how good of you to come."

There was a slight pinch of annoyance around the man's face but he covered it well, inclining his head in deference.

"Yes, your man claimed you wished to discuss a matter of grave importance with me."

Biddeford smiled, enjoying the feeling of his lip curving. "Yes, I believe you shall find it most interesting that I have met just recently with several members of His Majesty's privy council. Tomorrow, this petition that I am finishing will be introduced and put to a vote. I believe it shall pass and the recently ennobled Baron Harrow will find himself placed under house arrest until it can be determined why my ward has not returned to my side. It is entirely possibly the man will have to answer for imprisoning her. After all, I am her guardian, and there is no reason why she would not want to return to me."

Lust flashed through de Canis's eyes and his lips curved with it. He tilted his head and looked toward the window for a moment.

"I believe there is time to prepare our little gathering for the evening." He turned his face back to Biddeford. "But if you cross me, be sure you will pay for it, my lord."

The viscount frowned but he wanted Bessie too much to risk offending de Canis. "How will you get the girl here?"

De Canis grinned. "Simple really, we shall let her think she is being invited by Justina." He pointed at the quill. "Pick that up; you have an invitation to pen."

Biddeford did as instructed. It was odd, his temper should have been irritated but he discovered that he was far too excited to take offense. Anticipation was making him giddy, and he had to force himself to listen to what de Canis wanted him to write. The man truly did have confidence in his potion because there was no way they would gain success otherwise. He dipped the quill into the ink several times before the parchment was ready to be sealed. By the time the ink was dry, his cock was rigid. It had been a long time since he had suffered an erection longer than a few hours. That's what a mistress was kept for, to keep a man from having to be distracted by his cock. Today he was going to wait for release. Bessie

Portshire was going to ease the stiffness from his swollen flesh this time. By the week's end, he would have her wed and installed in his bed for at least a month.

And he would also have his ward back, too. Satisfaction warmed him almost as much as lust did. He discovered that he enjoyed the combination far more than anything else.

"Come, Mother! The table is set for our supper."

Justina didn't think that she would ever grow tired of hearing her son's steps as he came running down the hall-way. The day had flown far too fast, each hour feeling like only a few precious moments.

She could not stop thinking about the parting that was sure to come with the dawn. She told herself to savor the day, instead of dreading what was to come. There would be plenty of time to grieve once her son was safely on his way.

Outside it was gray, with thick clouds pressing down from the sky. The temperature never grew to anything that might be considered warm, and as the sun began to arch back toward the horizon, Justina found herself happy to be able to dress completely once again.

She followed her son's footsteps down a long hallway and around a corner until she could smell the scent of food in the air. Her belly gave a rumble, making her laugh softly beneath her breath, for she had neglected to eat in favor of spending time with her child.

Justina froze in the doorframe, her gaze drinking in the sight before her. It was not a grand hall, not if one compared it to Whitehall palace. The room was large enough for several tables and there were four of them pushed against the walls. A single trestle table was set with pewter plates and linen squares. Two large candelabras sat in the center with candles burning brightly over the table.

What stole her breath away was the sight of Synclair sitting at the table. He wasn't at the head of the table but sitting next to the chair her son was eagerly climbing into while Nan stood behind him with a watchful eye. The nurse pushed the heavy, X-framed chair toward the table once Brandon was seated.

But it was Synclair who reached over and dropped the waiting linen into her son's lap. Brandon looked up with a smile on his lips that showed off the gap where his missing front teeth were. Synclair leaned down and whispered something in his ear that made her son fill the dining hall with musical laughter.

Sweet God, she loved Synclair even more in that moment.

The table was everything she had ever been denied. It was simple and more beautiful than any she had ever dined at because of its lack of pomp and arrogance. The servant stood behind it, waiting to serve the meal, and they lacked the stiff posture she had seen her entire life. Arlene had spoken truly when she said that it was nice to have someone in the house to serve. The housekeeper was busy peeking beneath the lid of a soup bowl, while a young girl stood at the back of the room where the doorway to the kitchen was. She waited there for Arlene to give her a silent signal to carry back to the cook when the master of the house was ready for the next dish. The girl didn't look haggard as so many at court did. There was no fear on her face that she might earn a sharp slap tonight if she was slow or clumsy. Instead she smiled and toyed with her apron while she waited with a look of happy anticipation on her young face.

"There you are, my lady. I am beginning to think that you never eat." Synclair rose, his chair scooting back with a loud sound. Justina sunk into a curtsy and she discovered that she truly meant the respectful lowering of her body.

"Why do you stand, Sir Synclair?" Brandon asked the question, his face turned up to the man he sat next to.

"Because respect is earned, Brandon, and your mother has mine."

Respect . . .

It was a word she had heard so often and yet, it seemed to be nothing but a hollow shell. She straightened and walked to the table, her gaze on Synclair and the way that he waited for her, on his feet while his staff watched. He didn't miss her wonderings. He lifted up one hand and offered it to her while his eyes filled with determination.

"Come, Lady, and have a taste of what manner of life I am asking you to share with me."

"Did you ask my mother to wed with you?"

Synclair smothered a laugh and his face turned slightly dark as though he had forgotten that her child sat so close. He looked down at Brandon.

"Indeed I did, so be a good lad and help me convince her that I would make a fine husband."

Her son wiggled in his seat. "Would that make you a love match?"

Justina caught her lower lip with her teeth while taking the last chair at the table and sitting down. Synclair lowered himself into his chair at the same time.

"I believe it would." He was answering her son but his gaze moved back to her, and there was a flash of emotion in his eyes that humbled her.

"I believe you should wed Sir Synclair, Mother."

Justina shook out her linen cloth and laid it over her shoulder. "I will take your wise advice into consideration."

Synclair placed his own cloth over his shoulder and the moment he did, there was a snap from Arlene's fingers. The meal began but it lacked the rigid pomp that had always sickened her at court. Here, Synclair teased her son and shot her hot glances between bites. The table was not quiet but often the center of laughter and good humor.

A taste of the life he offered?

Justina very much feared that it was like poison, one dose was all that it would take to snuff out the tolerance she had for the life that Biddeford forced her to live.

Her wrist was still stained orange.

Justina sat in the slipper tub and rubbed her skin, but the stain was not washing away. Today she was bathing behind the kitchen, in the bath room. It was warm from the hearth, but in the summer months the heat would be too much and the windows along the top of the wall would be opened to allow some of the heat to escape.

Tonight it was perfect, though, and the warm air felt good against her skin that had been just a bit chilled for most of the day. She lifted a square of linen and rubbed it against a piece of soap for several long moments before trying again to wash the orange tinge from her skin.

"I didn't think it would stain."

The wash square dropped into the water as she jumped in surprise. Synclair stood in the doorway, blocking much of the light and making it difficult to read his expression, but sensation tingled along her skin just from knowing that he was near. Her flesh was instantly more sensitive, her skin becoming warmer and her heart increasing its pace by small degrees so that she began to draw breath faster.

"Well, I suppose it is a comfort to hear that you are not in the practice of chaining women to your bed."

He snorted at her comment and she heard his boots against the stone floor. She recaptured the square while resisting the urge to cover her breasts. Heat rushed into her cheeks, drawing a soft hiss from her.

Damn her body's illogical responses!

Synclair chuckled softly at her. "What troubles you, Justina? I find it charming that you blush for me." He reached out and stroked a finger along the surface of her hot face.

"I am not some girl who should be so undisciplined."

"Still, I think it looks quite well on you, an honest emotion." He wasn't wearing his doublet, and he began rolling up the sleeves of his shirt until they were past his elbows. There was something intimate about the moment, a slant to his eyes that made her feel admired.

He plucked the linen from her fingers and gripped her wrist. "Neither are you that advanced in years, Justina. Your father wed you far too young."

He pulled her wrist toward him and began to wash her arm. Sensation shot through her and she felt her nipples drawing into tight nubs.

His gaze went directly to the rose-colored points.

"Sixteen is not an uncommon age to be married." Justina heard her own voice waiver, betraying that she had no faith in her own words.

He continued to wash her arm, working along the underside before picking the soap up from where it was floating on the surface of the water and rubbing the wash square against it again.

"I can wash myself."

He flashed her a grin. "But you will enjoy it more if I wash you."

"A wife washes her husband, not the other way around." The words were out of her mouth before she thought about them. Synclair sent her a look that was full of challenge.

"But I am not your husband, am I, Justina? Nor have you agreed to marry me, so you shall have to continue to be only my captive lover, and I may do with you as I please."

He caught her other wrist and smoothed the cloth over it. The soap made the fabric glide across her skin, and having his gaze on her heightened her awareness of everything. Her skin was becoming increasingly sensitive. She shivered with enjoyment as he swept the cloth up to her shoulder and along her back. Once there, he applied more pressure, his fingers beginning to massage her back.

A soft sound of enjoyment crossed her lips. She couldn't hold it in, and she leaned further forward to allow his hands to work lower on her back.

"It's rather unfair that women wash their husbands but they never repay the service." He chuckled softly. "For I enjoyed giving you service, my lady."

"I agree." There was nothing else to say, not when his hands felt so good against her body.

"Ah . . . did I hear you declare that you agree with me, sweet Justina?"

She lifted her head and looked back over her shoulder at him.

"You did, and gloating is not something a lover does."

He slid his hands around to cup both her breasts. "Is that better?"

His fingers were slick with water and soap and her nipples were highly sensitive. Pleasure went through the tender globes as he toyed with the tight peaks.

"It is." She turned around, folding her legs beneath her so that she knelt in the tub. Now she could toy with him in return, and she reached out to begin rubbing her hand over his cock. She could feel it growing harder behind the fabric of his britches. Lifting her head, she rose up so that she might whisper beside his ear.

"Do you prefer it when I agree with you, my lord?"

His expression was pensive. "Sometimes."

She straightened her back and pressed her mouth against his. Just a brush of her lips against his, a teasing, flirting motion that drew a soft sound of male approval from him.

He suddenly stiffened. The water on his hands glistened in the candlelight. He opened his waistband and discarded his pants with swift motions.

"But I admit that I enjoy the challenge you so often throw at me, Justina." Determination edged his tone, touching off excitement inside her, but she cast a look at the door and noticed that it lacked a bar to keep it secure.

"Someone might come in."

His shirt followed the pants, baring him completely. He reached down and slid his hands beneath her arms to lift her onto her feet.

"I shall have to make sure you are making enough noise to keep them outside the doorway."

"Synclair, that is too wicked a thing to say."

He yanked a length of toweling off the table that was set against the wall and quickly dried the water from her skin with it.

"Even if I mean it, Justina?"

"Especially if you . . . um . . ."

His eyes glowed with passion, and her throat tightened until not another word could make it past.

He suddenly laughed and wrapped the toweling around her several times.

"I mean it, but I will bend to your will and take you back to my chamber where the door is solid."

He grabbed his britches and stepped back into them. That was the only concession he gave to his modesty. A moment later he tossed her over his shoulder and strode without a care from the bath room and through the kitchen.

Someone dropped something when they passed, and

there were several gasps that made her cheeks burn scarlet. But it was the giggles that she heard faintly drifting down the hallway that truly horrified her.

"Synclair, this is absurd!"

He began climbing the stairs and used one shoulder to push open the chamber doors.

"Aye, but its fun, too. I am beginning to see why the Scots cling to their ways. I never enjoyed chivalrous behavior quite as much as this."

He tossed her into the center of the bed and she bounced several times in a jumble of hair and toweling.

"I see now why the stories tell of those harems using gold chains on their slave girls."

Justina pushed her hair out of her eyes and fixed him with a narrow stare.

"I don't find the topic amusing. It was barbaric to chain me."

He pressed his hands down on either side of the bed, his weight pressing the coverlet down.

"Oh, it is very serious in the harems, too. How else would a man keep multiple women for his own pleasure if not by chaining them?" He crawled onto the bed and captured the wrist that was still stained orange. A soft kiss was pressed against the discoloration and then another until he had kissed his way to the delicate skin of her inner wrist. He lingered there, teasing it with a lick and then a carefully controlled bite. She jumped, unable to control her body. Pleasure speared through her from that nip, jolting her like a bolt of lightning did to the eyes on a dark night. It was felt as much as seen.

"It delights me to think you could not take any steps to avoid conceiving my child."

Justina gasped and pulled her hand from his grasp. Of course, she gained her freedom only because he allowed it.

"So that was your game."

He turned over and sat back on his haunches. His cock was swollen and tempting her with the promise of deep satisfaction once again. All she had to do was stop thinking, stop talking, and fall back into the cradle of passion once again.

It was so very simple.

He lifted one finger up. "I also wanted you here when I returned with Brandon."

She pouted at him. "That is unfair. I cannot remain cross with you when you mention bringing my son here."

"Good."

Victory edged the word and Justina pulled the toweling up to cover her breasts. "Nor can I remain in the grip of passion."

He muttered something beneath his breath and the profanity pleased her. Synclair's gaze lowered to where her beaded nipples raised the soft fabric of the toweling. Something flickered in his eyes that sent heat back into her belly. She was beginning to know the look and her body recognized it, and there was no question of returning to passion's hold. Need rose up to surround her while her lover contemplated her bare form.

"If it's difficulty you are having remaining in passion's grip, perhaps I can employ a few tactics that I learned in the East to place the odds in my favor. Those Moors have some very interesting ways of entertaining all their women."

"Moors? You met some?"

He chuckled and the sound was husky, hinting at something that her curiosity wanted to know. There was a dark promise flickering in his eyes, and it sent a quiver through her. The court was always full of rumors of the East. Stories of debauchery and sexual acts that made Henry the Eighth look like a puritan.

"Do they truly have harems with hundreds of women?"

One of Synclair's eyebrows rose. "Some men do, and they keep those beauties satisfied."

"But . . . how?" She shouldn't ask but she just couldn't stop herself. "One man can only do so much . . ."

"So much fucking?"

He left the bed and walked over to the table that sat next to the wall. Her curiosity kept her gaze on him as he lifted the lid off one chest and searched for something inside it. He drew a fabric-wrapped bundle from it and turned to display a wicked grin.

"What is that?"

He held up the bundle and wiggled it back and forth on his way back to the bed.

"This, my lover, is a toy from a harem."

She scoffed at him. "I doubt it. Some merchant probably just wanted you to pay more for it."

"Ah, you doubt my skills at shopping." He placed it on the bed between them and she couldn't help but look at it. There was something about the way he was grinning that sent excitement flowing through her veins. She was becoming addicted to being his lover because it allowed her to enjoy bed sport, something she had never thought possible. It drove up her excitement, making her breathless with anticipation. Her clitoris was throbbing between the folds of her slit, eager to be stroked until she climaxed again.

She was becoming addicted to him, just as she knew she would, and yet, for the moment she did not care to worry about it.

"With so many women to please, the Moors have invented a unique way to keep them all satisfied."

He unrolled the fabric and she gasped when she looked at what lay hidden inside. The toy was made of marble and looked exactly like an erect cock. She had heard that many of the statues found in the ruins of Rome had full phalluses but this was only the male organ itself, carved with attention to detail. The head was flared just like a real cock and the veins ran down the length of it to the base where the wrinkled skin of the sac was etched into the stone. A long wooden handle was inserted into the base of it, making it a statue of a cock and only that.

"I hear the women compete against one another to win these for their use for one evening."

"What use?"

He chuckled and she felt her eyes widening. "Can't you guess, my sweet? All of those women, doing nothing but waiting on the favor of one man. I hear that a harem master often takes more than one of his concubines to bed at the same time. Can't you imagine how that might build a woman's passion?"

Justina felt her lower lip go dry with anticipation, but that did not mean that she was going to allow him to silence her with his words.

"So why did you buy that phallus? Are you planning on keeping several mistresses?"

He picked it up, holding it by the handle so that the candlelight illuminated it. His eyes narrowed as he contemplated her.

"No. Yet I do plan to make sure that my wife is completely satisfied in my bed."

Justina shook her head, scooting farther back toward the headboard without thinking about it. Her passage was suddenly hot and eager.

"Are you denying that you shall be satisfied, or that you will consent to be my wife, Justina?"

He followed her and captured one of her legs by laying over it. He dropped the phallus and stroked the inside of her thigh with one large hand. He spread her wider with that hand, until the folds of her sex separated.

"I enjoy the sounds you make when my touch pleases you."

That was difficult to believe, and yet his tone convinced her in spite of all her years full of examples of men taking pleasure from women without returning it.

His eyes flashed with something that was white-hot. His fingers reached her slit and began to tease the sensitive flesh. Just a light touch but it sent shivers of delight across her belly and up to her breasts. A small whimper crossed her lips.

"Ah, the first sound." His fingers brushed across her slit again, this time lingering and stroking the folds until he had coated them with the fluid easing down from her passage.

"I believe we shall have to see how many more I might coax from your lips."

His fingertips delved deeply until he found her clitoris. The small bead was throbbing with excitement and he fingered it, gently drawing another sound from her. It became impossible to do anything but experience the pleasure his touch ignited. Her hands clutched at the bedding and her hips arched up toward his touch.

"I believe I have discovered a portion of the Moors' fascination with love toys." Synclair's voice was dark and rich with promise. Justina lifted her drooping eyelids to look up at his face and gasped when she discovered his gaze centered on her spread slit. He was watching his finger as it teased her clitoris. Hunger brightened his eyes and his lips were thin with desire.

He lifted his eyes to lock stares with hers. There was such ferocious determination in his eyes she almost feared him.

But he chuckled softly and drew his finger down the center of her slit to the opening of her passage.

"Do you still not trust me, Justina?"

His finger circled the opening to her passage, sending short little jerks of need up into her belly. She felt empty, the walls of her passage yearning to be stretched around his length.

"Is that what this is? A test of my faith in you?"

He thrust one thick finger up into her body and she gasped. Sensation spiked through her, dragging her closer to the edge of climax but dropping her abruptly short of the cliff's edge.

"Yes."

His tone was deep and rough. She opened her eyes to find him watching her with eyes flickering with flames so bright she would have sworn she felt the heat burning her face.

"I want to hear you cry out with pleasure while you know that I am taking none for myself." His finger returned to the top of her slit, pressing down on top of her clitoris and wringing another cry from her.

"I want you to surrender, Justina, and take every bit of pleasure I give you, and I want to listen to you enjoy my touch without my own enjoyment interfering."

It was too much to resist. His finger was pressing just hard enough to send her into a pulsing storm of need without granting her relief from the waves smashing into her. Her eyes closed and she arched up to his hand, seeking out the last bit of pressure that she craved, but he withdrew his touch, making her hiss with frustration.

"Stop teasing me, Synclair!"

"Only when you ask me for it, Justina." Her eyes opened wide and she discovered him watching her while he held the phallus mere inches from the opening to her passage.

She wanted it. Craved it deep inside her, and yes, there was a part of her that wanted to know he pleasured her while gaining none himself.

She wanted to be the focus of his attention.

"Yes! Give me pleasure, Synclair! Make me cry with it."

"My plan exactly."

He pushed the toy forward, the smooth marble slipping easily into her. She gasped because it was just as hard as his cock and yet not as hot. He must have warmed it with his body because it wasn't cold, either. Her passage took it eagerly, stretching as he pushed it deeper and farther into her. Her back arched to make sure she took the entire length and pleasure began to twist through her belly. He had built her need up so much that she could already feel it beginning to crest. The phallus filled her completely and that was all her body needed to take what it craved.

"Not yet, my beauty."

She was suddenly empty and frustration ripped a snarl from her lips.

Synclair chuckled at her and pushed the toy back into her body. She locked stares with him to discover no mercy in his eyes. There was nothing but determination and savage enjoyment of having her completely under his control.

"You will gain your pleasure when I decide, Justina."

"Bastard."

He pulled the marble length free in response, his expression unrelenting.

"Say you are mine, Justina, mine to do with as I please."

"No!"

That single word was born from the years of being forced to obey. She surged up off the surface of the bed, determined to resist being put in her place once again. Synclair captured her, pulling her struggling body to his and locking her in place before rolling her onto her back once more.

"I won't . . . I can't!"

He thrust his cock into her, filling her sheath with hot, hard flesh. His hands framed her face, forcing her to keep her eyes locked with his.

"You can trust me, Justina, for I will never take more from you than I give." His hands tightened, pulling her hair while his cock felt as though it was growing larger. "I love you. I always have."

His body bucked, shaking the bed as he began to ride her with hard motions.

"Oh God . . . yes!"

She wanted to scream; she wanted him to make her scream in spite of every reason she had to refuse such an outburst.

"No mercy this time, Justina! Do you hear me? I am going to take you."

"Yes!"

It was the only word her mind could form. Her body was a swirling storm of clashing sensations. Synclair pressed his hands flat on the surface of the bed and pushed his upper body away from hers. His hips were thrusting hard against her and she could hear their flesh slapping when it met.

"Wider . . . spread yourself for me."

His breath was raspy, and she didn't care if he was possessed of a demon that would devour her once he was finished, so long as he didn't stop. She lifted her feet and opened her legs wide so that he might drive his cock deeper and faster into her center. Her breasts were swaying with the motion of the bed. It was wild and she opened her eyes to see that Synclair looked more like a barbarian than any man she had ever seen.

The sight pleased her . . .

"More!"

She reached up and grabbed the headboard, lifting her hips up to meet every hard thrust. Her eyes closed again as her body's pleasure took precedence over every thought. Pleasure was twisting in her belly so tightly, it felt like it would snap her in two when it finally crested. Justina didn't care. All that mattered was the driving need to keep pace with him, to urge him faster and harder and . . .

Pleasure broke over her, tumbling her like a fallen tree in the grip of a storm. She twisted and thrashed as the climax tore through every inch of her flesh. There was no way to tell if it was pleasure or pain because it was so intense. Her heart threatened to burst with the effort of keeping pace and she cried out with enjoyment.

Synclair growled. It wasn't low or deep, it was a sound full of victory. His body bucked frantically a few final times before he shuddered and his seed began to spill deep inside her. He drove his length deep, intent on pumping it against the mouth of her womb. A second tremor ripped through her, deeper and weaker than the first climax, but her eyes flew open because she had never experienced a second climax before.

Her open eyes locked with those of her lover, mesmerizing her while the pleasure washed over her and left her lying helpless on the surface of the bed. If he had drawn a knife and made to slay her, she could not have moved.

His arms shook and bent until he was only an inch above her. Heat radiated off his body too hot to tolerate because her own body was so warm. Their breathing was raspy, filling the chamber with the sound of their panting. The bed jerked once again as he rolled over and landed on his back beside her. Her thighs ached when she moved them, surprising her because she couldn't recall noticing that her muscles were strained.

No, of course not, she had been too intent on the moment. On being possessed so very completely. Now there was only the rapture that coated her from head to toe; she couldn't think or move.

And she didn't want to either.

"Promise me that you will wed me, Justina. That is what I need to hear from your lips."

Justina groaned but Synclair rolled onto his side, propping one elbow against the bed and resting his head in the palm of his hand. One brief glance showed her that the man was not in the mood to be denied his request.

"I do not understand what drives you, Synclair. We are good lovers but that is not what anyone should choose a wife for."

He blew out a harsh breath and reached over to cup her chin when she would have looked away from him.

"I am not a boy, Justina. What you fail to grasp is the fact that I crave passion, deep, soul-shattering pleasure of the flesh, and I want a woman who can meet me in that desire. What I don't want is to keep a string of mistresses, discarding one after another and blaming them for the fact that true satisfaction requires a deep intimacy that is only found with a soul mate. I meant it; I love you."

She witnessed it shimmering in his eyes, and also the first hint of fear she could ever recall seeing in him. She couldn't endure that fear, her heart rebelled against every logical reason her mind offered up to refuse him.

"I do love you, Synclair. More than you might ever know. That is why I persist in telling you—"

His mouth covered hers, sealing her well-meant arguments behind a kiss that was sweeter than anything she had ever known. It cut through the harsh edges of reality and burned every rule until there was nothing except the man kissing her. She reached for him and clung to the man she loved while he kissed her softly and the night closed around them.

"That is why you must belong to me."

Synclair pulled the covers over them now that their bodies had slowed down enough for the winter chill to begin biting into them. Justina shivered and Synclair pulled her closer.

"Trust me, Justina."

She heard his voice in her dreams and couldn't stop herself from doing it.

* * *

Bessie Portshire was happy. She hummed a little tune of springtime while making her way toward Justina's chambers. There were personal guards for the Viscount Biddeford standing at the entrance to the area, but she did not allow them to concern her. Most of the higher nobles set their retainers to securing the area around where they lived in the palace. Her own father did the same.

"I am here to see the Lady Wincott."

"The lady's chambers are on the right, third door."

The men did not bar her path. They didn't even look directly at her but kept their eyes on the hallway in back of her. Bessie smiled and counted the doors before lifting her hand and rapping softly on the third one. She glanced back down the hallway and was grateful to see that she had escaped everyone who seemed to be forever clinging to her skirts. She drew a deep breath, eager to spend the evening with someone she wouldn't need to guard her expression against or consider each word before she muttered it. Sometimes, being the daughter of a duke was exhausting.

The door opened and a maid stood there with her head bowed. Bessie entered quickly, intent on having the door shut and enjoying some rare privacy. The maid closed the door with a soft sound before she walked to a table and began pouring a glass of mulled wine for her.

Bessie could smell the cloves, and it made her smile, for it touched off memories of evenings spent with her mother when she was still too young for court. She missed those simpler winter days.

"The mistress shall attend you shortly, Lady Portshire. Lady Wincott requests that you enjoy the wine while you wait." The maid brought her the goblet on a small tray, the scent of other spices growing stronger as the servant drew close. Bessie picked it up and sniffed at the dark brew. She detected a hint of nutmeg and cinnamon along with the cloves. Considering that it was not a feast day, such spices were a treat. She sipped at it and smiled when she tasted sweet sugar. Her mother had always feared that her teeth might rot because she liked sweets too much, so sugar had always been locked away and only allowed for celebrations.

Bessie drank more of the wine, enjoying the way it seemed to coat her tongue. The maid disappeared on quiet steps while Bessie continued to enjoy the wine.

"Wait."

Francis de Canis placed a hand on Biddeford's chest to keep him from entering the room where Bessie was nursing her goblet of tainted wine.

"Give it a bit to do its job."

"I want her to know that she is being drugged." Biddeford pushed the hand aside that de Canis had put on him. "I have wasted a great deal of time courting that girl. It will be very satisfying to watch her fear when she hears that she will lose her wits."

"The potion doesn't work that way. She will be as impressible as a child, open to suggestion, but easily frightened, too."

The viscount made a disgusted sound beneath his breath.

De Canis shot him a hard look in return. "You shall have all the nights for the rest of her life to bend her however you see fit. Tonight you need to tumble her without there being any sign of rape. Do try and be a little appreciative of my ability to deliver that to you for something so small as bringing your ward back to court."

Biddeford ground his teeth together. "As you say, you have delivered so far, everything that you promised."

"I always do."

There was a sharp sound from the other room as Bessie stumbled and knocked a bowl off the edge of the table.

"Oh my . . . how did that happen?" Her words were slightly slurred and she giggled instead of worrying about the mess she had made. She began to hum and even lifted her skirts so that she might dance along with her tune. De Canis laid a hand on the viscount's shoulder and leaned closer.

"Remember, instruct her like a child. Give her gentle suggestions, and she will follow them."

Biddeford walked into the chamber and smiled. Bessie was still dancing across the floor, her humming growing louder as de Canis's potion took her deeper into its grasp. She was dancing with more passion now, her skirts bouncing as if she were at a spring festival. She turned and caught sight of him.

"Sweet mother of Christ! My Lord Biddeford, I did not hear you arrive!"

Her eyes were wide, and she blinked rapidly as though attempting to clear her mind, but de Canis had spoken true; the potion was firmly in command of her. Bessie suddenly frowned.

"You are in your shirt and hose, sir." Instead of being alarmed, Bessie smiled and then giggled. She extended her hand and pointed at his knees. "I can see your garters very well, indeed I can!"

Biddeford smiled. The sides of his face actually felt tight because so few things actually made him happy, but he was tonight because Bessie was staring at his state of undress exactly like a child who found it amusing and not a young maiden who would expect to recoil in fear. Her wits were completely dull. He stuck one leg forward.

"Do you like these garters? I find the color most pleasing." He kept his voice low and soothing and Bessie responded perfectly.

"Why yes, I do think them most grand." She stepped forward and frowned when she tripped over the hem of her gown.

"This dress is so cumbersome."

Biddeford felt his smile grow wider. "Perhaps you should take it off, my dear."

Bessie's face lit up with approval. "Yes, that would be nice but I cannot reach the laces."

"I can."

She clasped her hands together and turned around in a quick motion that made her skirt bounce.

"That would be most kind of you, and then I might show you my garters. They are very pretty, too."

"I would like to see them, my dear girl . . ."

Biddeford chuckled but reached for the forgotten goblet of wine. He poured more of the tainted brew into it before offering it to Bessie once more. She took it happily, drinking it so quickly that some of it poured down her chin.

"I shall be most happy to help you unlace your gown, my dear girl."

There was pain.

Bessie gasped, the burning pain ripping away the fog that seemed to blind her so completely. She gasped and tried to lift her eyelids to see what was holding her down. Fiery hot pain ripped through her passage again, far worse than any monthly cramps had ever been. She didn't understand and she couldn't seem to twist away from the hard flesh causing her such torment.

But it moved, leaving her while her eyelids still refused to lift. She wasn't sleeping, she could feel the heat of another person, feel it pressing against her own skin and then her passage was split open once more.

She gasped, her eyes opening wide.

"Now you will wed me, Bessie."

"I won't . . ." Her voice was unclear, her tongue feeling like it was swollen. She wanted to argue but the fog returned, trapping her mind in its folds and pulling her down into its white mist where the only thing that she was sure about was the hard flesh invading her passage again and again until she felt a hot stream of fluid fill her.

"You'll be my wife and bear my children, for your virgin's blood is spilled . . ."

Evil. Bessie had never heard a voice of pure evil before, but she did in that moment. Surrounded by suffocating mist, all she could do was shiver as she listened to the laughter.

It was evil, so black, that she feared for her soul.

CHAPTER TEN

Footsteps pounded down the hallway at dawn.
Synclair jerked awake and pushed Justina over to the far side of the bed before she completely awoke. She tumbled to the floor, smacking her knees against the hard surface at the same time she heard Synclair pull his sword from its sheath.

"My lord! We've riders on the road!"

Captain Repel pushed the doors in without knocking, making Justina grateful that she had the bed to hide behind. He didn't spare her even a glance but had his full attention on Synclair.

"They are flying the King's colors but there is an entire contingent of them."

Synclair snarled something beneath his breath. "I will be there in a moment."

Captain Repel didn't stop long enough to offer his lord a bow. The man was on his way back out the door, the sound of his spurs echoing in the hallway. Justina stood up instantly, climbing over the bed and sliding onto her feet next to Synclair. He was already stepping into his britches and she gathered his shirt up in her hands so that she could push it over his head when he looked up at her. He didn't bother to tuck the tail in but sat down and yanked his boots on with hard motions of his hands.

"Get dressed and find Brandon. I have too few men here to secure the house and safeguard him."

"But surely there is no danger. Captain Repel said it was the King's men."

Synclair stood up, his face set in a hard expression. "The King is not directing his men these days. I should have sent Brandon north yesterday." Synclair sent her a hard look. "Have Arlene hide the boy and silence the servants about him."

The lament in his voice horrified her. He was gone a moment later, leaving her to battle the dread that began swarming through her. Arlene appeared in the doorway, her linen cap missing and her apron tied only at her waist and not pinned up over her bodice.

"Mistress, we needs dress you in a hurry. The yard is filling with men all suited up in armor. I believe they plan to occupy the house."

Two maids came through the doorway with their hair still trailing down their backs.

"Bring my son to me. Bring him here immediately and tell no one that a child slept beneath this roof last eve."

Justina watched one of the maids hesitate but a quick snap from Arlene's fingers sent the girl back out the door. Icy-cold fear wrapped its fingers around her heart. Only she was torn between her worry for Brandon and her concern for Synclair. She loved them both more than herself, and even feeling the horror flooding her, she still could not lament it.

Dressing had never taken so long, nor had she ever detested the layers so much before.

"Mother, who is coming to our house? I saw the archers from my window."

Her son was still in his nightshirt, the maid holding him and the coverlet from his bed. The girl had not wasted any time in obeying her order, but simply scooped Brandon up along with the bedding to keep him warm.

Thank God!

"Arlene, you must take my child and conceal him."

"Mistress?" The head of house looked startled, wrinkles appearing around her eyes as she tried to understand the fear lacing Justina's voice.

"My guardian is a depraved man, Arlene. He sins against nature and must not have my son. Do you understand? Lord Harrow was to send my son north today to protect him. The court is no place for an innocent boy."

The housekeeper gasped, covering her mouth with a hand while her eyes filled with horror. She made the sign of the cross over herself before she began sputtering.

"Oh, the wickedness of the palace! We've heard tell of it but I never wanted to believe."

"Believe it, Arlene; I swear it on Christ's sweet mother."

The head of house reached out and scooped Brandon up into her own arms. "I'll see to the boy. You may place your trust in me."

"Mother? What is going on?"

Justina fought the tears that threatened to spill down her cheeks. She reached out and laid her hand on her child's cheek. "You are going to be the best boy and do what Arlene tells you now, Brandon."

"But I don't want our visit to be over, Mother."

"Neither do I, Brandon, but you must not be seen here. Now be my lion and show me how brave you are for you have a journey to begin."

"Like a knight on a quest?"

She cupped the side of his face in her hand, shuddering at the feel of his tender skin against her palm. "Yes, my lion, exactly like a knight who must be strong and do the duty he has been charged with."

"I will not fail you, Mother, or Sir Synclair. I want to earn his respect, as you have."

"I have faith that you shall, my son. Nan will be with you."

Arlene began turning to the doorway, and Justina gained only a glimpse of her son nodding while he watched her with wide eyes over the housekeeper's shoulder. Justina jabbed her hairpins into her hair, caring nothing for the pain. Each moment felt too long while she finished dressing. There was only one defense left to safeguard her child and that was to appear before anyone entered the house and learned that Brandon was there.

She ran through the hallways and down the stairs the moment her French hood was pushed down to cover her head. Just as her son had said, the yard was full of armed men and the archers stood just beyond the gate with the bows in hand. The men wore three-quarter suits of armor and they were, in fact, flying Henry Tudor's flags in the early morning light.

It was a desolate sight. The yard full of snow and the King's messenger standing in front of Synclair while he read from a parchment he was holding open. From the bottom of the paper, crimson ribbons dangled, fluttering in the morning wind to confirm that the parchment was signed and sealed.

"Lord Harrow, you are henceforth restricted to this house until it does please His most royal Majesty, Henry Tudor, to rule upon your transgression against the Viscount Biddeford's ward, the Lady Wincott."

"He has done nothing to me."

The man reading the parchment looked up, his eyes peering at her from beneath the visor of his helmet. The fingers holding the parchment open were encased in armored gauntlets, telling her that Biddeford had kept his word and sent his wrath down upon her for daring to displease him. The entire yard was full of men who were going to break her for her disobedience, and she felt icy dread close around her heart because she would not suffer herself. No, the viscount would force her to watch while the man she loved was punished, possibly put to death for her sin. It was too horrible to comprehend but the royal guard lifted his chin and spoke to her in a hard voice that pierced the disbelief trying to smother her.

"Lady Wincott, you are summoned to court by His Majesty's privy council. You will accompany my men to Whitehall palace immediately."

"She's a woman; leave this between us men. I will accompany you to the palace." Synclair snarled at the messenger wearing the King's colors, but the men behind him drew their swords and held them ready. Justina saw Synclair's hand tighten around the pommel of his own sword but there were far too many of the King's men. But she could feel his rage. Justina could see it etched into the hard expression on his face. The King's man hesitated, even stepping back in the face of Synclair's anger, but he looked behind him, noting the men who stood ready to back up what he wanted, and straightened his back.

"You are placed under house arrest, my Lord Harrow. The King's seal is upon this order and these men are here to enforce the will of the King! The Lady Wincott is summoned to court, not you. The Lady shall accompany us and you will restrict yourself unto this house with half my men left here to ensure that you abide by the will of the King."

"The Lady remains." Synclair growled the words but the men holding the swords began to push forward, their boots crunching against the snow that had frozen during the night. Justina watched it all, as though time itself was caught in the grip of the winter ice. It was too much, the

impending horror of watching Synclair fall beneath the
weapons being pointed at him, too much for her to witness.

"I will go with you."

Synclair reached out and closed his fingers around her
wrist. He pulled her to him and she stepped across the distance between them so that she might whisper next to
his ear.

"Please release me. I beg you, Synclair, do not make me
witness your death. There are too many of them." She
pressed a kiss against his cheek. "I *trust* you to keep your
promise."

He jerked, his eyes flashing at her words. Understanding darkened his eyes and she shivered with the knowledge that she did indeed trust him to see to her son. Tears
stung her eyes but she moved away from him, her eyes
pleading with him to release her.

His hand didn't relax, not until she was a full two steps
from him. Fury danced in his eyes but his fingers lessened
their hold and finally unlocked to free her.

"I will see you soon, Justina, I promise you that."

Each word was edged with rage. It sent a shiver along
her skin that had nothing to do with the frigid weather.
The knight she had witnessed riding so confidently through
the night was staring at her through a blaze of anger that
she knew would not be kept contained for very long.

"You shall keep to this house, Baron Harrow, by order
of the King."

Synclair growled. "You already said that, man."

The paper crinkled behind her, the King's man crum-
pling it between nervous fingers. He stepped back and
pointed other men toward her. No one wanted the duty
of moving too close to Synclair, but the men standing in
the yard wanted to be gone quickly, before the knight
used the sword clasped so confidently in his tight fist.

Justina felt the men reach for her. She shrugged their touch away, hissing at them while she forced herself to turn away from the man she loved.

It hurt worse than anything she might have imagined. But the tips of the swords being pointed at him gave her the strength to move away from him. The only pain that would be worse was to see his blood staining those weapons.

She would rather see her own upon the steel.

Instead she felt her heart beating while she forced her feet to keep taking steps that sent pain through her with each crunch of the ice beneath the soles of her boots. The pain continued to grow as she was assisted up and onto the back of a horse. Her breath made white clouds but she was certain that the reason was the bitter chill coming from her heart. It was freezing solid like a lake, while she looked back to see Synclair watching her with eyes the same shade as ice. She would have sworn that she heard him inside her thoughts, for she certainly felt his rage.

But that did not stop the King's men from turning toward Whitehall palace. They took her with them, but what finally sent the tears in her eyes spilling down her cheeks was the sight of half of those men remaining. They began to march up the stairs and into the house to begin their occupation of it. Who knew how long they would stay? Or if Synclair would escape further punishment for keeping her.

The Viscount Biddeford had many powerful friends, and it was very possible that Synclair might be sent to the tower. More than one man had lost his head for charges that were frivolous. Her heart ached more and she began to pray.

It was the only hope she had left.

Traveling was hard.

The roads were packed with snow that had frozen during the night. It made the horses struggle to make the distance to Whitehall, the animals fighting for every pace while the men marching were forced to follow behind in narrow columns, or break ice themselves.

The men in their armor must have felt the chill cutting into their flesh and it disgusted Justina to think of so much suffering for such an inglorious cause.

Well there was one thing that was worth going out into the winter weather, and that was the fact that her son was left behind, secretly safe. She did trust Synclair with more than her own welfare, but with the most important thing to her heart.

You love him . . .

Justina tightened her grip around the reins and tried to force her mind onto logical thoughts. Somehow, she seemed to have lost the ability to view her life in terms of what was best and most reasonable.

Love was an insanity . . .

She'd heard that said by too many to count, the Church, her father, and many other knowledgeable men. Yet none of it changed how she felt, and she realized that she did not lament the affection warming her heart.

It was the thing that kept her alive while the winter ice kept the forest and the rest of the world its prisoner. In her heart she felt that love warm away every shred of despair, leaving only a deep ache for the separation she must suffer.

That thought sobered her, for it was an all too familiar one. Whitehall came into view and she cast her gaze onto it. A deep shudder shook her, distaste welling up inside her until her stomach was nauseated with it. She doubted that she had ever loathed a place so much as she did the palace her horse was carrying her toward. Already the roads were beginning to be used by those intent on spending the day currying favor within its walls.

All Justina saw waiting for her was more demands. Rebellion rose up inside her so thick, it threatened to choke her, but she didn't struggle against it. She suddenly understood how women chose death over dishonor. They did it because they loved and that feeling was far more important than even continuing to breathe. Still, the face of her son rose from her thoughts and she couldn't help but be happy that she had suffered her years as a wife, for it had brought Brandon to her. Surviving had offered her the chance to taste Synclair's kiss, and in spite of the ache burning in her heart now, she could not wish away the hours she had spent wrapped in his loving embrace. They had been the most precious ones of her life.

She would cling to the memory and hold it dear while the palace grew larger and the scent of unwashed bodies grew stronger. Along with the people moving toward Whitehall were the animals that took them there. In the grey winter morning, men badgered their beasts forward, while mothers lectured their daughters from inside closed chairs that were held between horses on long poles or sometimes carried by men. Now that the roads had frozen, carriages were kept in the stables so that the wheels might not be damaged by the ice. Men sat in the saddle, wearing fur-lined half coats with the collar turned up to protect their necks from the wind. They all struggled to reach Whitehall and the promise of power that it beckoned with. All Justina thought when she looked at the majestic building was that it was the most horrible sight she had ever seen.

But her escort carried on, moving steadily forward until they took her beneath the raised gate and into the lower courtyard. One man offered her a hand to dismount from her horse and her feet landed on the frozen ground in the yard. She could feel the ice through the soles of her shoes and it sent her lips up in a small smile.

The chill, she decided, was very fitting.

★   ★   ★

"The Lady Wincott, my Lord Biddeford."

"Ah yes, thank you, Captain."

Justina felt her eyes narrow with suspicion, for Biddeford sounded more cheerful than she could recall him being in a very long time. On another occasion, she might have even found his words polite, possibly charming, but she knew the man too well. The King's man even looked surprised by the pleasant greeting, but he inclined his head and left before the viscount had time to alter his mood.

Justina remained still and watched the viscount. He stood in the midst of his grooms with his hands outstretched so that the men might dress him. They moved around him on hushed steps while securing his cuffs and waistband before a velvet doublet was brought forward and eased up his arms. Another groom began to use a small silver hook to pull the buttons through their holes. In spite of the daylight making its way through the open window shutters, candles were burning on the long table near the wall. Justina stared at the waste, disgusted by the greediness that had Biddeford expecting more light than the winter day provided. She noticed every detail that failed to measure up to Synclair and there seemed to be no tolerance inside her for the shortcomings. But she had to give Synclair time to send her son north. A few hours, but they felt like months now that she knew that the man in front of her would very shortly lose his grip on her. Patience, she needed patience, and it felt like she had none at all.

"I am pleased to see you, my dear."

Justina fought the urge to choke. Biddeford turned to look at her, his lips settled into a smirk that at least she knew well. There was also a familiar look of triumph in his eyes that warned her the man was scheming, as he always was.

Just a few more hours . . .

Justina swallowed her rebellion and dug her own fingernail into her hand to keep her from speaking the truth. There was another thing that she had enjoyed full well while with Synclair—the ability to speak freely. Silence was essential, for Biddeford would assume that she was properly fearful of his wrath. She kept her lips pressed together but heard another male voice speak up from the other side of the chamber.

"I find myself very happy to see you as well."

Every muscle along her back tightened in pain. Francis de Canis sounded as insidious as her memory recalled, and he chuckled, the sound drawing her around to face him fast enough to make her skirts twist. She knew too well what his tone meant and every inch of her flesh refused the lust shining in his eyes. De Canis read the rebellion in her gaze and it made his lips twitch in enjoyment. Justina had to fight back her disgust for him. His lust for her was an ugly thing, even more so now that she knew how it felt to be loved.

"There now, you see, Francis? I have delivered what I promised. My ward will be residing at Whitehall for the rest of the winter."

Justina clenched her hands into fists, every inch of her flesh repulsed by the man running his gaze over her. The lust in his eyes sickened her but it also inspired a flare of rejection that was too hot and too large to ignore.

"I will not lie with you, sir." She turned to look at Biddeford. "Nor with anyone that you attempt to direct me toward."

The viscount's eyes narrowed but Francis de Canis laughed. His voice echoed between the walls of the chamber while his face reflected how much he enjoyed her rejection.

"Good. That will make the moment so much more satisfying when I come for you, my sweet Baroness. You have my promise that you will not see it coming."

The viscount cleared his throat, drawing de Canis's gaze to him.

"I am not finished gaining what I desire. Did you bring the man or not?"

De Canis didn't bother to mask his disgust over Biddeford demanding more attention. "He's on his way."

There was a scuffle beyond the outer doors to the viscount's chambers and de Canis turned to open the doors wide. Several rough-looking men hurried another man inside and closed the doors quickly behind him.

"This is most improper, I say!" The man wore the longer robe of the Church of England. His cap was sitting somewhat askew as he was sent another few steps toward the viscount by a solid shove.

"Most improper, I tell you! What is the justification for this rough handling?" His face was flushed red, and he was sputtering with his outrage, words failing him, but that didn't keep him from glaring at every man in the room. Justina felt a tingle cross her nape when he turned his eye upon her and she lowered herself. The man was a bishop and held a great deal of power in his own right. Biddeford was acting a fool to treat the man so, but that only sent another shiver down her spine. There was a look of victory in the viscount's eyes that warned her that the worst was yet to be revealed.

"Forgive me, my good Bishop, but I am intent on righting a great wrong that I have done and I need your blessing."

"A great wrong? Sir, having your ruffians drag me from my morning prayers is a great wrong! There is nothing of man, no issue of earthly life, that is of greater importance than kneeling in penitence to my Lord each morning before I do a single other thing. To do so is to place man above God and I shall not do such a thing."

The viscount made a noise beneath his breath that at last struck Justina as familiar. She tilted her head and looked at him to see him frowning at the bishop. His arrogance was truly overgrown now, for he wasn't even repentant in the face of the man of the Church. Only the King was above the Church, and even the great Henry Tudor had asked the Church for what he wanted.

Biddeford didn't seem to care very much about the bishop's displeasure. His grooms were still working hooks and buttons, while another stood quietly waiting with a hat perched carefully in his hands, awaiting his lord's pleasure. The bishop snorted and turned toward the closed doors but de Canis blocked his way, earning another smothered sound of outrage.

"Remove yourself from that doorway immediately or risk the wrath of the Church!" The bishop shook a thick finger at de Canis.

"My matter is great, sir, and you will be compensated for your time." Biddeford snapped his fingers and his secretary held up a solid gold coin. The flash of bright gold made the bishop snap his lips shut with a small click of his teeth. Obviously even being a humble servant of the Church didn't keep him from thinking twice when it came to choosing between his morning prayers and solid gold.

Perhaps *soiled* was a better word. Justina had to bite her lip to maintain an expressionless mask over her features.

"I trust that your outrage is sufficiently appeased, sir?"

Justina had to quell the urge to smile yet again. The viscount was too arrogant by far. Bishops had a great deal of power under the King's new English Church and they enjoyed it every bit as well as Biddeford liked his position.

The viscount might just discover that he was not the only one with a large ego and the power to flaunt it.

The bishop drew himself up stiffly, his nose rising into the air. "Matters of God are not for hire nor negotiation."

"Nonsense, of course you can negotiate. I require you to perform a wedding, sir. Is that not a service you do provide?" Biddeford looked at his secretary and the man held up a second coin.

Justina felt a prickle of foreboding invade her. Dread began to twist through her as she looked about the room.

"I will be most agreeable to giving you the blessing of the Church, once you are in a church, sir."

"That will not be possible. I need to wed here and now before the gossips have anything to sharpen their tongues with." The hat was placed on the viscount's head and he made a small sound of satisfaction while admiring his appearance in a mirror. He turned when he was finished inspecting his reflection to find the bishop frowning at him.

"My good Bishop, this cannot be the first early morning wedding that you have performed in order to cover up an excess of nighttime passion."

There was a poorly smothered laugh from de Canis. Biddeford snapped his fingers at his secretary.

"My good man has all the papers penned and with your seal on the matter, there will be no need for any gossip about Bessie Portshire and her lack of virtue this morning."

"What have you done to Bessie?"

The viscount turned a deadly glare to her. "You shall remember your place, Justina! Do not mistake my good humor for any manner of forgetfulness of what trouble you have put me to these last few days." He snapped his fingers once again and pointed his secretary toward the long table that ran along the wall.

"The women in this country still do not appear to know their place."

The bishop began nodding. "A woman should have a husband and follow his direction. That is God's order."

The viscount slowly smiled. "Perhaps we should have a pair of weddings this morning. How does that strike you, Francis?"

"I want guardianship of her son, too."

Biddeford scoffed at him. "You ask too much. I am keeping that boy and his fortune. You can wed her and gain her widow's thirds but I will not transfer the guardianship."

"Where is Bessie?" Justina didn't bother to protest about Biddeford's suggestion that she wed de Canis. The man wouldn't listen to her will in any event. What ate at her too much to ignore was her rising fear for her friend.

He clapped his hands and his grooms snapped to attention. "Bring me my bride! Bishop, name your price but set your signet ring into wax and wed me, for I have spent the night in sin with Bessie Portshire."

"The Duke of Portshire's daughter? Are you mad? That man is known for his affection toward his only daughter."

"An affection that smothered her, I tell you! I have paid her court for many months and her father's jealousy has been a barrier between us until last night when we took solace in each other's company."

"That is a lie! Bessie refused your suit, she told me so."

Biddeford chuckled, the sound sending a shiver down Justina's back for she knew it too well. The cruelness that she had so often tasted from his hand had clearly been dealt out to her friend.

The curtains were shoved aside and Bessie stumbled into the room. She wore only a tattered chemise that was stained brown with her own virgin's blood. The girl's hair was pulled from its neat coif in many places and she stumbled on one shoe. Justina gasped and caught her friend before she collapsed onto her knees. Bessie shook, quivering like a dry leaf in a strong wind. Her hands were as cold as ice and clutched desperately at her arms, while her eyes were full of wild fear.

"I . . . can . . . can . . . not . . . remember. . . ." Her voice was dry and hollow. Justina looked at her closer, for the pupils of her eyes looked too large. It was unnatural and the scent of spices on her breath brewed suspicion in Justina.

"What did you give her, Biddeford? You have used foul means to do this deed."

The bishop looked up from where he faced the door. His face drained of color as he took in Bessie's stained chemise.

"What matters is that I have had her, and there is no bruise upon her to prove rape."

"That does not mean it wasn't rape, sirrah!" Justina spat out the insult without any hesitation. Brandon had Synclair now, and she would trust in her knight to safeguard her child. That knowledge allowed her to cast aside the chains that had bound her in obedience to the horrible creature standing in front of her.

"Bessie is not in her right mind and that ensures foul means."

The viscount's lips twisted into a smirk. "But she is quite well and truly deflowered. There are witnesses to her loss of virtue which makes it very much in her interest to wed me."

"Before the rest of the court learns the colorful details of last evening." Francis de Canis spoke up, his tone full of enjoyment. "And be very sure that they will know of it, in graphic detail, if the Bishop does not wed the couple immediately."

"No . . . don't. . . ." Justina soothed her friend's arms, feeling her temper rise up in defense of the kindhearted girl.

"You are both villains of the worst sort."

Biddeford turned his back on them and pointed at the bishop. "I have had her and there is no sign of rape. Marry up!—now, or face the scandal that this event will produce in this court."

"A scandal that will darken your name."

The viscount turned a furious look at her but Justina refused to remain silent. No woman deserved to be bound to such a man.

"I do assure you that I will survive the storm of gossip." He turned to look at the bishop. "Bessie will no doubt cry at her father's feet and swear that it was all my fault. He is far too soft with the girl, otherwise she would not have been able to spend the night here, with me, without being discovered. Think of the example it will set for everyone if she doesn't have to wed me."

The man of the Church folded beneath the authority in the viscount's voice. The bishop walked to the table and the parchment that had been placed there by the secretary. He picked up a candle and set it beneath a stick of crimson wax so that it dropped in shiny wet tears onto the parchment.

"You must not seal that document. This is foul business."

The bishop lifted disapproving eyes to her.

"Women are best wed. They need a husband to keep them from the path of sin. It is your place in this life, and to argue against it is to abandon your immortal soul to peril. I agree that her father is too soft with her. Better to make sure that others will not attempt to stray from the narrow path of righteousness."

He turned his hand over and pressed the face of the

ring, where the crest was, into the cooling wax, setting the seal of the Church onto the official document that would forever bind Bessie to Biddeford as his wife, his chattel. Only his fellow lords of the privy council might overturn it, and they certainly would not take any action against one of their own. Bessie's father might be a duke but it would still be a horrible battle to gain a divorce, and such action would stain her forever.

"Now kneel and receive the blessing of the Church."

Biddeford plucked the parchment off the table instead, staring at it while his lips rose into a wide smile.

"Thank you, Bishop, you may go now."

"But the blessing . . . you have not taken your vows."

"I don't care. Marriage is a business, man. I care about the contract, not the stupid words of fidelity that no man ever keeps. Get you gone. Your seal is what I needed."

Biddeford's secretary offered the gold and the bishop took it.

"Now go, I have a bride to enjoy."

De Canis didn't wait for the bishop to comply. He stepped forward and grabbed the man by his robe and sent him out of the chamber doors that the grooms held open. Those same servants shut the doors the second the man was on the other side of them, the solid oak shutting out his outraged stuttering.

That sealed Justina and Bessie in a room with two men who were laughing in glee.

"Wine! To celebrate my new bride and her fortune! Be gone, Tomas, you have served your purpose."

The grooms hurried toward the interior doors, intent on pleasing their master quickly. The secretary followed them, eager to take the freedom his master offered. From the other side of the door there came a faint pounding and the muffled sounds of the bishop still protesting. Francis de Canis laughed and sent his fist into the door. The wooden panels shook violently and the sound instantly stopped the protesting from the bishop.

"Be gone, Father! Unless you want to kiss the bride. I intend to," De Canis exclaimed.

Bessie moaned, a pitiful sound that drove a spike through Justina's heart. She knew what the girl was feeling, had endured it when her father turned her over to a man the rest of the world called her lord and master. Biddeford was laughing and walking toward de Canis with his hand outstretched so that they might clasp wrists and congratulate one another on bringing Bessie to her knees.

Justina refused to tolerate it. She had lived too long on her knees and refused to remain there.

The parchment was lying forgotten on the tabletop. Justina moved to it and thrust it at the fireplace beyond the table. The paper fluttered and landed on the bed of coals that was left from the fire that had been laid last night.

But it wasn't far enough inside the fireplace.

Justina reached for a long iron poker and angled it at the parchment.

"Stop!" Biddeford howled with outrage but she didn't turn to look at him. Justina kept her eyes on the parchment and leaned over further to try to push it into the coals with the poker.

A moment later she was slammed into the wall, her face scraping along the rough stone, but she was grateful for the pain because the stone kept her from being pushed head-first into the fireplace. The long iron pole in her hand lodged against the place where two bricks were set against one another, making her hand and arm remain behind her because her grip was so tight on the iron.

She heard a harsh gasp and then there came a rough gurgling sound next to her ear, accompanied by the touch of warm fluid on the skin of her neck. A harsh curse filled the chamber a moment before the weight crushing her against the fireplace was lifted off her back and the iron poker pulled from her grasp at the same time. Justina turned and gasped at the horrible sight of Biddeford gasping for breath while the iron rod went through his throat. His body drew into a mass of tight muscles, his hands forming talons before he fell over with a heavy sound and lay still on the floor.

She looked down on his still form and no lament rose inside her for the fact that he had died. There was nothing except for relief that her friend would not have to suffer him. A sense of justice filled her but a soft chuckle broke through her elation.

"Well, my sweet Lady Wincott, it seems that things have changed now."

Francis de Canis snickered low and deep, while he looked up at her from where he knelt next to Biddeford's body. He aimed a victorious look at her.

"You are going to please me, in every way, and fear my displeasure, for the day that you earn such, I will confess your crime to all and tell them you blinded me with witchcraft to keep me silent so long."

He meant it, every word, and the enjoyment of being able to say the words glowed in his eyes. Justina stared at his face, horror welling up to choke her, but there was no lament, for she wasn't sorry.

"It was an accident."

De Canis began chuckling, the sound more evil and eerie than anything she had ever heard. "But there are no witnesses, except for me and a girl who is wearing a stained chemise. Whom do you think will be believed about what happened in this chamber?"

Justina lifted her chin but she couldn't help step back when de Canis stood up and loomed over her, his lips fixed into a smile of glee.

"If you do not agree to my terms, I am going to wrap

my fingers around your throat, squeeze the life breath out of you, and tell everyone that I could not contain my rage over your crime . . ."

He stretched one hand up and toward her neck. Justina felt it before he actually touched her, her lungs drawing in deeper breaths in anticipation of being deprived.

"What is this?" De Canis asked the question in a tone that lacked all arrogance.

He suddenly stopped, a confused look taking command of his face. His hand never closed around her throat but stopped in front of her face before he looked down at his chest.

"It is your death."

Synclair's voice was edged with hard resolve but deadly quiet. De Canis touched the length of steel protruding from his chest with a single fingertip, a smile lifting the corners of his lips when he saw his own blood staining his skin.

Chapter Eleven

Justina felt her lungs burning but she still couldn't draw a breath. The hands that had so recently threatened to crush her throat closed into fists and then contorted until they looked more like talons. Francis de Canis looked back up at her face, his eyes still lit with life, but it began fading while she watched.

"Lady Wincott belongs to herself."

Synclair pulled his sword free and de Canis began to turn to him, but his body faltered and crumpled to the floor before Synclair finished wiping the blade free of blood. Her knight used the carpet to clean his sword with a swift motion that spoke of practice. Synclair kept his gaze on the man he'd just run through, no remorse on his face. Once he was sure that de Canis was dead, he looked at her and she gasped, air filling her lungs finally. There was a flare of victory in his eyes, but what stole her breath was the need shimmering there. She felt it pierce her heart because it was a reflection of what she felt for him.

"It is a death he so richly deserved." Synclair's voice was not as calm or controlled as his expression. There was tightly contained rage in his tone and he sent a look of disgust toward the crumpled form of Francis de Canis. "This world is well rid of his kind of filth."

"It was . . . too . . . kind."

Bessie spoke from where she sat on the floor. She had drawn her knees up to her chest and had her arms wrapped around them while she watched the blood seeping out of de Canis's chest. Her attention was focused on the dark puddle while her lips were pressed into a hard line. Justina understood that look. It was the same one she had given to her husband once fate had finally been kind enough to free her from his grasp. But there was a torment in the freedom, one that came from her own conscience as she questioned whether or not she was as large a monster for being glad that someone was dead. Bessie was struggling with that same thing while Justina watched.

"Yes, it was too kind." Sinclair muttered the words and Justina looked up to discover his eyes on her. "You said the same once." There was an understanding in his eyes that sent tears into hers.

No one had ever understood . . .

A soft whimper escaped her lips before she flung herself into his arms. Her knight didn't disappoint her. Sinclair wrapped her tightly against him, threatening to crush the breath from her with the strength of his arms.

Justina didn't struggle. She pressed her face against his neck, inhaling the scent of his skin while she trembled in his arms.

"You came."

"Of course I did." He angled his head back so that he might see her expression. "I cannot live without you, Justina, that is what my love for you means to me. I will follow you anywhere and without fail, no matter the obstacles that need to be moved in order for me to keep that vow."

"But the King's men . . ."

He snorted and set her down, so that he might slide his sword back into its sheath.

"They are young lads who have never been beyond the

palace walls. They know little of how to deal with a seasoned knight, much less how to contain me. It would not surprise me to ride back to my house now and find them all still drinking at my table while thinking that I am truly in my bed." He snorted. "As if I would retire so early without you there to entice me toward those sheets."

She scoffed at his jest but couldn't quite become cross with him. She was still quivering with joy, her eyes blinking rapidly while her mind tried to make sure that he was not an illusion conjured up from her desperation. "I'm grateful for that."

Something crashed to the floor, making a horribly loud sound inside the chamber. Synclair jerked around to see the grooms returning. A silver tray lay on the carpet, rich red wine spilling out of a decanter to mix with the blood puddle on the floor. She had never seen so much blood in one place; it flowed from the two bodies and covered the floor while soaking into the Persian carpet beneath the table.

They looked to one another, neither of them certain what to do. A heavy fist pounded on the outer doors, shaking them.

"Open these doors for the Duke of Portshire!"

"Father!" Bessie fought her way to her feet but she shook, looking too frail to remain standing. The grooms all stepped back, guilt turning their faces dark. They looked at Bessie and the harm that they had known was going on. Justina watched as they stepped back even farther into the shadows of the chamber.

Synclair crossed over the center of the room where the bodies lay. There was an ease about the way he walked among the newly dead that sent a shiver down her back, but once again Justina discovered no lament in her for that fact. She was glad that he was not some paper knight such as Biddeford had been, a man who had proudly displayed his title but had never seen true battle nor bled during the earning of his spurs. Biddeford had been knighted because his family expected it and the King wanted something from those powerful relations. He had fallen to a true knight.

Synclair opened the door, stopping the pounding, but he stood in the doorway, blocking the view of the chamber with his body.

"You will not care for what you discover here, my Lord Portshire."

The Duke of Portshire was not hiding behind his men. The man stood in front of them, his doublet not even fully buttoned.

"Stand aside, Harrow. I have found you an agreeable fellow but I will see my daughter. That bastard of a bishop claims he married my Bessie to the Viscount Biddeford."

There was no mistaking the fact that the duke was furious to hear such news. His tone was sharp enough to cut through leather.

"You may want to choose who accompanies you, my Lord. She is not dressed properly."

There was a low growl from the duke but he made a slashing motion with his hand and several of his party turned around instantly. They continued to guard his back while only his immediate personal guards remained at his side. Synclair stepped out of his path and Justina watched the duke take in the scene inside the chamber. He didn't show his emotions on his face but his eyes filled with the flames of rage.

"Close the door." His voice snapped like a whip and the grooms jumped in the shadows. The duke's men had the door shut before the cowering servants moved. Bessie's hand twisted around Justina's while her father looked over the mess that she was. The duke knelt down to stare at both Biddeford and de Canis.

The duke suddenly looked up at Synclair. "You killed de Canis?"

"I did. He was reaching for Lady Wincott's neck."

"I wish I had killed Biddeford, but he impaled himself on the poker Justina was trying to use to burn the marriage agreement the bishop sealed."

The duke snapped his fingers and one of his men picked up the parchment where it was lying on the floor in front of the fire. The duke shook the ash off it and read it quickly. Justina watched his face tighten even further. He looked at his daughter once again.

"Lady Wincott, I find myself in your debt."

"But . . . this is murder . . ." One of the grooms finally found the courage to speak up. The duke snapped his head about to look at the man.

"Murder? It is not murder when the dead are villains! Now make yourself of use and fetch my daughter a dressing robe. According to this parchment, she is your mistress and heir to your lord's estate since the man is dead."

"I want nothing of his touching me."

The duke made a low sound beneath his breath as the servants hesitated. "Find something among Lady Wincott's belongings!"

There was a scuffle as the grooms all tried to leave the chamber at the same time. They ran into one another, pressing their comrades against the doorframe in their hurry. Justina could hear them running across the stone floor toward her chambers, the doors slamming open because of how fast they went. It didn't take long for a dressing gown to be returned, but she jerked it out of the groom's hands and eased it up Bessie's arms herself.

"Now fetch her some wine."

"No!"

Bessie snarled out the single word and her father's face darkened. He reached out and grabbed a handful of the doublet of the groom closest to him. The man's feet skidded against the floor as the duke lifted him up by one hand.

"Fetch my daughter some wine, man, and make very sure that it is fit for the King himself or answer to me."

The duke released the groom and the man stumbled while attempting to gain his footing.

"I couldn't stop my lord from feeding the girl what he did . . . none of us could . . . we're servants . . ."

"Nonsense! You could have run to my chambers instead of allowing me to hear of this from a bishop's lips! One of you worthless creatures should have done something to prevent this evil from being done, and by God's grace I will not listen to your pitiful excuses! You are a man, not an animal that cannot reason and see foul play for what it is!"

"But we didn't kneel for the blessing, Father. I am not wed."

Bessie sounded desperate but at least her voice was steady instead of slurred. Her gaze was becoming sharp as the last of the toxins released her.

"Your friend was right to attempt to burn this parchment, Bessie. The lack of a blessing is irrelevant now that the bishop is complaining about the matter to any who will listen." Another snort came from the duke. "With winter's chill around the palace, there are many, many interested in hearing the tale. You are wed now and it appears a widow. You need the protection of marriage since the entire court will know of this business before sunset." The duke turned to Justina.

"I discover myself in your debt as well, Lady Wincott, but I am envious, too, for I would have enjoyed killing your guardian myself."

"It was not intentional. He tried to stop me and impaled himself." Justina looked down to where blood was staining her bodice. It had trickled over her shoulder in a thin stream. "I do not lament it."

The duke snorted. "Well, we shall keep this wedding parchment and take what we can from the villain. It will give me great delight to set my lawyers upon his estate."

"I do not want to be called Lady Biddeford."

The duke turned a hard look upon his daughter. "It is far less of a burden than what you have already been forced to bear. Would that I might have spared you this, Bessie, but it is time to discover if you are strong enough to rise up from the fire or die because of the sting of its burn."

Bessie made a sound beneath her breath that was very much like a snarl. "I'd have killed him myself the moment my wits cleared. That foul potion robbed me of my strength and my mind, but I have it back now."

The duke offered his daughter a short nod. Justina made sure that Bessie didn't find any pity on her face either. That was not what the girl needed. Justina recalled that all too well. Bessie would have to be strong if she wanted to rise above the night that had passed.

"I'll be fine, better than fine, in a few more hours."

Justina met her friend's eyes and witnessed the turmoil in them. "I believe that you shall, Bessie. You are no weak-kneed girl after all."

There was a commotion outside the doors, the large wooden panels shaking as men were jostled up against them. The duke's men instantly turned to defend their lord. Justina gasped as Synclair sent her back across the chamber with one hard jerk before he planted himself in front of her with his sword in hand. Bessie stumbled along beside her because Justina was still holding her hand. Both women found themselves pressed against the wall as the doors gave way.

Some of the duke's men fell to the floor when the door gave way behind them. But the men attempting to gain entry froze when they saw the tips of swords being pointed at them from inside the chamber.

"Lower your weapons for the King's men!"

The knight leading them held his hands up so that the men behind him knew to hold their advance.

"Sheathe your weapons in the presence of His Grace, the Duke of Portshire!"

The duke's men did not abandon their stances. The ones who had fallen to the floor rolled over and quickly joined the men who had entered with the duke.

"Enough!" The duke raised his voice, the sound almost deafening in the confines of the chamber. "The King's men may enter. I have nothing to hide."

Swords lowered but not before the men guarding the duke looked over their shoulders to confirm that it had been their master who bid them to abandon their position. The bishop who had sealed the wedding document pushed his way through the King's men and gasped when he laid eyes on the two bodies still lying on the floor of the chamber.

"It is true! I did not want to believe the tale even as the man who told it to me swore it was so! Murder, there has been murder done here, I say!"

Justina felt her blood chill. All of the relief that seemed to have settled on her was ripped away as she watched the King's men look at the bodies lying on the floor. They looked at everyone in the room, their gazes touching on the blood staining the back of her gown and down the front, too. The bishop looked at her and pressed his lips into a hard line of disapproval. Synclair stepped between her and the man even as Justina reached out to stop him from shielding her.

"I ran de Canis through, and the Lady Bessie Portshire is the witness who will tell you that the man was intent on killing Lady Wincott at the time."

"It is true!" Bessie shouted, but her words only drew more frowns from the King's men.

"Enough! A peer of this kingdom has been murdered. It is a matter for the privy council." The King's man looked at the armed men standing in the hallway. "The Baron Harrow and the Ladies Wincott and Portshire shall be placed under strict guard until the council decrees if they shall be taken to the tower."

Justina though her heart might stop. Too many who went to the tower never left it alive. Her freedom from Biddeford might be very short-lived if she was convicted of murdering the viscount. There would be far too many who felt she had good reason to seek his death.

But that was not what sent dread through her. It was the sight of Synclair being relieved of his sword. Pain slashed through her because of every noble thing that she had ever witnessed him doing. He was a knight and that sword was his by the deeds he had done. To witness it being stripped away was more horrible than anything Biddeford had ever forced her to do. It felt as if her heart might stop because the pain was so great, but it was not yet the most painful.

Everything began moving in slow motion again. The King's men surrounded Synclair, their expressions betraying their fear of the knight, but he walked forward, complying with their sanctioning of his person. Justina followed but her guards turned her down a different hallway, tearing her away from Synclair. The pain became unbearable in that moment. Synclair must have felt her distress for he turned and his face became a mask of rage when he saw that she was heading in the opposite direction from himself. The men escorting him suddenly faced their fear as he resisted their direction, sweeping two of them to the floor with one powerful motion of his arms.

"The Lady Wincott goes with me!"

"That is impossible, my Lord Harrow!" It was the bishop

who spoke, his voice carrying authority. "She is not your wife."

Synclair's face became a mask of rage and she heard him growl across the space between them. His body tensed as he prepared to lunge at the bishop.

I will overcome any obstacle that is between us . . .

His words echoed in her mind as she witnessed the determination on his face. He would do it, do anything it took for her.

"Then marry us!" Justina didn't care if her voice echoed down the corridors.

The men surrounding her were far too trusting of her gender. By the time they realized her intention, she had slipped between them and was running back toward Synclair.

She stopped at the bishop and forced herself to look at him in spite of the sounds of struggle coming from Synclair and his escort. She fell to her knees, her gown billowing out because she sunk so quickly. She was uncaring of her own pride in that moment, how she looked was irrelevant. She didn't care about all the practicing that she had been taught as a child to ensure that she never moved without complete grace. All that mattered was making the bishop do as she wished.

"You said women need husbands and I agree! Wed us, my lord Bishop, this moment. I beg you."

"As the lady says, wed us."

The bishop looked surprised by Synclair's words. The guards trying to hold him back released him and he crossed the space between them and knelt beside her.

"But . . . my Lord Harrow . . . this is not a church . . ."

"All of Whitehall was a sanctuary before it became a palace." Synclair reached over and grasped her hand. "Marry us here and now because the future is too uncertain to leave sin on either of us. What matters is the

Church's blessing, not the vanities of this world, only that we submit to the Church's will."

"I will witness it."

It was the Duke of Portshire who spoke up. He stepped closer and snapped his fingers. A moment later his men carried a small table out of a nearby room and sat it down next to the bishop. Someone set a candle on it, with its flame flickering brightly. The bishop's manservant stood nearby with the bishop's box of wax and other important items. He looked at his master and waited for the man to indicate whether he should place the box upon the table or not. Justina felt her heart racing while that moment drew out longer and longer.

"My secretary will draw up the papers while you give the blessing."

The bishop looked around to discover that he was the center of attention. His face flushed and his teeth worried his lower lip, but his eyes flickered with growing excitement, and he raised his hands into the air while his voice began the first verse of their wedding. The stone was hard beneath her knees and there was not a single note of music or pleasing scent in the air from incense or bees wax candles.

But the man kneeling beside her made it the most perfect moment of her life.

The moment the bishop sealed their wedding document, the guards gestured them off their knees and down the hallway again. The men charged with the duty of escorting them did it quickly, marching them toward a chamber. They shut the doors behind them with the nerve-shattering sound of an iron lock.

Synclair chuckled, making Justina turn to face him. His face was transformed by a smile that split his lips and reached all the way into his eyes.

"Have you gone mad?"

One of his eyebrows rose. "Your tone is less than respectful, *Wife*."

Justina froze, her emotion unsure in that moment. Sinclair's smile faded. He reached across the space between them and cupped the side of her face tenderly.

"Do not look so alarmed by the word, Justina, for it brings me much satisfaction." His fingers gently stroked her jaw and along her lips. "And happiness."

She shivered, emotion rippling through her along with his touch. "I couldn't bear the idea of being parted from you, especially since we may not live much longer."

He snorted and his hand dropped away from her face. "We shall see about that. It was justified action."

"Anne Boleyn was innocent of the charges against her, too."

Synclair offered her another sound of male disgruntlement. "Have a bit of faith, Wife. We are still breathing."

He turned to look at where they were. The chamber was of good size but still dark because the window shutters were closed. Synclair unhooked his sword belt now that his sword was missing and dropped it over a chair.

The sound of the bar being pushed up on the other side of the door made them both turn toward it. The doors opened and the Duke of Portshire stood there for a moment while his gaze found Synclair.

"You are not a man I want to surprise on a day like today." The duke offered a grin along with his words.

"I will not complain for I saw a goal of mine accomplished, one that was very dear to me."

Synclair didn't look at her but she still felt cherished. More so than she could ever recall in her entire life. The duke nodded and walked into the chamber. He swept it with a quick glance before snapping his fingers.

"This chamber needs a bit of comfort since it will host

a newlywed couple." Servants began to carry bundles in through the open doorways. "Lady Harrow, the guard has graciously agreed to escort you to my chambers where you may bathe in privacy. Lord Harrow and myself need a bit of time to discuss the trial."

The word *trial* stuck in her throat. Justina was reluctant to leave but more afraid of offending the duke if she refused him.

They needed his support.

"That is very kind of you." She lowered herself before turning toward the doorway and the men waiting to escort her. There was no doubt in her mind that she was about to take the most expensive bath of her life, for it had surely cost the duke plenty to bribe the guards.

In spite of the apprehension attempting to choke her, Justina felt her lips turning up into a genuine smile.

Lady Harrow indeed.

Now she just needed fate to be kind enough to not have her executed before she had the chance to enjoy her husband. It was certainly something she had never expected to do.

The Duke of Portshire clearly knew how to express his gratitude. Justina returned to a chamber that didn't resemble the one she had left at all. It smelled fresh now, the window shutters having been opened to allow the breeze to carry away any smoke left lingering. The bed was made with a brocade coverlet and there were plump pillows in creamy pillow cases. The table was laid with pitchers of wine and fresh milk. A tray held dried fruits and thin, delicately rolled peppered meats. It was expensive fare, fit for only the highest nobles or those with a great deal of gold to spend. The Duke of Portshire was obviously more than a titled noble, but a knowledgeable businessman, too.

"You are too quiet."

Synclair was watching her. His blue eyes had been trained on her since the moment she stepped back into the chamber with the guards at her back. Justina discovered herself grateful to be locked behind the doors because at least she had privacy.

Except from her new husband, that was. But he had not spoken, only watched her every motion, and she discovered herself becoming uncertain of him.

"I am struck silent by the fact that you are now my wife."

Justina found herself in almost the same position but there was too much turmoil to remain silent.

"I hope you are pleased." Her voice was low but not soft enough, for he clearly heard the uncertainty in it.

"How could you doubt it, Justina?" Synclair didn't raise his voice much above a whisper but it cracked like a whip. He crossed the space between them on silent steps and captured her in an embrace that betrayed just how tense he truly was. His lax demeanor of the last hour had been merely a sham. Her hands landed on his biceps and she could feel the tension in his muscles.

"What did the duke say?"

His hand smoothed up her back until his fingers clasped her neck. He leaned down and sealed her mouth with his, kissing her harder when she tried to twist away and continue asking questions.

"Synclair . . ." She succeeded in getting one word out and she heard her husband snarl.

"We are not going to spend the remains of this day— our *wedding* day—talking about what the future holds, Justina."

"I cannot be at ease while I worry about our fate."

He released her and walked toward the bed. He sat down on the edge and used a bootjack to pull his thigh-high boots off.

"It will be my fate, not yours. Only I will answer to the lords of the privy council on the morrow."

Justina felt her eyes widen. She flew across the space between them and placed her hands against his cheeks.

"But I killed Biddeford; it is my trial to face."

Synclair growled at her, his arms clamping around her. He rolled onto his back and took her along with him in one swift motion that stole her breath. Justina landed on her back with his hard body alongside her. Synclair rose above her, his expression tight.

"It will be mine to face, Justina, because I shall shelter you, and now that you have wed me, you will allow me to protect you." His hand cupped her chin, his fingers smoothing along her jaw and up to her cheek. It was a tender touch, the opposite of his tone, but she realized that Synclair had always been a combination of strength and tenderness with her.

"Do you still fail to understand how much you mean to me, Justina? You are the only woman I have ever been unable to ignore. You stick in my thoughts when I should be devoted to other matters. I hear your sweet voice at night and smell your skin when I close my eyes."

He lowered his head and nuzzled against her neck. She heard him draw a deep breath and hold it for a moment before softly exhaling. His hands threaded through the strands of her freshly washed hair and she felt him quiver against her body.

"I would rather die than watch you walk out of here tomorrow to face those charges."

He lifted his head and she witnessed the emotion shimmering in his eyes. "If you wish to please me, then hold me and make love with me and *trust me*."

Synclair didn't allow her to answer. His mouth claimed hers in another kiss that stole her breath. She reached for him and for all the things she had forced herself to leave behind for the better good. Desperation sent her hands stroking over every inch of his body, not content to merely feel only part of him. She needed more, craved more, but she wasn't alone. Synclair stripped her dressing gown away, his lips trailing kisses down the column of her throat and onto her chest. His hands slid up and over her belly until they cupped each breast, sweet sensation flowing through her while she quivered with anticipation of his kisses reaching her nipples. Each one contracted until it was a hard point, the skin more sensitive than it had ever been before. Synclair didn't rush and Justina heard her own little cries filling the room.

"That is the best thing I have heard from you this day, my lady."

His voice was husky and edged with need. He leaned down and she felt his breath brush one puckered nipple. Sharp desire spiked through her and she arched up off the surface of the bed in her quest to feel his mouth on her flesh. Synclair pressed her back down, his lips closing around the puckered point as his tongue took a swipe across the very top of it.

A soft cry passed her lips and she heard him chuckle. "I believe we should conduct all of our conversations in bed, madam. We seem to agree often when we are bare and alone."

"I think we need to stop talking completely."

He lifted his head and brushed the hair back from her face. She couldn't suffer the distance between them and reached for him. He covered her body, her thighs parting to allow him to settle where she craved him. The head of his cock nudged against the opening of her passage, discovering her wet and eager already.

"Because it prevents you from thinking of the outcome of the trial?"

"Because I want you and I don't care what is happening

in the world, so long as we may forget about it." She gripped his biceps and lifted her hips so that his length filled her completely. "So long as you do nothing save shelter me, I care not what else is happening."

"Exactly my plans, Lady."

He pulled free before thrusting back into her. The bed moved along with their motions and Justina let the pleasure tear her away from every thought beside the hard body holding hers. Pleasure crested and they clung to one another for long moments until they began to tease and touch again. The sunlight reached in long fingers across the floor of the chamber before it faded completely, leaving them with nothing but the glow of the candles. Synclair never extinguished those flames. They flickered throughout the night while he held her, his embrace becoming everything she had told herself she might never expect from any man.

It was perfection.

Dawn invaded their chamber and along with it came tension in the arms of her husband.

"I wish I might bid you remain in bed but I do not wish you to be seen by others as I enjoy you now."

Synclair rose and began to dress. Justina followed him, taking time to pull a chemise over her head before she began to help him dress.

"No argument today?" He looked at her while she went to retrieve his doublet from where it hung on the back of a chair.

Justina offered him a smile. "The very first time that I laid eyes upon you, I was impressed with the fact that you were a true knight. It is part of you and something that draws me to you. I would not have us argue this day. Let us speak of love instead."

He waited until she had buttoned the doublet all the

way to his chin before slipping his hand beneath her chin and locking gazes with her.

"Because you fear that it might be our last day? Well, Lady, I am a knight and one who is willing to risk everything I have for victory."

He was cocky and arrogant but she smiled at him even as she shook her head at his vanity. He chuckled and a solid smack landed on her backside when she foolishly exposed it to him.

"Get dressed, Wife! The day has broken and we've matters to attend to."

Justina didn't get time to dress before there came a solid knock on the doors. She shrugged back into the dressing robe that was lying forgotten on the floor. The Duke of Portshire offered her a brief nod before Synclair strode across the chamber to join him. Her knight never looked back but faced his next challenge with every bit of courage and determination that she had come to expect of him.

Two maids filled the doorway once the men departed. They lowered themselves before entering on silent steps. They both had their arms piled high with items that they laid on the long table before one approached her with a silver comb and began to apply it to the tangled mess her hair had become throughout the night. She eased the comb through the knots until every strand lay smooth. The maid braided and pinned it up while her companion began to bring her stockings and garters, shoes and underpinnings. They dressed her in a warm, winter dress that was made of sturdy English wool. It was lined in silk to make it soft against her neck and arms.

The doors opened again and another pair of maids entered. One carried a small tray with dishes on it that were covered with newly pressed linen squares. The other girl held a kettle that she took to the fireplace and hung it over an iron hook that she then pushed over the newly rekindled flames. Justina felt her stomach knot with tension so tight, she was certain she could not partake of any of the food.

"Mistress?"

Justina turned and gasped. The tray did not hold food. The small box that she kept her herbs in was sitting there, the lid resting beside it and the wooden mug that she used to brew her morning drink in.

"The Lord Harrow instructed that this be brought for you."

The tray held one last item and it was a small, folded piece of parchment. A wax seal closed it and she lifted it up to look at the crest of the Harrow family. Her fingers shook when she broke it and opened the letter so that she might read the message inside.

Trust is earned, Justina, and not by only one gender.
I will place my faith in you and hope that you will welcome
our child just as joyfully as I will.

Tears welled up in her eyes, refusing to be held back. She pressed the letter to her lips before picking up the linen that had covered the box to wipe her face with.

"Take it away. I have no need of it."

The maid lowered herself and turned to go, but Justina suddenly thought of Bessie.

"Wait. I have another use for that box." The maid turned around to face her.

"I will take it to my friend. She may have need of it."

There was a twinkle of understanding in the maid's eyes, but Justina didn't linger over it. Bessie needed the choice, and she would offer that to her friend.

For she was finished with taking the herbs. Fate had finally granted her the rarest of things, a husband she loved. But the day loomed ahead with dark fears of what the council would decide. Biddeford had been a powerful man but the duke was as well. There was no true way to guess at the outcome; there was only the solid truth that the issue would be decided over far more than just the facts of the matter.

Justina walked to the door and the men waiting to escort her to the privy council chambers.

"I am ready, Gentlemen, but if you please, we shall stop and collect Bessie Portshire along the way."

Justina used her polished manners and meekest voice to convince the guards that she was nothing but a submissive woman. She lowered her eyelashes and peeked up through them at the senior guard. He crumbled in a moment, nodding agreement and gesturing her forward.

CHAPTER TWELVE

The Duke of Portshire wore his formal robes with the white fur collar. Resting on top of that fur was his knight of the garter chain, the Tudor roses medallions linked together with knots, and suspended from the center was an emblem with St. George slaying the dragon. Every member of the privy council was dressed as finely and the room was silent in spite of the fact that every inch of space was being used. So many had arrived to hear the proceedings that many of the ladies' hooped slips were crushed, but still no one left.

"And so, my fellow lords, I say unto you all that Francis de Canis is a villain of the worst caliber! He has slain my son-in-law of a single day and left my only daughter a widow. Would that I might demand satisfaction from this assembly, but the man is dead by the hand of a fellow lord that I owe a debt of gratitude to."

The duke paced along the length of the table, his cape flaring out from his ankles. "I entrust the fate of Lord Harrow to your noble charity but know this . . ."

He held one hand up in the air. "I do applaud his deed, so condemn him and consider myself condemned as well. Francis de Canis murdered the Viscount Biddeford in front of my daughter, and I could no more have stayed my hand if I had been there."

Bessie tightened her grip on Justina's hand. They stood together, watching the proceedings. The lords whispered among themselves but Justina didn't fail to notice the relief that crossed more than one man's face. Francis de Canis had worked for most of them, and they were happy to know of his death because it would forever seal his lips. The Earl of Hertford rose and the whispers died instantly.

"My Lord Portshire, we find your words moving and the Lord Harrow innocent of wrongdoing in this matter. Furthermore, I shall add my condolences to your daughter. The marriage is valid and shall there be any issue from the union, the inheritance conferred."

Many of the lords pounded the table in agreement.

"There shall be no issue." Bessie spoke in a soft voice but each word was solid. She was more of a woman now, hardened by the circumstances of fate. Ones that Justina knew very well. Synclair was released from the custody of the King's guard and stopped to clasp the wrists of many of the members of the privy council.

"Will you retire to the country now that you are wed?"

Justina heard the lament in Bessie's voice. "Yes, and leaving you shall be my only regret. But know that it is truly a large one."

Bessie sighed. "I shall miss you but do not worry so much about me. I am no longer such a child and will not be taken in easily again. There is a blessing in this affair. I will not be forced to wed now. Everyone believes I had a secret love match with Biddeford and that gives me a shield to hide behind."

She smothered a harsh sound of scorn. "I shall enjoy taking my pleasure from him."

Justina clasped her friend's hand. "Love can truly be a blessing. I've discovered that recently. I hope you have the chance to learn that for yourself."

Bessie shook her head. "I want naught to do with suitors. For the moment I must contend with the viscount's nephew. The man has sent word that he intends to claim the title. I expect him to be very unhappy to hear that I shall hold my widow's thirds from the estate."

Bessie Portshire looked too pleased by that knowledge. Justina ached for her friend for there was bitterness burning in her eyes that she understood so very well. The girl was clinging tightly to her anger, just as hard as Justina had once clung to the notion of not trusting her heart to anyone.

She looked up to find her husband striding across the large receiving room toward her. Her breath caught in her throat and she felt her heart fill with joy. She cast a last look toward her friend.

"Try and trust again someday, Bessie. If you find the right man, it will be worth your heart. I swear it for I have learned that lesson recently and I am glad of it. More happy than I ever believed possible."

Justina felt Bessie watching her as Synclair took her hand and raised it to his lips. It was only a brief kiss, one that broke no rules of chivalry or even hinted at impropriety, but she felt it burn a path up her arm and into her chest.

"My lady wife, I believe I am about to give you an order that it will displease me very much to hear you object to."

"And what might your will be, my husband?"

His eyes glittered with hard purpose. "To leave this court immediately."

Justina smiled and sunk into a low curtsy. "As my lord does command."

She didn't care about the roads, or the icy cold that made her nose hurt. Justina took to the road the moment

Synclair and his men were ready. She looked back at Whitehall and the only thing that she found pleasing about it was Bessie.

"She will find her own way, Justina. That one has strength inside her."

Justina kept her eyes on the palace. "I have never been so happy to leave a place that so many find the center of the world."

"Change is coming to Whitehall, and I for one am glad to be gone before the storm breaks." Her husband's voice was thick with emotion for the King he had served so long.

The wind blew in a strong gust and her horse danced nervously. Justina felt the chill penetrate the thick wool cape she wore and slip beneath the hood to raise the hair on the back of her neck.

"I am sorry, Synclair."

He stiffened and tore his gaze off the palace. "Do not be. I have what I came here for."

Her husband sent his stallion forward and Justina followed. They covered the distance between the palace and his house, eagerly anticipating a warm kitchen to warm their fingers. Arlene came out onto the steps when she heard them approaching and the housekeeper lifted her arm up to wave in welcome to them.

It was the most perfect greeting Justina had ever received. It lacked pomp and courtly flare and that pleased her greatly.

Synclair lingered only a single night beneath the roof of the house. His holdings were further to the north and he patted her bottom, interrupting her slumber before sunrise.

"I am awake, sir, have done with tormenting me."

His eyebrow rose and she scoffed at him. "Begin that

conversation, sir, and we shall not be leaving this bed-chamber."

"I believe I shall enjoy a country life with you, Justina." He reached out and hooked a hard arm around her waist to pull her against him. His breath was warm against her neck as he angled his head to press a kiss to the sensitive flesh.

"I will look forward to hearing you abandon those courtly manners in favor of a less restrictive lifestyle."

Justina pressed her hands against his bare chest to push him away but he only allowed her a few inches. "Does that mean you have a taste for a wife who speaks her mind?"

"I enjoy hearing you demand what you like in our bed."

She felt a soft shaft of desire move through her. "I shall remember that, unless you have forgotten your desire to leave so early this morning?"

"No, I have not, but I am sorely disappointed that I cannot enjoy your sweet body right this moment."

He released her and stood up. Justina savored the heat in the bed for a moment more before she followed and shivered on her way toward the fire where the embers still glowed. She froze when she passed the table and saw her box sitting on it.

"I meant what I wrote, Justina. Would you like some hot water before we depart?"

She heard the need in his voice and her heart ached to fill it, just as he had filled so many of her own.

"No. That is not what I need or crave. Leave the box behind, it belongs at court."

Synclair nodded, his eyes shining with satisfaction. "Get dressed, woman, we've ground to cover."

It took them three days to reach his holdings. Justina gained her first look at Bentwood Castle by evening's light. The towers were ivory and rose four stories into the air. The lands that surrounded it were covered in snow

now, but come spring there would be crops growing there to fill the place with life. When they rode into the courtyard, bells set along the walls rung out to welcome the lord home.

"Mother! Mother! I am very happy to see you!"

Justina gasped and discovered Synclair watching her.

"You said you sent him to Curan."

"I couldn't risk having anything you knew becoming the truth, not when you left my side to go to the palace without me."

There was a hard glint in his eyes that spoke of just how much he disliked the action she had taken to protect her child. Justina returned it with steady confidence.

"My trust was well placed, I see."

He snorted at her. "That is most unfair, Lady. You know how much hearing you say that means to me." He reached up and clasped her around the waist to lift her from the saddle.

"And you know how much I mean it."

"I do, Lady, and I love you even more for it."

Brandon pushed his way between them, his excited voice cutting through their conversation. Synclair hefted the boy up and placed him on one of his wide shoulders.

"Welcome your mother home, Brandon. She is now my wife."

Her son hooted with glee. "Does that mean we are to be a family, Sir Synclair?"

Her husband reached for her hand and she felt his fingers wrap around her own.

"Indeed it does."

Henry the Eighth, King of England, died on January 28 in the year 1547. Synclair received word of the King's death a full month after the fact but he didn't lament the distance that had caused him to receive news so delayed.

Synclair offered the royal messenger a firm nod. "You have my gratitude for braving the winter chill to bring me this. Go to the kitchens and my staff will make you welcome."

The messenger lowered himself before moving off toward the promise of a warm meal and a cheerful fire to melt some of the ice off his boots.

"What news did he bring?"

Justina appeared in the doorway, her nose wrinkling at the chill in the room. Synclair lifted his chin and offered her a grin, the one he always gave her when she tried to tell him that his solar was too cold. Campaigns in France had been far colder. His grip tightened on the parchment and he heard it crinkle.

Well, those campaigns were history now, and the woman in front of him represented a happy future that was all the warmth he would ever need.

"The only news that could have come from Whitehall. Henry has died and Edward is crowned King."

Synclair stood up and left the message behind on the table. He walked across the room and pulled his wife into his embrace. She settled easily against him, her hands resting on his chest.

"I am sorry."

"Do not be. Henry was my past and I am very happy in the future . . . with you, my love."

She smiled and stretched up to place a kiss against his lips. The motion pressed her body against his from foot to shoulder and he felt the gently rounding shape of her belly. Synclair reached down and smoothed a hand between them, stroking over the tiny beginning of what would be his child once summer arrived.

"My body seems to recall exactly what to do when I am with child." Justina ran her own hand over her belly. "I swear that I did not grow so large, so quickly, with Brandon. At this rate, you will not be able to kiss me on May Day without leaning over to reach me."

"I will suffer the neck ache gladly for I refuse to endure without your kisses."

Justina smiled at him; it was radiant and emotion shimmered in her eyes. She lifted her hand and placed it on the side of his face.

"I love you." She reached down and captured his hand and placed it back on her swelling belly. "I trust you."

Her husband's eyes lit with satisfaction and victory. Justina only smiled, for she had finally come to understand. Fate was delivering happiness in large amounts and she intended to savor all of it. Her husband cupped her chin in his hand while his gaze studied hers.

"As I promise you, Justina, you will be mine but most importantly . . . you will enjoy it."

"You are arrogant, sir."

He leaned down and placed a soft kiss against her lips. "I am in love, madam, and I know no other way but to pursue what I crave."

"I pray you never change."

If you liked Mary's story, try her other books available from Brava!

In Bed with a Stranger

Brodick McJames is an earl in name only. To secure his clan's future he needs an English wife. Mary Stanford, daughter of the Earl of Warwickshire, will suit perfectly. He's never met her, but what matter? She'll grace his bed eventually, and once she bears his child he need see her no more.

Anne Copper looks just like her noble half-sister, but she was born illegitimate, and can never forget it. The best she can hope for is to stay a serving girl in her own father's house. But when Lady Mary finds herself betrothed to a Scot, it seems there's a use for Anne after all. . . . The woman who arrives in Alcaon is not what Brodick expects, and the passion that grows between them promises far more than a marriage of convenience. When fate draws two together, it may take more than a noblewoman's plot to part them. . . .

In the Warrior's Bed

Cullen McJames will not have his honor sullied, certainly not by his clan's nemesis Laird Erik McQuade. So when McQuade tells the Court of Scotland that Cullen has stolen his daughter's virtue, Cullen steals the daughter instead.

Since his brother wed a fetching lass, Cullen's been thinking he too needs a wife. A marriage could end the constant war between the clans. And looking on Bronwyn McQuade but once has put her in his dreams for a week. . . .

But Bronwyn won't go quietly. She won't be punished for what she did not do. Nor is she eager to live among the resentful veterans of McQuade wars. And however brave and beautiful a man Cullen may be, he has much to learn about a woman's fighting spirit. But as Bronwyn will discover, he has much to teach her as well. . . .

Bedding the Enemy

Laird Keir McQuade is a newcomer to his title, and has much work before him to restore the McQuade honor. Finding a wife is an excellent start. He's duty-bound to go to court and swear homage to his king anyway, a perfect opportunity—were not court women trussed in stupid fashions and corrupted with false mannerisms. Of course, not every lady hides behind a powdered face. . . .

Helena Knyvett may be a daughter of the aristocracy, but in truth she is little but a pawn in her brother's ploys for power. Her smallest acts of defiance carry a heavy price. But one honorable man among a crowd of dandies could give her all she needs to change her fortunes—and set her free. . . .

Among the ruthless ambitions of England's powerful, love at first sight is a dangerous game. But the treachery, scandal, and treason that follow can unleash as much passion as it does adventure. . . .

A Rearranged Marriage

Lord Curan Ramsden is home from war, and eager to claim his betrothed. And he arrives just in time—his bride's father has summoned her to London, to wed another man. But Bridget's father promised her to Curan, and Curan means to have her. Especially now that he sees the luscious young woman she has blossomed into. He'll just have to convince Bridget, somehow, that her heart is more important than her duty. . . .

Bridget Newbury has always done her duty—to her parents, to the church, to the man they selected as her betrothed. She knows what could happen if she disobeys her father. The king has put nobler women to death for lesser trespasses. But she was promised to Curan first, and his kisses are very tempting. . . .

My Fair Highlander

Jemma Ramsden is a wild thing in a noblewoman's body—so thinks Gordon Dwyre, Laird Barras, watching her galloping on horseback through her brother's lands. Bold, headstrong, beautiful: the perfect bride for a lusty Scots warrior. He might be able to convince her, too, if she would hear his suit. But Barras doesn't wait to be handed what he wants. When he's forced to rescue her from English ruffians, he makes sure she stays safe—by locking her in his castle.

Jemma is hardly an eager captive. She has no horse and no freedom, and she is an Englishwoman in a hostile Scots keep: a stranger without work or friend. Barras seems determined to charm her—even tempt forbidden desires, a daring game that leaves Jemma desperate for more. But with passion, love, and a new life within her grasp, Jemma is in more danger than even she knows. . . .